# Wayward Sisters 2

# BENITA TYLER

ISBN 978-0-9856964-8-1

First Edition 2019

Published in the United States by
Beloved Daffodils Inspirations
700 E. Firmin Street, Suite 188 Kokomo, IN 46902

# Dedication

This book is dedicated to those men and women who have gone down a wayward path or two to pursue their dreams while hoping that God had their back. Although we may find ourselves living in disappointment, unforgiveness, and under scrutiny, I encourage you to be of good cheer! The truth is, when we turn our hearts toward God and included Him by asking Him to reveal what He would have us do while living on this Earth, we will find ourselves fulfilled and will remain on the path of endless possibilities while avoiding wayward paths and snares set up by our adversary whose malicious intent is designed to halt God's Plan for us.

Matthew 7:2

*"For in the same way you judge others, you will be judged, and with the measure you use, it will be measured to you."*

# Acknowledgements

Special thanks to my husband, manager, and hype man Cedric Tyler. I thank my father for what he didn't provide, and my mother for what she did, as both made me the beloved daffodil that I am and the inspirer of others ready to bloom. I thank my beautiful children, who were with me through the good and bad seasons of life. (Ahmad, Jasmine, Quadree, and Cenia) With special thanks to my stepchildren who also love me through successes and failures. I'm providing a legacy for my beautiful family through my writings. Thanks to my fans for believing in me and purchasing my books and attending my yearly Released to Live Life Out Loud Conferences.

# Table of Contents

# Sisterly Love Prevails 2

"In the midst, love finds us complete and whole, a love so powerful and pure. Although we allow other's scrutiny and opinions to penetrate our thoughts, we begin to evolve when we believe that God designed us to engage with our sisters who make us stronger. Together we experience a sweet surrender grounded in the fruits of redemption. Tranquility fills the air while beautiful butterflies remind us that we are free and love is restored once again."

–Benita Tyler

# Chapter 1

# Wayward Truths

## (Terrance's Plight)

S leep had eluded Keisha for weeks, and restless nights were promised after the city of Albuquerque, New Mexico had come under siege. While lying wide-awake in her king-size sleigh bed, she rolled over to look at her alarm clock that sat on her nightstand. Keisha was restless and felt annoyed. It was 3:30 a.m. but felt closer to midnight, when she'd first gone to sleep. She got up to get a drink of water believing that it would settle her nerves. Her younger brother Terrance had relocated to the city of Albuquerque after finishing high school some years earlier, and now the city he had come to love was under a state of emergency.

Keisha paced the floor in anguish while pleading with her inner spirit for a little more faith in God, knowing that "worrying" was something God frowned upon. Growing up in church taught her many things, including that faith is the substance of all things hoped for. Keisha's father was a prominent Baptist pastor, making it absurd for her to pretend that she was not aware how faith worked. However, Keisha couldn't help her disobedience, knowing that her baby brother was in harm's way. Terrance's fate was something that stayed on her mind, *I don't know what I'll do if something happens to Terrance,* she thought. Although they had been able to maintain a close bond after he'd moved, she prayed he'd return home to Pittsford someday.

Keisha felt an eeriness in her spirit, resulting from staying up a lot later than usual, glued to the television and listening to the continuous news coverage on the chaos brewing in Albuquerque. The African-American community was up in arms, and the lives of young Black men who lived in the area were in danger. Keisha prayed day and night that Terrance wouldn't become a statistic of police brutality. However, every detail being reported by CNN's Don Lemon said otherwise. Don Lemon weaved a tale of horror and urged all African-American males listening to lay low until things returned to normal.

Keisha turned off the television and fell to her knees to surrender to the Holy Spirit, who in turn assured her that Terrance would be okay. Her lavender housecoat draped her beautiful tile floor as she clutched her cherished Bible that had once belonged to her deceased father. "My God, thank You in advance for protecting Terrance!" she yelled over and over again. She felt the fullness of the Lord and believed in His promises. While still exhausted, she stood up to wash her tear-stained face. She decided it would be better to wait until morning to call Terrance and check on him. She crawled back into her bed and fell asleep within minutes of her head hitting her plush pillow.

Throughout the day, Keisha's goal was to remain in peace so that she wouldn't alert her beautiful mother Victoria or her sister Jada about the problems Terrance faced. Her mind was like a roller coaster consisting of good and bad thoughts, forcing her to continue to pray that the violence and killing would cease. The notion that the upheaval was so close to Terrance's neighborhood shook her to the core. Over the years, Keisha had heard similar stories of unjust circumstances that had occurred in African-American communities throughout the United States, such as the Rodney King incident that had happened in the early 1990s. Mr. King, a taxi driver, had become famous after being brutality beaten by members of the Los Angeles Police Department when they attempted to arrest him. It was disgraceful! Those officers had taken an oath to protect and serve the citizens of Los Angles no matter their color.

While growing up, Keisha and her brothers were reminded of this by their parents, who purposely moved to the city of Pittsford, New York as a means to shield their sons David and Terrance from discrimination.

However, the harsh reality was that all police officers didn't share the same sentiment required of them to protect and serve. Those were the kitchen table conversations that took place in the Williams household, and the Reverend always shared his own stories of being harassed as a young boy by rogue cops on more than one occasion. However, Terrance was the rebel who had always had his own ideas and beliefs about how to keep himself safe and how to obtain happiness for himself. His sheltered upbringing had backfired and had caused him to believe that prejudice didn't exist since Pittsford was a minority-friendly city that gave him a false sense of inclusion. He believed that life was that way everywhere, but he was wrong.

David and Terrance were popular in their community, and being the sons of a prominent pastor benefited them. Terrance's views clashed with the Reverend on almost everything. When Terrance graduated from high school, he received a scholarship to play basketball at the University of New Mexico and he didn't hesitate to accept it. He had purposely applied to colleges that were as far away as possible to let the Reverend know that he planned to find his own way in the world despite his disapproval. Terrance was adamant about not following in his father's footsteps and becoming a pastor. He believed that basketball was all he needed to launch himself into a future career in coaching and working with the youth, and he was right.

Keisha turned the television back on to see if there were any new developments. She listened as Kate Baldwin reported that The Head Bangers, a well-known local gang that was notorious for criminal activities such as selling drugs, terrorizing neighborhoods, womanizing, and murdering their own people, vowed to protect their turf and were adamant about getting revenge for the death of their homeboy, Antoine Davis, a seventeen year old who joined the gang at the age of fifteen. The breaking news stated that Antoine had been murdered after engaging in a heated argument with a rogue cop who had pulled him over after he had run a red light.

Antione thought he was being harassed and tried to make his point by arguing with the cop who thought his combativeness had crossed the line. He warned Antoine to be quiet or he would be arrested. However, the unthinkable happened and the rogue cop pumped four bullets into Antoine's chest. The news of another Black youth dying at the hands of the police spread quickly, and his cohorts sought revenge with anyone who opposed them by rioting and confronting those who they perceived to be the enemy. Albuquerque's "finest" happened to be the enemy and had become the target, and it was anyone's guess when the mayhem would end. Keisha prayed that no one else had to lose their life in protest, but she knew better.

Meanwhile, back in Albuquerque, Terrance had become enraged after hearing about the mayhem. His anger had intensified after he realized that some of The Head Bangers being vilified were youths who he had mentored as children at the city's community center. He couldn't believe his eyes, as he watched them throwing caution to the wind to fit in with the more notorious gang members who wanted revenge. He feared for their lives and wondered how they were willing to exchange their unbridled emotions for a piece of unobtainable justice, a risk that he knew wouldn't pan out for them. They had to know that all the rioting in the world wasn't going to bring Antoine back or help them to settle the score, but it didn't matter. Police profiling was common in their neighborhoods. However, getting a rogue cop charged legally for committing illegal acts was few and far between. The Head Bangers sought to send a strong message to the cops this time around that things had to change. Their sentiment was shared by most of the African-American males in the community who were fed up with losing loved ones.

They were unwilling to continue to accept the police brutality, or worse, being killed for being Black. The nonsense needed to stop, but who would be able to make the positive changes needed?

Terrance believed that he was his brother's keeper and was willing to take up their plight since they were unable to defend themselves. He had some influence with some of the members of The Head Bangers who saw him as the "lucky homey" who had escaped the life of a street thug. He wanted to help change their corrupt hearts before it was too late and went down the street thinking that he could convince at least one of them to turn from their wayward ways. However, when he arrived, he could tell that he was going to have to approach them with caution, knowing that if he said or did anything wrong, the entire situation could escalate. He didn't have much time before the SWAT team would be dispatched to the area, so he had to think fast. The smell of burning buildings filled the air, and he gasped while trying to clear his throat. Terrance noticed that several of the storefronts had already been destroyed. The members of The Head Bangers recognized his vehicle and hurried over to it to form a circle around it as a means of intimidating him. He slowly rolled down his driver's-side window, not knowing what to expect.

"Hold up, Trey. It's me, homey!" he yelled. "I just want to talk to y'all. I know things are fucked up out here, but it doesn't mean we need to destroy our own neighborhood," he reported while trying to reason with them. However, nothing he said was working, in fact, his words heightened their emotions and he could tell they weren't in the mood for sermons.

"Don't nobody want to hear that bullshit you're talking right now, Terrance," Trey blurted out. "Get the fuck out of here, homey!"

"Wait! Hear me out," Terrance pleaded. "Setting shit on fire and ruining our community isn't going to bring Antione back. We've got to do things differently if we ever expect shit to change like going to the state house to protest peacefully like those who came before us. That's the only way for a Black man to stand a chance of having his voice heard."

"Man, you *got* a hearing problem? We ain't got time to listen to your psychological bullshit! We gonna get even with them punk-ass motherfuckers one way or another, and if you keep running your mouth, you gonna be the first bitch to catch a bullet. You done forgot where you came from, homey," the ringleader Mookie said.

"That's where you're wrong, Mookie! I'm came down here as soon as I heard about Antoine. I didn't want to see anything happen to anybody else. Hell, I've known most of you since y'all were boys and I mentored Trey and Wayne. Why y'all tripping!" Terrance asked, still fearing for his life.

"Step out of the car, and you got two minutes to make your point," Mookie told him.

Terrance exited his car, and from out of nowhere Mookie sucker punch him and began yelling a slew of expletives at him. Terrance fell backwards and landed flat on his back. He tried to get up and regain his composure, but he panicked after he heard what sounded like gunshots.

"Oh, shit!" Terrance yelled before rolling underneath his car to take cover. He could hear the sound of footsteps fleeing in all directions and sirens blaring as the gang members tried to avoid being arrested. He laid still for what seemed like hours while examining his body, and he was relieved that there was no blood on his hands. He was in a state of paranoia while choking on the intensely thick smoke that filled the air. Windows were bursting out from the intense heat all around him. He crawled from underneath his car, knowing that it could blow up at any second. He kept low to avoid being seen by the cops and ran toward his apartment. His legs were wobbly and his heart was beating out of his chest, but he didn't let that deter him. Once in front of his apartment building, he climbed the stairs that led to his front door and began frantically banging on it, hoping that his girlfriend Sarah would let him in quickly. With each passing moment, he remembered to thank God.

Sarah was shocked by Terrance's appearance and inquired, "Babe, what happened to you?"

His left eye was nearly sealed shut from the blood and swelling. She could tell by the frantic look on his face that something terrible had happened. She allowed him to lean on her shoulder as she almost dragged him to one of the chairs in the kitchen. Sarah ran to the linen closet, grabbed a washcloth, and made a cold compressed to help reduce the swelling.

Terrance attempted to catch his breath long enough to answer her, "Those thugs tried to kill me! I could've been burned to death, but I was lucky that my car didn't blow up," he said.

"Oh, my God! Terrance why did you go down there? You should've called the police."

"Damn-it, Sarah! How was I supposed to do that? A better question would be why in the hell would I? You have no idea what Black men in this country go through when dealing with the cops. You've been listening to the damn news all week, and you mean to tell me that as long as we've been together you still can't see the forest for the trees. It ain't easy for a Black man in dem streets since the cops can shoot us down in cold blood without consequences! Your naïve bullshit is driving a wedge in our relationship, and I'm tired of putting up with it."

"Terrance baby, I've tried really hard to understand what you've gone through, but you don't make things easy by lashing out at me."

"I'm always breaking things down for you? The truth is — I've changed. I don't feel the same way about you, and I refuse to keep dealing with this shit."

"Honey, you can't mean that. I've really tried to be here for you, but you won't let me. What else am I supposed to do to show you that I love you and that I understand there is racism?"

"Bullshit! You only care about what's best for 'Poor Little Sarah'. I wish you had my back like you say you do. You and this city have become a nuisance. I'm out! I'll be moving back to Pittsford with my family where I belong."

What seemed to be a thousand tears ran down Sarah's face, and Terrance wasn't sympathetic toward her. In that moment, he realized that he had reached the crossroads and that she was no longer the woman for him. He desperately wanted to talk to Keisha, knowing that she was worried about him since the news being reported had gone viral. Keisha was the only person he trusted and who understood him. As teenagers, they were inseparable; nothing could change that. Keisha had always vowed to have his back no matter the circumstances, and they didn't allow the distance between them to destroy their bond. Terrance was proud of her and the way her ministry had evolved. She had always encouraged him to come home to help in the family ministry, and believed that he had stayed away too long. Terrance needed his family just as much as they needed him.

There wasn't a morning that went by that Keisha didn't fall down on her knees to thank the Lord for her answered prayers. She prayed a similar prayer for their half-sister Jada who had agreed to move to Pittsford from Dallas after the death of their father. Keisha believed that her world would be perfect if only she could convince Terrance also.

Terrance was the rebel of the family and the one who went against the grain. He wanted no part of his father's ministry and thought that following in the Reverend's footsteps was out of the question. However, the Reverend relied on his faith, believing that both of his sons would eventually carry out his legacy. David, their older brother, was well on his way to matching the Reverend's ability to pack the church on any given Sunday because of his masterful preaching. He and Keisha were now co-ministers. In Terrance's opinion, there were other platforms available to him to use his gifts to minister to the youth. Keisha recalled how combative Terrance would become whenever she mentioned the family ministry. The Holy Spirit convinced her that today was the day for a miracle, and she needed to contact Terrance. "Hey, Terrance, how are you? I've been listening to the news, and things are really crazy out there. I've been glued to the television and must admit that I'm concerned about my baby brother, so I'm calling to check on you and to ask for a favor, but you gotta hear me out?"

"What is it, sis? You know I'll always listen."

*Well, here goes,* she thought to herself before sharing, "Jada decided to move home, and... well... I was hoping that you'd consider moving back too? I really miss you, and, to be honest, we could use your help. I've tried really hard to play down my concerns about you to Mom and David. When they ask me if I've heard from you, I tell them that you're fine. What do you think?"

There was a long pause before Terrance answered. Her suggestion forced him to consider everything his family had gone through along with his current situation in Albuquerque. It hadn't been that long ago that the Reverend passed away and Keisha had been involved in a near fatal accident. Family had always been important to him. His relationship with Sarah hitting the rocks had forced him to make changes, and suddenly the thought of moving back home wasn't such a bad idea.

Keisha wasn't sure if she'd heard him correctly when he responded, "Why not?" so she asked him to repeat himself before she screamed, "Oh, my God!"

Her cell phone fell, as her hands trembled from hearing the good news, and she quickly bent down to pick it up.

"Terrance. I love you so much. I'm thrilled that you're ready to come home. I've prayed and dreamt about the day the four of us would be together. Mom is going to be so happy. We love you so much."

"Well, sis, to tell you the truth, I've been considering coming home for some time, especially after your accident. The thought of losing you scared me to death. If something else were to happen to you, I wouldn't forgive myself. Besides, I'm not in love with Sarah anymore. Take a breath; I know that's a shocker. She's become a pain in my ass. She can't identify with my issues as a Black man. I had to plead with her to come to Pittsford when you were in a coma, but she refused to go, claiming that her work was more important than me having a family crisis. She nags me every time I want to go out with my homeboys and criticizes the work I do with the youth, saying it's worthless. I want a woman who's down for me no matter what, and Sarah's not it. Her time is *UP!*"

"Wow! It's a good thing you didn't marry her. No worries, Terrance. I'm sure you'll find someone who'll appreciate you once you settle in back home."

"Sis, I'm open for love but not right now. My main focus will be the ministry and the youth. That's what motivates me and brings me joy."

Keisha listened as Terrance shared his dissatisfaction about life in Albuquerque, and she thanked God for urging her to call him. With their pressing conversation out of the way, she decided to take a much-needed nap, as worrying about Terrance had caused her to become fatigued.

She slept for what seemed like hours but was awakened by the smell of her mother's pot roast, a smell that everyone in the family had come to know. Victoria's pot roast was delicious. David had convinced her to prepare it, thinking it was the perfect way to celebrate Jada's decision to move home. Keisha took a quick shower, before putting on a pair of jeans and her favorite novel T-shirt. She hurried into the kitchen to keep her mother company while she put the finishing touches on dinner. When she walked in, she noticed that Jada had beaten her to the punch and was already in the kitchen with Victoria, engaged in what seemed to be a private conversation.

Jada stopped abruptly in her discomfort and changed the subject, "Keisha, it's about time you woke up," she joked.

"How was your nap? You were snoring so loud that we almost needed to put in earplugs," Victoria told her.

"Refreshing! Ha-ha... sorry that you had to put up with my snoring, but I slept like a baby. It's been a long time since I've been able to do that ever since Dad died. I struggle with sleep because I want the best for our family and for Dad to be proud of me, so my mind is always racing."

"Mine too, Keisha, and I was just telling Mom that. I'm so grateful that you push me out of my comfort zone and for the love and support you all have given me."

"Oh, I'm so proud of both of you both. Keisha, your father has always been proud of you, so there is no reason for you to be restless. Jada, this has always been your home, and we couldn't be happier that you are here," Victoria reminded them.

Victoria excused herself to tend to her roast. By then its delicious aroma had filled the air. She added potatoes, green beans, carrots, onions, and her secret spices, into the large roasting pan before preparing her famous macaroni and cheese, asparagus, and homemade dinner rolls. Earlier that afternoon, she had placed an order for an oversized apple cobbler from the families' favorite bakery. Patti's Bakery was their *"Go to"* place for pies, cakes, cookies, and other delicious desert items. Victoria swore that the owner was one of the best bakers in the city.

With everything nearly finished, Victoria left the kitchen to change her clothes. Her closet was packed with lovely clothes, and she knew how to put herself together, especially on Sundays. Being a versatile woman, she also loved to cook for her large family and for her friends who always invited themselves over to dinner. Keisha and Jada monitored the food in their mother's absence. Victoria returned wearing a beautiful flowing blouse with a floral print paired with black slacks and a pair of Tori Burch sandals.

While waiting for the rest of the family to arrive, Keisha decided to call her girlfriends Natalia and Megan to invite them to dinner too. They had become fixtures at the Williams dinner table and whenever invited they jumped at the chance to be included.

Keisha called Megan first to invite her, "Megan, what's going on? I was hoping that you had some free time to join us for dinner," Keisha said.

"Tell me your mom is cooking her scrumptious mac and cheese and I'll be there," Megan replied.

"Girl, I wouldn't be calling if she wasn't! Everyone knows how much you love it," Keisha joked.

Keisha hung up to call Natalia who surprisingly answered on the first ring, "I already knew why you were calling since it's Sunday in the Williams house and time to eat dinner, so I'll be right over," and Keisha signaled to Jada to add a few extra table settings to their large dining room table. Victoria insisted that they use her best china since she deemed this dinner to be a special occasion. Jada put a few extra bottles of Moscato in the refrigerator, knowing how much her family loved wine. When the doorbell rang, Keisha ran to answer the door. It was Natalia and her sons Juan and Marco.

Natalia said, "Keisha I'm glad you called. We were sitting around watching college basketball and had just declared how hungry we were. I hope you'll excuse my rudeness for not mentioning that I was bringing my boys, as you know they love Victoria's cooking too."

"Of course it's okay! Mom always cooks plenty of food, and besides, I wouldn't turn my godchildren away, and I wanted you guys to share in our celebration of Jada moving to Pittsford for good. You guys are part of this family too, so come in and make yourselves comfortable. Dinner is almost ready," Keisha said.

Before Natalia and her boys could get settled, David and his lovely wife Loretta walked in with Asia and Aleyah, and David announced their presence like he always did, "The Williams clan is here, and we're ready to eat," he said with authority. The girls ran to their grandmother and exchanged pleasantries with her and the rest of the family. Victoria offered them some of her festive fruit punch, as it was her way of setting the mood for the evening before they sat down to devour her delicious meal.

"I'm here," Megan announced as she walked in without knocking. She went into the dining room where everyone was already seated, and David led them in grace, "Father God, in the name of Jesus, we ask that you bless this food we are about to eat. Let it nourish our bodies, and let us affix our hearts and minds on You today and every day. Amen."

David announced as he went back for seconds, "Mom you've outdone yourself again. This pot roast is the bomb!"

"Thank you, son. I know how much you love it."

"Yes, Mrs. Williams, I couldn't wait to get the mac and cheese, and everything else tastes delicious," Megan added.

Victoria blushed while receiving their complements. After dinner, the family congregated in the kitchen as always, especially when the Reverend had been alive. It was their way to celebrate one another and had become a tradition that would live on. The sound of music filled the kitchen along with lots of laughter. Megan shared her memories of their high school days, a time when they had competed against one another for the lead roles in their high school plays. Over the years, whenever she did things that became contentious, the good memories always outweighed the bad.

They ended up singing some of the memorable songs. Before the night was over, David encouraged everyone to bring their individual prayer petitions to the light. He wanted to pray for them, believing that the stress of everyday life might be weighting on their hearts. He had always been the catalyst for the family, encouraging healthy conversations and prayers. Jada didn't hesitate to raise her hand, as she wanted to give a praise report.

"David, I praise God for bringing our family together. My heart is overflowing, and it's a joy to be accepted by all of you. I ask God for His continued favor on our lives. I've been praying about my upcoming book tour and have asked God to show me the right time to ask if my family would accompany me on the first leg of my book tour. I realize that everyone has busy schedules, but it would mean the world to me. I've spoken to my agent who has scaled my book tour down to four cities — New York, Philadelphia, Chicago, and Boston. What do you all think?"

"Girl, you know I will clear my schedule to go anywhere you need me to," Keisha said.

"Just let me know the dates, sis," David chimed in.

"Jada, if it's okay, I'd loved to travel to all four cities. It would be my honor to stand in for your father who was very proud of you," Victoria told her.

Jada was thrilled after hearing how eager they were to support her. It was something she had dreamt about and had always yearned for. David asked them to join hands as he prayed for Jada's success and the family's travels. He paused for a few minutes afterward to ask if anyone else had petitions or praise reports they wanted to share, and to his surprise, Juan raised his hand. He hardly ever spoke when they prayed together.

"It's my mother," he blurted out. "She's worked so hard to turn her life around since the death of my father, but I think there's something missing in her life. It a soul mate! I would like to see her fall in love and get married again," Juan declared.

Natalia was shocked and embarrassed. She'd had no idea that he'd felt that way. Her going on with her life and remarrying was something they'd never discussed. She believed that marrying again was out of the question with teenaged boys to raise. "Son... your embarrassing me! I can't believe you want me to get married again," she said.

"Of course I do, Mom! You deserve a good man, and so does Aunt Megan and my godmother too," he joked.

"Oh snap! Juan is calling you single ladies out. I guess somebody needs to put a ring on it! Y'all ain't getting any younger," David teased.

Everyone burst into laughter, knowing that the Wayward Sisters' biological clocks were running down and that Keisha, Megan, and Natalia could benefit from having a significant other, as none of them were currently in a serious relationship. Considering their brains and beauty, it was questionable why they were still single. It was apparent that a few handsome bachelors were missing out on dating these amazing women who downplayed their interest in being in a serious relationship.

"I don't need a man!" Keisha protested.

"Speak for yourself!" Natalia recanted.

"I know I do!" Megan joked.

"Keisha, do you remember when you were in college and all you talked about was the beautiful Vera Wang's wedding dress you would wear before turning forty?" Victoria asked.

"Yes, Mom! Can't a girl dream?" Keisha snapped.

David brought the conversation back to order and started to pray again. He prayed for God's grace and for husbands for Natalia, Megan, and Keisha. There was a feeling of love in the air as they embraced one another. Victoria suggested that they partake in the scrumptious apple cobbler she had brought earlier. She topped it with vanilla bean ice cream and it was delicious! They ate the entire cobbler. Megan and Jada helped to clean the kitchen while talking about the things they had in common. Keisha pulled David aside to tell him about the conversation she had earlier with Terrance. She told him that Terrance planned to relocate to Pittsford. David wanted to tell their mother the good news but decided to wait. Terrance vowed never to come back because he believed that the Reverend had choked the life out of his dreams. He believed that his father had hated him, so he went out into the world to prove that he could live his life on his own terms without his family. Keisha and David were happy that life experience had the power to mature people, and it was evident that Terrance had changed.

"Guess who I finally convinced to return to Pittsford?" Keisha asked.

"Not the kid who swore he'd never live in this city again. You're not talking about my baby brother, Terrance, are you?" David asked.

"Yes, in fact I am. He's moving home in less than a week. Things in Albuquerque aren't going so well. He is finally realizing that Sarah isn't more important than his family. I don't know about you, but I can't wait for him to get here," Keisha said.

"I feel the same way! Terrance belongs here with us," David proclaimed.

David announced that it was getting late and that it was time for his family to go home. Natalia and Megan decided that it was time for them to go too. With the house empty, Keisha and Jada help Victoria tidy up before going to bed.

When Keisha woke up the next morning, she went for a quick jog in Pittsford Park. It was still something she enjoyed doing. She had gotten a lot stronger since going through rehabilitation. Now she was able to take long runs like she did before her terrible accident. Dressed in her favorite jogging attire, she hurried over to the embankment just like the hundred times before and kneeled down to pray. She prayed for her family's goal and for the ministry to evolve. She also prayed that Terrance could be encouraged to help David with the men's ministry. Her last prayer was for him to continue working with the youth in Pittsford and those with mental health issues, something that he was equipped to do with his many years of experience. The church needed someone like him. She and David had worked hard to keep the church's youth program going, since it was something near and dear to the Reverend's heart. He had blessed so many youths in the community, and he and Terrance loved helping the youth, one of their similarities they failed to acknowledge. Having Natalia and Megan onboard was nothing less than a miracle too. Keisha prayed for everyone to do their part to keep the family's historical church relevant, anointed, and packed every Sunday.

Many thoughts ran through Keisha's mind as she jogged through the beautiful park. She thought about how she was going to pull off the spectacular Mother's Day event she'd been planning for her mother. She wanted to honor her since she believed that her mom was nothing less than the perfect mother. Victoria had taken care of them despite the small blemish on her impeccable record for keeping secret for years the fact that the Reverend had fathered an illegitimate daughter. Victoria's sweet, compassionate, and kind nature caused family and friends to do anything for her. The event would be held in the church's Family Life Center, a cozy place where the congregation and community gathered for festive events and delicious catered meals after most services. Keisha couldn't wait to get home, as she wanted to share her ideas with Natalia and Megan and to recruit them to help.

Meanwhile, back in Albuquerque, Terrance was busy packing his belongings and tying up loose ends. He had experienced a few restless nights and decided to be a man by having an adult conversation with Sarah, believing he owed it to her. He wanted to better explain his reason for ending their seven-year relationship and bailing out on her after their explosive argument. He wasn't comfortable having the conversation, knowing how Sarah was if she was still nursing her wounds. She couldn't believe the man she thought she'd spend the rest of her life with was breaking things off for good. They'd shared what she believed was a good relationship that had begun years earlier when they had been college sweethearts. Although their relationship had been complicated over the years, she desperately wanted things to work. She wanted Terrance to take things to the next level by marrying her. However, his plans were different, and she was no longer a part of them.

He vowed to dedicate all of his time and attention to the youth by drumming up support from community leaders with their financial support for tutoring and sports programs once he settled in Pittsford.

Sarah reminded Terrance every chance she got that he was wasting his time pouring into the lives of the worthless youth who she had seen as disrespectful. He considered her assertion to be offensive, and the more she repeated those negative things, the more disconnected he became. He walked into the living room where he found Sarah sitting on the couch and started to speak. However, she interrupted him by mouthing off. Having a civil conversation with her was out of the question.

"You should've listened to me. I told you those punks were going to turn on you one day, but no, you just kept on believing you could save them. Now you have the audacity to leave me after I've stood by your side for all these years, waiting patiently for you to marry me," Sarah mouthed off.

"You don't know what the hell you're talking about. Those 'punks' that you constantly disrespect have the right to receive the same opportunities as their White counterparts. You're so full of shit and you act like it don't stink. That's why I'm not marrying your ass," Terrance asserted.

"I can't wait until your sorry ass comes begging for my forgiveness, because by then I will have already given all this goodness to one of your homeboys!" Sarah bragged.

"Screw you, Sarah!" Terrance replied.

"I hope you plan on taking care of the remainder of the lease. You do realize that we will lose our security deposit, don't you? But go ahead; act like a jerk and run back to your snooty family. Just so you know, I already have a side dude who's giving me what I need," Sarah said.

Terrance ignored Sarah, which caused her to become even more irritated. She jumped off the couch, ran to the front door, and slammed it. Terrance was proud of himself for finally telling Sarah the truth. It felt good to put her in her place, which was something he should have done years ago. He grabbed a cold beer out of the refrigerator, turned on the stereo, and began celebrating his breakup. He planned to walk out of Sarah's life just as fast as he walked in it, taking his happiness back. Their failed relationship was conformation that leaving Albuquerque was a good decision. He had some loose strings that he needed to take care of, like putting in his resignation at the Community Center. Being a respected member of the community and being known for overseeing one of the finest mentoring programs in the city made his leaving bittersweet, but he knew that there was equally meaningful work waiting for him back home.

Terrance took care of his unfinished business before purchasing a one-way ticket to Rochester, New York. He called Keisha to let her know that he would arrive on time and to let her know that he already had a ride.

Terrance boarded the plane for the three-hour flight. He purposely chose a window seat so that he could get a last glimpse of the city he loved as they departed. A woman with a crying baby was seated next to him. He usually welcomed his seat mate, but this time he felt a little stressed and wasn't in the mood to chat or try to help console a crying baby. He buckled his seat belt and closed his eyes for a nap for the duration of the entire flight and woke up to the voice of pilot's welcoming them to Rochester. Terrance grabbed his overhead bag and exited the plane quickly. It felt good to be back on East Coast soil. He couldn't wait to get his hands on a slice of New York Cheese Pizza at one of the concession booths in the airport. The taste always put a smile on his face and reminded him of home. He followed the crowd to the ground level to claim the rest of his luggage. He had a renewed sense of belonging after being greeted by his favorite cousin Lamar who volunteered to drive him to Pittsford.

Lamar had parked illegally to wait for Terrance to come out to the arrival area. As they put his luggage in the trunk, they were approached and rushed by airport security who reported that a ticket would be issued if they didn't leave within minutes. *Welcome to New York* Terrance thought to himself.

Lamar was happy to see him and relished the fact that he was back home to stay. They had always enjoyed the other's company and were close.

"Hey, man, I finally made it back to the place I swore I'd never return to," Terrance said.

"Terrance, man, you know you belong here with us. It's good to see you," Lamar gloated.

"I know, this time I plan to stay! I've have missed you guys," Terrance told him.

Terrance and Lamar had grown up together and planned on picking up where they had left off. On the drive to Pittsford, Terrance talked Lamar's ears off about Sarah and all the other stress he'd been under while in Albuquerque. Lamar knew that Terrance was a simple man who didn't entertain a lot of drama, so he wasn't surprised by Terrance's long rant. Terrance talked about everything under the sun, from his childhood to what he wanted for Christmas.

Lamar was exhausted by the time he pulled into the Williams driveway. However, he noticed that Terrance seemed sad and was experiencing some mixed emotions, with most of them stemming from unpleasant childhood memories.

Terrance vowed to push through his feelings as he grabbed his luggage from the trunk and thanked Lamar for picking him up. He walked into his family's beautiful home.

"Home sweet home," he said under his breath as he walked through the front door. He nearly pushed his mother Victoria out of the way when she leaned in to give him a loving hug. However, she understood that he probably needed a few minutes to compose himself before engaging with her and the rest of his family.

When Terrance walked into his bedroom, a stream of tears rolled down his face. He closed the door to avoid anyone seeing him in such an emotional state. There was a sense of masculinity oozing from the walls of his bedroom that hadn't been disturbed for many years. His room had remained exactly the way he'd left it. Although he had been home twice since high school, once to attend his father's funeral and the other time to support Keisha after her near fatal accident, he hadn't been able to muster the courage to go inside and instead had slept at Lamar's house. He had assumed Victoria and the

Reverend would've remodeled his room by now since he was so adamant about never returning. However, a sense of peace was now his to claim, knowing that they would always love him despite his defiance. Standing there alone and vulnerable, he could feel his father's presence. He thought about how silly it was for him to have thought that moving so far from his father held the answers to the disdain he felt for him, but he had been wrong and had to ask God for forgiveness. Embracing Pittsford and the opportunities it would bring was going to be an honor and a challenge that he was ready for.

# Chapter 2

# Wayward Opportunities

## (Jada's Good Fortune)

Jada's move to Pittsford caused her to experience a renewed feeling of purpose and confidence. She was feeling on top of the world, and so far, things were perfect. She couldn't believe how supportive her siblings were, and to top it off, her new book, *My Unforeseeable Future: From The Eyes Of A Child,* was quickly climbing the charts to become a New York bestseller. Her relationship with her sweet stepmother Victoria had proved to be a lot better than she had imagined. Prior to meeting her Pittsford family, there was a big hole in her heart that only God could fill. Feelings of depression and anxiety were beginning to dissipate and were being replaced with by love and security.

It didn't take Jada long to value many of the same things that were important to her siblings, such as jogging in Pittsford Park and providing ministry to anyone who needed it in the city. After a good night's sleep and a feeling of refreshment, she jumped out of bed and took a hot shower before getting ready for a morning jog. However, there was an unusual nagging feeling in her gut that she couldn't describe way deep down in the pit of her belly. She felt an urgency to get to Pittsford Park in a hurry but wanted Keisha to tag along, knowing that she was the perfect person to help ease her mind. She knocked on Keisha's door, even though she didn't think she was home. Keisha always rose at the crack of dawn to get her day started and was definitely a morning person. There weren't too many mornings that she missed her morning jog. Jada was caught off guard when Keisha actually opened her door but didn't waste time asking her to join her for a jog.

"Hey, Keisha!" Jada said enthusiastically. "I was hoping that you had some available time to go with me for a jog in Pittsford Park. I've been uptight lately and need to get rid of some nervous energy. I don't think it's a good idea for me to be alone. My head feels like it's going to explode," Jada reported.

"Wow, girl, you're really on edge! I got my jog in early this morning. I also had an encounter with the Holy Spirit that stopped me dead in my tracks. I even cut my run short to rush back to my office to download the word I had received. Girl, I can't even begin to explain everything I received, but the Lord revealed some great things. Oh, by the way, I've been meaning to sit down with you to explore how we can benefit from your gifts in our ministry. You bring so much to the table. I believe that you will be an inspiration to women all over the world, because it's fresh perspectives like yours that help women stay motivated and get them fired up," Keisha said.

"Sis, you're right about that! I've learned that it's best to share your plight with others, especially if you do it for the right reasons. Most women benefit when they are willing to be transparent. Testimonies are what helps us to live our best lives," Jada said.

"Jada, you're wiser than most people your age! I've got to head back over to my office. I have no doubt that God will protect you. Perhaps you'll have a spiritual experience too, so be sure to keep your heart and mind open and let God reveal His plan," Keisha reminded her.

"Believe me; I can use all the help I can get from the Lord right now!" Jada admitted.

"Give me a hug, sis. We can talk later," Keisha told her.

Jada walked into the kitchen to grab a bottled water. As she stood in front of the refrigerator, she suddenly had a fantastic idea, "Breakfast in bed!" she blurted out. She considered how nice it would be to serve Victoria breakfast in bed with a hot cup of her favorite herbal tea, a banana, along with a blueberry muffin. She poured some hot water into the kettle and placed it on the stove to allow it to boil for a few minutes. The steamy water brought out the best aroma from the herbal tea bag that she placed firmly in the bottom of the crystal teacup. She added a teaspoon of sugar, knowing that Victoria liked it that way. She then took a blueberry muffin out of the breadbox to spread some cream cheese on it before arranging the items beautifully on the breakfast tray. She carried the tray to Victoria's bedroom, and to her surprise Victoria opened the door before she could knock. She looked beautiful without make-up and began smiling from ear to ear once she realized that the lovely tray with the breakfast items were for her.

"Jada, what have I done to deserve this?" Victoria asked.

"Mom, you're being here for me is enough," Jada told her.

"Honey, I have prayed for years that you'd feel comfortable enough to call me Mom. I have always been here for you and appreciate you making me breakfast," Victoria said.

Jada gave Victoria a loving hug and kissed her on the check. "You're welcome! I wanted to do something nice for you since you work so hard to take care of everybody else," Jada said.

She excused herself to head over to Pittsford Park. Jogging there was a ritual for the Wayward Sisters and brought solace to them. It was the place that had carried them through some of the most difficult times of their lives. However, the best benefit was the beautiful bond they had established with one another. Pittsford Park was their place of reckoning whether they visit together or alone. Back in high school, Keisha had always bragged about her encounters with the Holy Spirit. It was a vital part of her spiritual journey. Lately, Jada was experiencing much of the same, but she was also still consumed with worry. Now at the embankment, she took a few minutes to stretch before jogging the familiar route that Keisha had taught her. As she jogged, she envisioned herself doing great things in her family's ministry. She prayed that God would give her the strength to make it through her book tour. Her life had drastically changed, and she credited prayer for that.

Jada continued to run at a steady pace, and then all of the sudden the clouds opened up to a beautiful skyline. She looked up in amazement and heard a familiar voice, "Daughter, welcome home." It was the voice of the Holy Spirit, and His words resonated with her and penetrate her heart. She had seen herself receiving accolades for her current and future books, and she couldn't get home fast enough to share her experience with Keisha. For that reason and many more, she vowed that Pittsford Park would forever be her spiritual oasis.

As Jada drove home, she couldn't help but to reflect on God's words, and she couldn't stop smiling. It was great to get a confirmation, letting her know that she was exactly where she needed to be, but it didn't negate the fact that she remained consumed with fear about what was nagging her spirit. After she pulled into the driveway, she raced through the front door and didn't bother to shower or even change her clothes. She peeked her head into Keisha's office, and there she sat.

"Keisha!" she yelled. "OMG! You were right! Today I received a word from God because I remained open to hearing His voice. He told me the very thing that I needed to hear, and it was so surreal! I ran the familiar route that you taught me, and as I rounded the corner near the embankment, I felt a warm sensation that consumed my entire body in every area with vigor. Then I heard, 'You're home, daughter.' You don't know how important that breakthrough was for me, and to your question earlier, I've been thinking a lot about our family's ministry. I'm willing to do everything in my power to help, but I need your help with something first. I can't concentrate because I'm consumed with emotions about what's bothering me. I have some unfinished business in Dallas. I left my grandma, Ms. Emma Jean, to come out here with y'all, and I owe it to her to tell the truth about my intentions. She's been the only person I've had in my life that I could depend on. She's taken care of me the best she could. I love my crazy grandma, and I don't mean to sound disrespectful. It's just that she has a way of making me feel really bad whenever I don't do what she wants me to. She'll probably be furious when I tell her that I'm choosing my father's family over her. Do you have any advice?" Jada asked.

"Jada, first let me say that I'm so happy that you had an intimate experience with the Holy Spirit in the park today. Sis, we would never ask you to do something that makes you feel uncomfortable, and I thank you for trusting me enough to come for advice. I wish I had known that this decision was causing you so much heartache. We want you to be happy and to feel supported. However, I really think you're underestimating your grandma. I'm sure she's been preparing herself for this news for a long time. I'm even willing to bet that she'll say that she understands and gives you her blessing without a fight. Do you need me to fly back to Dallas with you so that you can tell her in person?" Keisha asked her.

"No, not exactly! Did you already forget about my book tour? We'll be leaving soon, and I don't have time to fly back to Dallas to deal with her, but I've contacted my roommate to take care of the issues with our apartment. I'm so grateful that she was able to find a person to take over my part of the lease. I've dreaded calling my grandma because she'll probably go off on me. She has a sharp tongue, and you'll hear about it if you make her mad," Jada said.

"You're going to have to ask the Lord to help you find the right words. You could always let her know that she is welcome to come out here for a visit. I would love to meet the woman who took care of my little sister all of these years. Call her right now. I've got your back," Keisha advised.

Keisha could tell that Jada was nervous, but she also understood how important it was to make the call to get closure. She wanted to support Jada the best she could by suggesting that they pray first. Afterward, Jada felt confident enough to make the call. She removed her cell phone from her pocket and dialed her grandma's number. Ms. Emma Jean always took a long time to answer her phone, allowing it to ring five or six rings. She still had a house phone and was usually in the back room sewing or reading trashy romance novels.

"Hello, Grandma. This is Jada," Jada said.

"Jada, I was wondering when you were going to call me. You know better than to let me worry. I didn't want to brother you and figured you must be having a good time. Is everything alright?" Ms. Emma Jean asked.

"Yes, Grandma. I'm okay. I've been meaning to call, and your right; I've been having so much fun with my siblings and Victoria. They've been so supportive and loving! They have encouraged me to stay in Pittsford, and to be honest, it's what I want to do," Jada said as her voice began to tremble. To ease the tension between them, she quickly changed the subject. "Oh yeah, Grandma, I almost forget to tell you about my sister Keisha's ministry. She's an amazing woman and is so powerful. She reminds me of our father when I used to listen to his sermon tapes that he sent me. Their church is packed every Sunday, and I'll bet there's at least a thousand members who eagerly sit in the pews to hear her and David speak. She wants me to join the ministry team, but I would like your blessing first before I give her an answer," Jada reported.

"Jada, I knew the day you left Dallas that you wouldn't be back. The Williams seem like good people, and I'm grateful that you are forming a bond with each one of them. Honey, don't you worry about me. I'm not angry. I'm happy for you. I just wish you had called me a lot sooner. I wasn't sitting here trying to guess what you were doing, and I can't blame you for wanting to be with them. Besides, I will come up there to check on you whenever I get the notion, right?" Ms. Emma Jean said.

"Yes, Grandma. Keisha told me to make sure I let you know that you have an open invitation. Thank you so much for understanding. I promise to have you come visit soon. Grandma, I love you so much," Jada told her.

"I love you too, baby, so you go ahead and be with your family. I'll be fine. Make sure you keep in touch. I'm so proud of the young lady you're becoming," Ms. Emma Jean said.

Jada was relieved that she had faced her fears by telling her grandma about her plans to remain in Pittsford. It made her happy that her news had been accepted without any drama. She didn't know what she would have done if the conversation had gone badly. Keisha reached for Jada's hands to pray for new beginnings and for her grandma to have peace. After they prayed, Keisha changed the subject by asking Jada for more details about her book tour?

"My agent sent me a text this morning to confirm the cities on my book tour. The first stop is in Manhattan at a posh café. I've never been to the Big Apple, but I'm excited to see the place that everyone loves. You lived there too, right?" Jada inquired.

"Yes, New York is my happy place. I went to college at New York University, so I'll be able to show you around. I absolutely love it! I think you'll love it too. When I lived there, I didn't get the opportunity to show Mom around or to take her to all my favorite places, but we will enjoy our time in the city, and I'm sure everybody will clear their schedules to go," Keisha said.

"To have my family with me as I kick off my book tour in any city is a miracle. I can't wait to experience New York as a family and do some sightseeing. This is a dream come true," Jada declared.

Jada excused herself to share her good news with Victoria. She yelled out when she entered the house, "Mom, where are you?" Jada called.

"What's going on, Jada? You look like an elementary school girl running from a bully on the playground," Victoria said.

"I'm just excited; that's all," Jada said as she attempted to catch her breath. "Can you believe that New York will be the first city on my book tour? We're leaving in a few days, and I hope everyone can come," Jada reported.

"I can't think of anything else I'd rather do," Victoria admitted.

Jada's emotions were all over the place, and she ran over to the church to talk to David. She loved the fact that the family's home was adjacent to the church, making it easier for them to interact with everyone throughout the day. Jada heard David talking when she approached his office, but she couldn't tell who he was talking to.

She yelled to get his attention, "Hey, big brother, are you in there?"

David stepped out of his office with Terrance close behind, wanting to see what all the commotion was about, but before they could ask, Jada blurted out her good news, "My book tour is confirmed, and we're going to New York first. Keisha suggested that we make it a mini-family vacation," Jada gleamed.

"Sis, I told you to name the date, time, and place and that me and my family will be there," David reminded her.

"Me too," Terrance said.

With her siblings and stepmother on board, Jada called her agent to confirm that she had received her text message and had gone over her itinerary. Things were going smoothly, but she couldn't stop thinking about the upcoming church service on Sunday. It would be the first time the entire family would attend a church service together minus the Reverend. Keisha and David were already feeding the congregation with uplifting sermons just as their father had been famous for. Keisha's brief brush with death hadn't stopped the church's momentum, and everyone expected Terrance to do great things with the youth ministry now that he was home.

Jada recalled her earlier conversation with Keisha and was considering specific things that she could do to help out. After her conversation with her brothers, she and Keisha walked back to the house and continued to chat about how she would help bolster the ministry. Keisha put on a pot of hot water for tea, figuring that their conversation could last for hours.

"So, Keisha, tell me what are your ideas for me? I'm dying hear your thoughts," Jada told her.

"Well, I was wondering how you felt about using your book as a platform to reach women in our church and all over the world. Our outreach ministry has grown so fast, and you could make a direct impact. I know you derive a lot of income from your book sales, but what would you say if I told you that your book has the potential to generate additional income streams? We could build some messaging around molestation to help reach young girls. There are a few women in our church who have been molested, and I believe, as a church, that we are responsible for doing everything we can to provide the tools necessary to address the trauma that women face. Sis, you have what it takes to resonate with them. They need to hear how you've overcome obstacles, if you're willing to share. I'd like to help kick off your book tour by having you deliver an inspirational message to our congregation tomorrow. I know it's a last minute request, but since we will not be here all week, I think it's fitting to get you pumped up. Does that sound like something you'd be interested in doing?" Keisha inquired.

"Keisha, I don't know what to say. Dad never believed that women had a place behind his pulpit, and you have fought really hard to prove yourself to him and to be taken seriously. I appreciate your passing on the baton, but I haven't earned that privilege. I wouldn't want to take away any time from your message. You and David are amazing! You've proved Dad wrong, and the congregation always looks forward to hearing you. They truly love you, sis," Jada told her.

"Jada, I won't disagree with you about that!" Keisha joked. "I make sure that every time I step behind the pulpit my messages edifies God's people, but you're no different than me; ministry is in our blood. Dad passed the gift on to the both of us. I want you to be a vital part of our family's ministry, and that means I can't be selfish. I have to share the spotlight. You have your own passion and can provide the congregation with something that David, nor I, can. This is why I'm willing to support you, little sister. What are you going to do with the opportunity?" Keisha challenged her.

"Okay, you've convinced me. I'll do it! I already have the perfect message prepared, but I better start practicing if I want to be effective. I promise I will not let you down, sis," Jada told her.

When Jada walked into her bedroom, her mind was filled with thoughts. She considered everything she had gone through over the years and how badly she wanted to make a difference in other people's lives. It took a long time for her to heal after being violated as a child, but she learned to surrender it all to God The Way Maker who made a path for her to live beyond her worst experiences.

"That's it!" she realized, "My message will be entitled, 'Truth in Awareness.'"

She pulled out her laptop and began typing some bullet points to help her to stay on message. She realized that she had a positive message that she wanted to share with the world.

Sunday mornings were always peaceful in the Williams household, but this Sunday morning was different. There were private conversations with the Holy Spirit, and challenges getting in the shower. However, once everyone was dressed, a feeling of peace came over them. They gathered in the kitchen to pray for one another before walking over to the church. David began the service with a riveting message, followed by Keisha who delivered a message about second chances, and finally Jada took the pulpit. Jada was nervous since she hadn't spoken to the congregation since Keisha's accident, but she realized that she needed to bring it. Jada began her sermon by sharing that she had been molested as a young girl and how that traumatic event had changed her perspective. She told them that she grew up a lot faster than most girls her age and explained how she never blamed her mother for not protecting her but did hold her accountable for neglecting her. She stressed the importance of being aware of their surroundings, their thoughts, and the people they allowed in their lives. The congregation listened intently to Jada and hung on her every word.

"When I was a young girl, my mother took a lot of risks, not only with her own life but with mine as well. The molestation I experienced at the age of eight forced me to learn a lot about myself. But, let's be clear that it was something a young girl shouldn't have had to deal with. As a teenager, I acted out sexually in the darkness of my own space, not knowing that my actions were a direct result of the decisions that a perverted man had made for me. I wondered what had caused my fingers to explore my private parts until I would bleed. My mind hated my actions, but my body needed them to feel normal. Then came one too many sexual encounters with boys who weren't worthy of my attention or my body. I snuck them into our home whenever my grandma had too much to drink. Through extensive therapy, I've learned that I can control my thoughts, feelings, emotions, and actions. This helped me to discover who I want to be in my life. We must take ownership of our actions and be accountable to ourselves. God has placed a strong desire in my heart to advocate against sexual violence and to teach other women and girls who have been molested that it isn't the fault of the victim. God will never, never, never, ever leave or forsake you. You must learn to forgive others, remembering that it's not our job to fix them, but it is our job to have awareness of who we are. People are broken and need God just like I do! It takes faith in knowing that you will be okay. If I'm speaking to you, I encourage you to let go and let God heal your heart. You must act today," Jada preached.

Jada's powerful message caused everyone in the entire congregation to jump to their feet with a thunderous applause. After church, everyone headed to the Family Life Center to enjoy a delicious catered meal. Several of the young women approached Jada to tell her how much her message resonated with them and to inquire where they could purchase her book. She felt encouraged, knowing that God was using her again in such a mighty way. Megan lined up too and waited patiently for her turn to talk to Jada.

"Jada, thank you so much for your courage. I know firsthand how difficult it is to relive the abuse you experienced. Keisha encouraged me to share my experiences with you. She says we have a lot in common. I was almost molested as a young girl. If it weren't for my little sister calling me, my mother's boyfriend would have raped me. What's worse is that my mother didn't even believe me."

Megan took a deep breath before continuing to share, "That ordeal caused me to act out sexually as a teen too. I became the butt of all the jokes in the boy's locker room during high school after having sex with several of them who were unworthy of my attention. Just like you, it took years of therapy for me to accept that it wasn't my fault. Thank you for sharing your story in such a candid way. I'm sure there are many other women in our congregation who live in shame and have stories similar to ours," Megan told her.

"You are more than welcome. I learned early in life to be candid, and writing my book has been the most freeing thing I could've done for myself. Sharing my truth was worth it. I've made it my life's work to help other women like me," Jada said.

"Keisha thinks we should collaborate to development self-help workshops for the men and women in the church. I think we could be effective, and it's a great way to utilize our talents," Megan added.

"Let's get together for lunch to brainstorm sometime soon," Jada suggested.

After spending a few hours at the Family Life Center, the Williams clan returned home. David and Loretta decided against coming over for dinner and cited packing for the trip as a better use of their time since they were heading out to New York in the morning. Keisha, Terrance, Jada, and Victoria spent the evening watching television together before enjoying some quite time in their own space.

Jada was excited about packing, but she needed to limit the amount of clothes she was taking on her trip. Her book tour included television and face-to-face appearances. She combed her closet for casual and dress clothes and picked pieces that would complement each other. She then called her agent to ensure her materials, books, props, and other necessities were ready to go.

The family needed to take two vehicles, since there were mostly women and they had a lot of luggage. David and Terrance complained about the heavy luggage but their complaints fell on deaf ears.

David, Victoria, Loretta, and the girls rode together, while Keisha, Terrance, and Jada rode in the other vehicle for the five-hour car ride to Manhattan. This was their first family vacation, and everyone was excited about supporting Jada. As they descended upon the last leg of their trip, the girls were restless and couldn't wait to get to their hotel. Aleyah and Asia were glued to the windows in the backseats while in awe of the Manhattan skyline. Aleyah wouldn't stop talking and continued to share her knowledge about the big city. She said New York measured up with her expectations. Her Mom and Dad laughed and teased her about how excited she was, and it could be heard in her voice as she kept repeating everything she knew.

"Wow, check out all those tall buildings," Aleyah said in amazement as they crossed the George Washington Bridge to enter Manhattan. She pointed at the tall buildings while describing their differences.

"I'm going to need a neck brace by the time we leave here," Asia joked.

"Me too," Aleyah responded. "My neck is cramping already," she complained.

The family didn't waste time checking in after having their vehicles parked by the valet at the New York Hilton Midtown Hotel. They had a few hours to spare before Jada was to arrive at the posh café to kick off her book tour. She called Amanda to let her know that they had arrived, and then they went to their rooms to rest and to change their clothes. Jada asked David and Loretta if the girls could stay in her room. It was her way of letting her big brother and sister-in-law have a few romantic nights together without their children. Asia and Aleyah were thrilled to hang out with their Aunt Jada, knowing that she was going to spoil them.

Jada and the girls met the family back in the lobby, and Jada looked gorgeous and ready to make her debut. Amanda sent a 'glam' team over to do her hair and make-up. She wore a beige camel coat with long, brown-suede boots. Underneath her coat, she was wearing a tan sweater dress that hugged her body perfectly. She felt confident after receiving their compliments. Victoria gave her a loving hug as they walked the few blocks necessary to get to the café. Once there, Jada introduced her family to Amanda, who quickly changed the subject and pointed out the droves of people who were waiting outside to meet her and get a signature copy of her soon-to-be bestseller.

She took a few family photos before excusing them so she could get to work. Keisha couldn't wait to put on her official tour guide hat and to make some suggestions about how they could spend their time while they waited for Jada. She suggested they go to a museum or to some of her favorite boutiques. Their evening plans included dinner with Jada and seeing a Broadway show afterwards. She heard that Kinky Boots, The Lion King, and Jersey Boys were all excellent choices. Keisha suggested that they secure their tickets early since the show usually sold out for the evening performances. With tickets in hand, Keisha guided them to her old stomping grounds that she frequented back in college, but her suggestion didn't get a rise out of them. She loved those boutiques, and they had fueled her love for fashion back in the day. The majority of them were scattered throughout the different boroughs of the city. They caught the F-Train downtown to SoHo to shop at the Chanel Store.

Keisha loved the jewelry, the flats, and the sexy high heels there. She told her family how she used to kill herself to get there even though she couldn't afford anything. David teased her but realized how hard it must have been not to be able to afford nice things back then. "Sis, you should've stuck with Target," he said jokingly.

"Boy, you know I have always loved me some Target too," she said.

Keisha purchased a few things for herself and for her mother. She made David carry her bags as they walked toward China Town to allow the girls to get some souvenirs. Terrance held Aleyah and Asia's hand as they made their way through the crowded streets, stopping every now and again to look at the merchandise. As they passed the stands, Asia told her Mom that she wanted this and that and her voice got louder as they passed the stands, but she remained empty handed.

"Mom, I want that backpack and that watch I saw back there," Asia demanded.

"Honey, I told you that we're going to look at everything first before I allow you and your sister to pick out a few things. Remember that we'll be here for a few days, so please slow down, sweetheart," Loretta reminded her.

Asia poked out her lips as she continued to admire all the trinkets.

Later that evening, they caught an Uber to reunite with Jada, who bombarded them with all the details of her eventful day and told them how she had signed at least five hundred copies of her book and had received multiple offers for speaking engagements around the country.

"I've had such an incredible day! New Yorkers are amazing, and I can't believe how they lined up in droves to support me. We sold a ton of books, and several marketing agents invited me to speak at their engagements over the next several months," Jada bragged.

"That's fantastic, sis? You certainly have that Williams blood running through your veins," David said.

"That's right, Jada! I told you that your message would resonate with the world," Keisha chimed in.

Victoria also didn't waste any time showing Jada affection, "I'm so proud of you," she told her as she gave her a tight squeeze.

Keisha said, "Jada, I bet your starving. We can grab a quick bite before heading over to the Al Hirschfeld Theatre to see *Kinky Boots*. If we have enough time afterward, we can shop, and I have plenty of places to show you guys."

"I am starving," Jada admitted, "and I appreciate all of you for supporting me. It makes me so happy!" Keisha took them to the Gotham Bar & Grill because she thought the variety of food options, such as steak, hamburgers, and everything else in-between, was their best bet. Asia and Aleyah order pizza and chicken fingers, while David ordered the biggest steak on the menu. Terrance went for seafood, while Victoria and Loretta ordered Cobb salads. Keisha surprised them by ordering nachos. She rarely ate unhealthy food options because of all the extra calories. David complained after he finished eating by saying that his fullness didn't lend itself to the stamina needed to walk. However, since there was still time before the show, Keisha suggested that they walk around the corner to her favorite boutique where the owner carried beautiful designer dresses for children. Keisha thought her nieces deserved new clothes, with all the upcoming family functions that were planned. Loretta's face lit up when she walked inside the boutique, as she loved all the beautiful pink and lace dresses for the girls to try on.

"Sis, you owe me one," David warned after watching his wife filling her basket with dresses. He could tell that they were expensive and knew he would have to carry more bags around the city afterwards.

"Yes, I know," Keisha giggled. "I expected you to complain about the prices, but you better start pulling out them credit cards," Keisha teased.

Victoria chimed in, "Don't worry, son. I'll pay half for the dresses for my sweet granddaughters."

"No, thank you, Victoria. We'll buy them. I set aside a budget for this trip, and that's why I told Asia earlier to be patient. The girls already knew they were getting new clothes," Loretta told them.

Terrance and David were relieved that they made it out of the store in one piece. Terrance helped David by telling them he needed to make a pit stop at the hotel to use the restroom. Surprisingly, he wasn't by himself, as the heaviness of their meals was getting the best of the girls too.

They told their mom they needed to use the restroom, and they walked as fast could to the hotel, skipping more opportunities to sightsee. Once at the hotel, they took a few minutes to freshen up before calling an Uber, requesting a large van to take them to the theater.

The show *Kinky Boots* was amazing. Jada and Keisha love it and couldn't stop raving about how good it was. They left the theater with smiles on their faces and vowed to see more Broadway shows that were on their list the next time visited NYC.

Over the next few days, the Williams family explored everything New York had to offer. Keisha took them to some of the well-known landmarks like the Statue of Liberty, Central Park, the Empire State Building, Times Square, and Rockefeller Center. By week's end, they were exhausted and ready to go home. Victoria planned to continue on with Jada as promised for the rest of her book tour in Philadelphia, Chicago, and Boston. She believed that each city was going to prove to be intriguing and couldn't wait to make new memories. The family packed up the vehicles and headed off to Pittsford, while Jada and Victoria took an Uber to the airport to catch a plane to Philadelphia.

The flight was on time and very brief. Amanda warned Jada about the possibility of larger crowds at Barnes & Noble in Philly. Her fans didn't disappoint her, as they emptied their wallets to purchase her fascinating book. Jada was amazed at how well her marketing team had done to get the word out. The crowds in the next two cities were also huge as well. Jada sold a lot of books and made a nice little nest egg. By the end of her tour, she was exhausted and ready to go home too.

She learned a lot about herself during the tour and realized that God had blessed her with a gift far more powerful than she could have imagined. However, Jada was conflicted about her career as a public speaker and author. She desired to work with her siblings in their family ministry. She realized that prayer works, and because she has a strong relationship with God, He will continue to direct her footsteps.

Jada and Victoria boarded a plane headed to Rochester, New York. Jada couldn't stop talking about their trip and how proud she was of herself. She and Victoria had plenty of laughs from the numerous quirky moments they had shared with the family in New York. They enjoyed each other's company and shared their feelings about a lot of things, including the Reverend. By the time the plane landed, they were in tears and felt consumed by what God was doing in their lives.

Victoria called David to have him pick them up. When he arrived, they gave him a tight squeeze and were happy to see him. He helped Victoria get in his vehicle before putting their luggage in the trunk. They talked David's ear off while sharing the highlights from the rest of the book tour, and he brought them up to speed on church business. Jada and Victoria were exhausted by the time they arrived home and needed a good night sleep to restore themselves after such a long trip.

# Chapter 3

# Wayward Relationships

## (Megan finds Love)

After returning from New York, Keisha had a difficult time getting caught up on her work. She was bogged down with church business and was working hard to get caught up. It was apparent that Megan missed her and their daily conversations where she had Keisha's undivided attention. There were several messages on Keisha's answering machine that still needed to be listened to, and they were all from Megan. Keisha decided to take a few minutes to listen to some of them. She wanted to find out what was so pressing that couldn't wait. Keisha noticed that each message was a continuation of the other with Megan rambling about her new love interest.

Her behavior was typical, and Keisha wasn't surprised. Megan had always sought her approval, but she believed it was going to be a stretch this time. As Keisha listened to the messages, she rolled her eyes and thought that Megan was repeating past behaviors that had gotten her in trouble. It was easy for her to throw caution to the wind when it came to men. Keisha thought to herself, *I can't leave this girl alone for a minute, and it looks like she done gone and fallen in love!*

In just one week, Megan had managed to be up to her old wayward ways and behaviors, causing Keisha to reflect on their high school days when Megan had pursued male attention that had nearly destroyed her. Keisha hoped history wouldn't repeat itself.

"I need to talk to this girl right away before it's too late," she said as she poured herself a cup of hot tea and waited for it to cool down before calling Megan, who picked up on the first ring.

Keisha started, "Girl, what's up with all these messages? I thought dating was off limits for now! You should be concentrating on your responsibilities at the church. We've got a lot of things on the schedule, and we need you to stay focused," she warned.

"Keisha, calm down! I'm not that same person anymore. Can't a girl share some good news with her best friend? Okay... where do I start? I bumped into the most gorgeous man I've seen in a long time. He's tall, dark, and handsome. Oh, I forget to mention he's a Black man, and you know that's something different for me."

Megan giggled before continuing, "You should see the body on this man. I can tell he works out. His name is Cory, and he came to the church looking for David last week. I told him that David was out of town, but he caught my attention when I heard him speak because his voice was so deep and sexy. He told me that he's a member of our church but that he hadn't been coming since the passing of your dad. He also mentioned that you guys grew up together," Megan told her.

"Girl, take a deep breath before you pass out!" Keisha teased.

"He said he wanted to talk to David about some ideas he has for our church, but of course he couldn't help flirting with me. He asked me out on a date, and of course I said yes. We went out that same night to The Village Coil Restaurant and have been talking every day since. He seems really sweet, but there's something about him that concerns me. He's gone through a nasty divorce and has a teenaged daughter. I wanted to run in the other direction when he mentioned the word teenager. They can be challenging, but I've learned from our teachings not to be judgmental. I'm concerned about his relationship with the Lord too, since it's something important to me. A man who loves the Lord is worth his weight in gold! The funny thing is, when I asked him about his personal relationship with God, he was a little vague. I think he was telling me what he thought I wanted to hear. He sure had a lot to say when he was talking about his job at a local advertising agency. He said that he and his ex-wife have joint custody of his daughter, who he refers to as a disobedient problem child," Megan reported.

Keisha patiently listened to Megan as she took her time to described every detail about her new love interest, although she didn't think the man who she was describing was worth Megan's time. She prayed that she wouldn't get hurt, but she tried hard not to impose her opinion during Megan's long rant.

"Keisha, I'm so happy that God sent Cory to me. He really is a good man, but I'm not going to get ahead of my skis on this one since the jury is still out. He's moving so fast and has already introduced me to his daughter Rhonda. She seems a little distant, but it could be that she's just not ready to share her dad with anyone. She reminds me of myself when I was her age. I think she's going through a dark period, but I don't really know," Megan told her.

"Girl, you need to be careful! You deserve love, but I'm a little concerned about this Cory character. His recent divorce and troubled teen makes me question the chances of him being a keeper. We need to pray about this guy," Keisha advised.

Megan assured her, "I told him that we should take our time to get to know each other."

"Good! If he's a God-fearing man who believes in honoring his woman, he will respect your wishes."

Keisha attempted to change the subject, but Megan only wanted to talk about Cory. Keisha recalled Megan's suicide attempt some years earlier that had resulted in a short stay in the mental ward where she was placed on suicide watch. The last thing she wanted to happen was for Megan to have a relapse. She'd come a long way and had recently completed Seminary School. Dealing with a "Drama queen" or hearing about a man with the wrong intentions was the last thing Keisha needed in her life.

"I can't wait for you to meet Cory. I'm sure you've seen him around the church or perhaps even his mother Sister Alexander," Megan said.

"Sister Alexander? Girl, that's my mom's first cousin. You can't possibly be talking about her son Dubs! He has a teenaged daughter named Rhonda and she's a hot mess. I remember going over my aunt's house when we were little. David and Terrance used to argue with Dubs all the time about who was the better basketball player. They had me laughing until my stomach hurt. Mom is always telling me about her conversations with my aunt, who worries about Rhonda and thinks that one day she'll get a chilling phone call from the authorities telling her that the girl is dead or something. She asks for prayer whenever offered," Keisha told her.

Megan commented, "I've never heard you mention that you have an aunt named Sister Alexander. What a small world!"

Megan took in everything that Keisha had shared. Then, all of a sudden, she burst into laughter while thinking about Cory's nickname, "Little Dubs, huh? I can't wait to tease him," Megan joked.

"Yeah, his real name is actually Derwin Cory Alexander. He was named after his father, but we always called him Dubs for short," Keisha reported.

"Keisha, I promise to take things slow now that I know Cory's backstory and that he's your family member," Megan said.

"God has the power to change things. I'm not going to judge him, but I am cautioning you to please be careful," Keisha replied.

"I know that you have my best interests in mind. No hard feelings, and I promise I'll be okay," Megan said.

Keisha ended their conversation and went back to work on the church business that had piled up. She also needed to put the finishing touches on the Mother's Day celebration. She wanted it to be extra special for her Mom. However, time had gotten away from her as she tried to shake off her exhaustion.

She took a hot shower and put on her comfy pajamas before climbing into bed where she fell asleep as soon as her head hit the pillow.

She was awakened the next morning by the smell of fresh homemade biscuits, a familiar smell from her childhood. The aroma teased her taste buds, and it didn't take her long to realize that Terrance was responsible for the goodness she smelled. While in high school, he would beg their mom to allow him in the kitchen so he could make biscuits and gravy from a recipe that had been passed down to him by Victoria's mother. After a lot of back and forth, he usually got his way. All of that practice made him an excellent baker, and everyone devoured his biscuits within minutes whenever he made them. The Reverend always complained about Terrance eating more than his fair share of them. Keisha laughed to herself at the notion that baking biscuits could cause tension in their family. She didn't prefer the thick gravy he made, and she would rather eat her biscuits drenched in warm apple butter. She hurried into the kitchen to make sure she got at least one of them.

"Morning, Terrance. I hope you saved some of your special biscuits for the rest of us," she joked.

"Of course! I baked a few dozen this time so we can freeze them and have them anytime, sis," Terrance assured her.

Keisha sat down at the kitchen table to go over her busy schedule with Terrance. She told him about her plans for the upcoming Mother's Day celebration and how she believed that their mom deserved a special honor for all the sacrifices she'd made over the years, as Victoria had been nothing less than the perfect mother, wife, and first lady of their church. Terrance agreed and offered to help out before dismissing himself to get ready for a meeting with the Pittsford City Council. He had been invited to talk about starting up a new initiative to help fatherless boys in the city. Terrance believed that he was the right man to lead the project and couldn't wait to share his amazing resume with them.

"Sis, I've got to run. I've been busy putting together a mentoring program for the youth in the city, and I hope to assist as many young men in our community as possible. This is important work to me," Terrance reported.

"I'm so proud of you, Terrance. I knew that your return home was going to be the thing to jump-start your passion. I can't wait to see the fruits of your labor," Keisha told him.

"Thanks, sis. I love you, girl!" Terrance told her.

"I love you more," Keisha replied.

Keisha had a couple of weeks to put things together and decided to get the faithful women of the church to assist her. She could depend on them since they'd helped out with every event that had been held in the Family Life Center. Victoria normally headed things up with her flare for decorating and being the perfect host. It was important to Keisha that she didn't find out about it. She contacted Sister Ernestine first, knowing that she would drop everything to get involved.

"Good morning, Sister Earnestine. I need you to roll up your sleeves once again to help out with this year's Mother's Day program. There is going to be a special tribute for Mom that will be fitting for a queen. She deserves it for being such a strong woman. Are you available to meet me at the Family Life Center this afternoon?" Keisha asked.

"Yes, Keisha. I'd love to help. Me and your mom go way back, and she has always been kind to me. Your mother doesn't know a stranger either," Sister Earnestine reported.

Keisha opened her laptop to pull up an excel spreadsheet with the Victory Baptist 2018 budget. She wanted to know how much money was left in the budget for special occasions. She loved the fact that the congregation celebrated the accomplishments of its members, especially the Pastor and First Lady. She was pleased to discover that the ledger showed a $25,000 balance. Keisha made a list of the items needed: a cake, fresh flowers, ice sculptures, a special guest speaker, and a light lantern team for the lantern celebration. She estimated that the cost would be close to $15,000, but she wasn't concerned about the cost depleting the account since the congregation loved fundraising and would soon replace the monies spent.

"Knock, knock. It's me," Sister Earnestine said as she walked into Keisha's office without really knocking, but she was not the type of person you wanted to challenge for having bad manners. "Keisha, I came as soon as I could, honey. What's so different about this Mother's Day celebration? I know you want to honor your mom, but we always pull out all the stops for her and all the other women. I have some ideas about special touches we can add for our First Lady," Sister Earnestine explained.

"This will be the first year that my mother will have all her children home at the same time, so it's important for me that we honor her the right way. She's been so good to us and the members of this congregation. You're not going to believe what I've come up with. I've hired a team to conduct a lantern celebration. Have you ever seen one? There're simply beautiful! It's a celebration where people come together and are given a personal lantern that is lit at the same time as others as they let go of their burdens by lighting up the skyline. I want everyone to light up the sky in honor of my mom," Keisha said.

"Oh, Keisha, that's such a beautiful idea! It's even more clever than the things I had in mind. What do you need us to do?" Sister Earnestine asked.

"I've put together a list of things that need to be purchased, and I've checked off the ones I've already gotten. We have a few more weeks to make things perfect. You and the ladies can take things over from here. I'll be responsible for the guest speaker and the lanterns. Remember, we can't allow Mom to find out, and she needs to believe that she's in charge," Keisha told her.

Keisha felt accomplished after delegating some of the responsibilities. Over time, she had learned the value of delegation and was happy to give away things to make her life easier. She needed to remain focused on edifying God's people through her partnership with David.

Keisha made a few more calls. She contacted her good friend, Valerie, who she had met a few years earlier, to assist her with securing her guest speaker. She and Valerie had spent time together during her recent trip to Dallas where she met Jada for the first time. Her reason for going there had been two-fold. She had desired to enjoy a leisure trip and explore the sights and sounds of the city while getting to know Jada, and she had wanted to participate in a highly recommended women's conference that she was asked to co-chair. She visited the famous Potter's House where Valerie was a member. Keisha dreamed of going there to hear T. D. Jakes preach in person. All her life, church folk had said that the Reverend's preaching style resembled T. D. Jakes.

Keisha hoped that Valerie's influence with the pastoral staff would allow her to schedule an appointment with Serita Jakes, the wife of Pastor T. D. Jakes, to ask her if she'd be interested in being Keisha's guest speaker. Valerie had served on a lot of committees where she had access to the First Lady. Keisha believed that First Lady Jakes was the perfect speaker. Valerie told Keisha about First Lady Jakes' compelling life story, and she had gone through her fair share of trials and tribulations. Her brother was murdered in front of his daughters, and she was a victim of emotional and physical abuse at the hands of her boyfriend. Her beloved mother died unexpectedly of a cruel disease, and she was crippled in a car accident. Her life was filled with disappointments, such as being teased as a child for being overweight. Her peers spewed words that whittled away at her self-esteem. While in college, she experimented with marijuana, sex, and alcohol. Keisha couldn't think of anyone better to inspire the women on a day that was all about celebrating the lives of women. In her opinion, women make the world go around, and she believed that First Lady Jakes would be able to speak strength and courage to her audience of resilient women.

Keisha was a big fan of women, especially those willing to tell their story with complete transparency. She too had been the underdog who had fought against male chauvinist views and literally had to go to battle with her father to prove that women have a seat at the table. She couldn't wait for the women to hear First Lady Jake's message if she was lucky enough to get her.

"Valerie, how have you been? We're having the ultimate Mother's Day celebration at our church, and I'm pulling out all the stops. I'm calling you because I need a favor, and lucky for me, you're the only one I know that can help," Keisha told her.

"Keisha, things have been great! I'm so blessed. The Lord has used me to deliver over one hundred speaking engagements since you were here. The money hasn't been bad either," Valerie joked.

"I know that's right! Do you still join First Lady Jakes for that monthly luncheon you were telling me about? If so, I'm wondering if you could put in a good word for me on a proposal that I have for her to be our guest speaker. I realized that she would prefer to be at the Potters House, but when she hears the details of what I want to achieve, I'm hoping she'll accept my proposal. I'm willing to pay her the going rate, and she will also receive a love gift. I guarantee that she will have some of the best food she has ever tasted because our women can really cook! They're from all over the world. I want you to come too if your calendar is free," Keisha explained.

"Keisha, I'm sure that you can imagine what a busy schedule First Lady Jakes has, but I understand why you want her to be your guest speaker. She is so impactful to those who hear her story. I won't see her for the next two weeks since she and the Bishop are traveling out of the country. I'm not sure when they'll be back, and I know you need an answer right away. I'll tell you what; I will see their daughter Sarah a few times a week and can run the idea by her. Can you go ahead and send over a high-level overview of your expectations, including compensation and accommodations, and I will see what I can do. Girl, you know I wouldn't do this for anyone else," Valerie said.

"Valerie, this means a lot to me, and I thank you for your willingness to help. I'll talk to you soon," Keisha said.

Keisha jumped for joy after hanging up. She prayed that God would give her favor and that First Lady Jakes would be willing to come. She called the lantern company to secure the five hundred lanterns needed for the event. Then she called Faith and Hope, a sister church located a few blocks away, to see if they would be willing to rent their spacious grassy area adjacent to their church. It was a great space for the women to release their lanterns into the night sky.

Victory Baptist didn't have the acreage necessary to host large outdoor events, so they partnered with Faith and Hope Church whenever possible.

"Pastor McKinney, this is Keisha Williams. We're having an inspirational event on Mother's Day. It's a lantern lighting celebration, and as you know, we don't have the outdoor space. I was wondering if you would be willing to rent the grassy area near your parking lot. It's the perfect size to accommodate all of our women," Keisha told him.

"Keisha, that sounds beautiful! I'm sure our women will be interested in joining you. I'll tell you what; if you are willing to allow our women to come, I won't charge you for the space. We have one hundred or so women who I know would love to participate. Let me know the cost of the lanterns and I will write you a check to purchase theirs," Pastor McKinney told her.

"Pastor McKinney, you have made my day. It pays to have good relationships with our sister churches in the community. It would be an honor to have your women participate. I will send an estimate of the cost for their participation. The plan is to release the lanterns at around 9:00 P.M. We will have our normal church service followed by a Mother's Day brunch. Then we plan to reconvene at your lot around 7:30 P.M. for prayer, song, and a few inspirational words before releasing the lanterns," Keisha explained.

"That sounds great, Keisha. I will be looking forward to receiving your estimate," Pastor McKinney told her.

Keisha thanked the Lord for His goodness and for the beautiful way things were coming together. She included Megan in her prayers too and asked God to look for ways to keep her busy with church business so she didn't have time for Cory. Specifically, she prayed for God to either change Cory's behavior or that He would deliver Rhonda from her wayward ways. It wouldn't hurt either if He decided to close the door by not allowing Megan to date Cory. Either way, Keisha was faithful that there would be a move of God on the things she petitioned.

Keisha decided to take a break, as she wanted to check on Terrance to see how his meeting with the city council had gone. She was encouraged after listening to him finishing up a call and overheard him telling the person on the other end that he could be counted on for bringing a fresh perspective to Pittsford and its youth. When he hung up, Keisha walked into his office to get more details.

"Hey, Terrance, I wasn't trying to eavesdrop, but it sounds like the city council likes what you bring to the table. Give me all the details," Keisha said.

"Keisha, I will forever be grateful to you for encouraging me to move home. Sis, I can't tell you how happy I am. There are some amazing people on the city council, and they're just as passionate about the youth as I am. We talked about mirroring some of the mentoring programs I chaired in Albuquerque. There are a lot of things that can be implemented in Pittsford. What's even better is they offered me a seat on the board along with a salary that I couldn't pass up," Terrance said.

"Terrance, I prayed without ceasing for you to have favor in all areas of your life when you came home. I'm so happy I could cry," Keisha said.

Keisha and Terrance embraced one another and found it difficult to let the other go. Having Terrance home again was a miracle and a confirmation that God is always in control.

# Chapter 4

## *Wayward Encounters*
### (Natalia's Surprise)

*N*atalia found it hard to ignore Juan's words about her getting married again that kept replaying over and over in her head. Deep down inside, she wanted to fall in love someday with someone special. She desired to have a man worthy of her love, since her first marriage to Carlos had ended in divorce. She had lost so much of herself by giving it to others, causing Carlos to suck the life out of her. Years had passed since his horrific murder, and she believed it was time for her to open herself up to the idea of love, although it was hard for her to admit that she was falling for Terrance and that her crush on him was consuming her every thought. However, she didn't want to deal with the fight for Keisha's approval. Lately the two had been spending a lot of time together, causing her to fall for his outgoing personality, confidence, and sexy body. She felt like a cougar since Terrance was younger than her. Nevertheless, she couldn't help fantasizing about being romantically involved with him. She found herself wanting to be wrapped in his muscular arms while lying underneath the sheets every night.

Terrance was attracted to Natalia too. He recalled her spending a lot of time at his house when she was a teenager in high school. She and Keisha had been rivals at first before becoming best friends. They were inseparable, but he didn't play attention to her like his peers and the older jocks did who drooled over her whenever she was in their presence. Terrance found playing basketball to be more interesting. Natalia was considered to be a "Hottie", and she enjoyed flirting with the boys too. They couldn't resist her, since she was, hands down, one of the prettiest girls to ever walk the halls of Pittsford

Sutherland High School. He recalled her getting pregnant shortly after graduation by Carlos, her deadbeat boyfriend, who she later married.

He considered engaging in a romantic relationship with her and started showing up at the church on the nights she had choir rehearsals. It was her angelic voice that people loved, and her ability to lead the choir made people pay attention. He hung around until the end to help her put chairs away, which gave him opportunities to flirt with her. Terrance believed that they had a lot in common, especially a love for children. He considered inviting her to tag along with him to visit a young teen boy who he was mentoring. His name was Leroy, and Terrance had met him in the church after hearing his foster mother's testimony about the struggles she'd had with taking care of him. Her gut-wrenching story of his agonizing home life caused Terrance to volunteer to help out.

Leroy had been molested repeatedly by his older brother and beaten beyond recognition by his mother for stealing a few dollars out of her purse. He ran away from her and was homeless until the system placed him in foster care. His foster mother was a faithful member of Victory Baptist Church. Since hanging out with Terrance, he was thriving in all areas of his life. His grades had improved, and he was a star of his high school basketball team. Terrance vowed to keep him on the right track.

Natalia sensed that Terrance was crushing on her too, but she decided to play coy. She admired his hard work ethic and the special bond he had with the youth in their church. However, more importantly, she was impressed with the relationship he'd started with Juan and Marco. She wanted them to have someone in their life who they could relate to. Juan and Marco enjoyed his company, especially when it came to a game of basketball every now and then. Terrance was in good shape for a man in his mid-thirties and could take the youth to the hoop with ease, embarrassing them. Natalia tried to purposely run into Terrance at the church to play a flirtatious game of cat and mouse with him.

Terrance was infatuated with Natalia and believed she was nothing less than a professional in her role at the church as choir director. Until recently, there hadn't been anyone other than an African-American to lead the choir known for its effectual and excellent singers. Natalia replaced Sister Jo, who had suddenly fell ill and was forced to retire. The choir and congregation loved Natalia because of her ability to keep things fresh and new by adding songs from the most captivating Gospel legends, no matter their nationality. She also had the choir record a couple of CDs, which were loved by Gospel music enthusiasts.

Natalia decided to call Keisha to give her an update on the choir's readiness for the Mother's Day celebration. She also needed her permission to purchase new choir robes and wanted to purchase them from the same company they had used over the years. When Keisha didn't answer, Natalia drove over to the church to talk to her in person, but of course, she had other motives too, like running into Terrance.

When she pulled into the parking lot, she noticed an unfamiliar white minivan parked in front of the church. There were car magnets on the side of the minivan that read 'City of Rochester Juvenile Division'. She wondered who the van belonged to but assumed that Terrance had something to do with it. As she passed the gymnasium, she saw several teenagers practicing basketball drills, and when she heard Terrance's voice, she stepped inside the gym. It was apparent that he had started working with the city and was mentoring the young men. He was too busy to notice her, so she decided to wait until after talking to Keisha to flirt with him.

She walked down to Keisha's office and found her sitting right where she thought she would be. Keisha had to be one of the hardest working people Natalia knew. She was able to multi-task, so Natalia decided to interrupted her to discuss her needs for the choir.

"Keisha, please tell me we have money in the budget for new choir robes. Our robes have seen better days; besides, we've been filling the pews with all of those new members, and a few of them are interested in joining the choir. They've been flocking in to hear you and David preach every Sunday. Oh yeah, and let's not forget that they love to hear the choir known for rocking the neighborhood. I'd like to think that I have something to do with that. We need to look the part while ministering in song to our congregation," Natalia reported.

"You're right about that! I love hearing our choir. How much do you think the robes will cost? I'll need a proposal right away to approve the funds," Keisha said.

"I will get it to you tonight. The members will be so excited. I'll let you get back to work. I know your busy," Natalia told her.

Natalia hurried back down the hall to the gymnasium to see Terrance. She pranced into the gym and could smell the sweat oozing from their skin as they engaged in a scrimmage. She liked the sweaty smell. The young men stopped in their tracks to check out Natalia and began slapping each other high fives and making catcalls at her. Terrance warned them to stop and to refocus on their scrimmage or there would be consequences.

Terrance enjoyed being a hands-on coach like the coaches he'd had in high school and college basketball. That coaching style had helped him become a star player, and some compared him to Allen Iverson who scored an average of 26 points per game. He wanted to share his knowledge with the youth. Terrance yelled out to the boys and told them to hit the showers so he could do his own flirting with Natalia. She pretended that she was looking for Juan and Marco since they had started spending a lot of time in the church gym, but Terrance forced her to admit that she was really there to invite him to dinner.

"Terrance, I'm glad you are here tonight. Juan and Marco have been bugging me about asking you over for dinner. Tonight, we're having Pork Chops with steamed veggies and loaded baked potatoes," she told him, knowing that she had inside knowledge about his favorite foods from all the years she'd spent at his family's dinner table. He loved to eat hearty meals and was a meat and potatoes guy.

"Hmm, that sounds really good. I'd love to hang out with Juan and Marco, and of course you too," he joked. "Maybe we could get into a ball game or two afterwards," Terrance said.

Natalia was thrilled that Terrance had agreed to stop by for dinner. She couldn't deny the fact that her crush on him was getting stronger even though he was her best friend's little brother. She wondered if her involvement with him would interfere with her relationship with the Williams family members, but on the other hand she thought he was worth the risk.

Natalia changed her clothes when she got home and then took some time to go over the music for the celebration before staring dinner. Although she had been the music director for less than a year, she prided herself in helping to make the Mother's Day service special. She wanted this years' service to be over the top and prayed that the new choir robes would arrive on time. The members deserved to look their best while sounding perfect. The congregation was going to be serenaded with several Gospel tunes, along with a modern-day rendition of "Oh Happy Day" that was once sung by the legendary Aretha Franklin. Natalia believed that it was the perfect song to get everyone in a celebratory mood. The choir would begin rehearsing the song soon, and she was excited.

Natalia had made some significant changes with the choir by capitalizing on the strengths of each member, a page she took right out of Hezekiah Walker's playbook with his flamboyant choir that always looked fantastic in their vibrant colors when they weren't wearing choir robes. She encouraged her members to try new things every Sunday and was great at highlighting the talents of the members who could belt out lyrics effortlessly. She wanted to make some changes to the original arrangement of "Oh Happy Day" by having three people sing the lead part and the choir sing the melody. Out of nowhere, she had a bright idea but wasn't sure how well it would go over with the people she needed to pull it off. She started reminiscing about all the fun she'd had with Megan and Keisha in high school in their theater class when they were forced to compete against each other for roles in plays. She believed it was fitting for them to pull their talents together and put them on display for the congregation to hear their perfect sound.

"Hmmm... Megan can lead, Keisha will follow, and I can come in at the end," she pondered. However, she wasn't sure if she would get their buy in but thought there was a chance since it was for a special occasion. She decided to share her idea with Megan first, knowing that if she agreed it would be easier to persuade Keisha.

Natalia pulled out her cell phone and called Megan who picked up on the first ring, "What can I do for you, Natalia?" Megan blurted out.

"Dang, can't a girl just call sometimes?" Natalia said.

"Yes, of course, but let's be honest; you never call me," Megan reminded her.

Natalia laughed, knowing all too well that Megan was telling the truth. She hadn't called her as much since they worked together as staff members at the church and saw one another every day. It wasn't necessary to call as much since texting was their preferred method of communication. Natalia told Megan about her ideas for the choir and the song she planned for them to sing.

"Do you remember the good old days back in theater class? We got scrappy every time we were forced to compete against each other for those lead roles, but we were all talented, and if I'm being honest, some of the best singers and actresses went to our school. I've been thinking about how nice it would be to showcase our talents to our congregation. It's time for us to show off our chops in a rendition of 'Oh Happy Day'. Trust me; they are going to love it," Natalia told her.

"Natalia, that's a really a good idea. Count me in. Besides, I've held on to my competitive spirit and plan on taking the crown," Megan teased.

"That's funny! The hard part will be getting Keisha's buy in. You know how adamant she is about keeping God's house in order. She doesn't go for any showboating or people serving their own interests," Natalia said, matter-of-factly.

"Yeah, but this is different, especially if you consider all she and her family have been through in such a short time. Keisha wants this Mother's Day to be special since all of her siblings are home. Our tribute will add to the celebration, and I think we are going to put a smile on everyone's face after hearing us," Megan told her.

"Your right. I'll ask her tomorrow," Natalia replied.

Natalia couldn't wait to talk to Keisha and get to choir rehearsal. She emailed her music director to ask if he had time in his schedule to work on their collaboration. She wanted it to be perfect. Natalia walked away from her computer to get some water when she heard the sound of an in-coming email. It was Trevor responding. He said that he had about an hour before choir rehearsal and wanted to know if that was enough time. She replied by telling him that she was looking forward to sharing her ideas with him.

Natalia trusted Trevor and believed that he was one of the most talented music directors she had ever come in contact with. Even though she wasn't a trained musician, she really had an ear for music and the chops to match. Her parents had kept her busy as a young girl with acting, and she enjoyed a level of success far better than her peers.

Natalia switched gears and started preparing dinner. She knew that her cooking needed to match her other talents if she wanted Terrance to remain interested in her since Victoria was such a great cook. After she finished cooking, she didn't hear from Terrance, which caused her some alarm so she went ahead and fed Juan and Marco. Although she was annoyed, she returned to reviewing the sheet music and assigning the parts they would sing before sharing it with Trevor, who insisted that she trust him with the arrangement. He told her it was going to be epic, and she believed it would be.

# Chapter 5

# Wayward Dynamics

## (Jada Learns the Truth)

*J*ada took her time getting familiar with Pittsford, and by now she was able to navigate fairly easily through the city. She even made friends with the neighbors on both sides. Her life seemed perfect, but if truth be told, she was missing her grandma. However, there were some deep-rooted painful memories associated with Ms. Emma Jean and life back home in Dallas. She didn't think it was a good idea for her to be stressed out and upset all the time. Jada recalled the conversation she'd had with Keisha about the open invitation extended to her grandma to visit. She believed that she was ready for her to visit but thought it might be a good idea to discuss it with Victoria first. Jada hoped that Victoria and her grandma would get along and would have a lot in common. She walked into the kitchen and was happy to find her beautiful stepmother standing in front of the stove cooking.

She didn't hesitate to bring up the topic, "Mom, can we talk for a minute?" she asked.

"Of course. I always have time for you. What's on your mind?" Victoria replied.

"I've been thinking about how nice it would be to have my grandma come out for a visit in a few days, but I wanted to get your blessing first," Jada said.

"Yes, your grandmother is always welcome. When do you plan to have her come?" Victoria asked.

"I'm not sure, but I was thinking that it would be really nice to have her see how we celebrate Mother's Day. I was hoping she could stay for at least a week," Jada told her.

"Honey, she's welcome anytime, and I would love for her to be here for Mother's Day," Victoria reported.

"Thanks, Mom! I think she'll like it here, so I'm going to go ahead and call her to make the arrangements," Jada said.

Jada was relieved after her conversation with Victoria, and she couldn't wait to call her grandma. She had so much she wanted to share with her. She was in a state of happiness, and it was becoming easier for her to push her negative thoughts down beneath the surface, but she didn't want to do that anymore. She wanted to clear up a few issues first with her grandma before she visited one, which was to deal with her feelings that she had placed on the back burner because they were too painful to talk about. Jada had some intense questions for her grandma about why she had been denied a healthy relationship with her mother. Growing up, her grandma had kept a lot of distance between them because she didn't trust her mother since she had been neglectful with her in the past. It always bothered Jada that her grandma had never said anything positive about her mother. Instead, she vilified her and seemed to focus on her negative behaviors. Her grandma's discord with her mother had taken a toll on her self-esteem, which explained why she had made so many bad choices throughout her life. She had been sheltered by her grandma and abandoned by her mother, making it difficult for her to trust people.

The thought of being denied the ability to talk to her mother had caused Jada a lot of unnecessary trauma. Her mother had been incarcerated for the last few years, which made it difficult for them to afford weekly collect calls. Whenever they did talk to her, an otherwise sweet conversation turned into a debacle. Ms. Emma Jean would hurl accusations and blame at her mother regarding some of her shady relationships. Jada recalled hearing Ms. Emma Jean yelling at the top of her lungs, "You don't give two cents about anyone but yourself."

She felt sad when they argued. The calls eventually stopped once Jada finished high school. It wasn't too long after that until her mother died in prison. The dreadful details of her mother hanging herself in her jail cell broke Jada's heart. It was the worst day of her life, and she carried the burden on her shoulders. What was even worse, her grandma denied her the opportunity to attend her mother's funeral. Jada was angry and felt robbed because she hadn't been able to get any closure, but she lacked the courage to challenge her grandma's decision.

Jada had the courage now and wanted to find answers, but she didn't want her grandma to think she was being disrespectful or ungrateful.

She called her grandma to talk and to extend an invitation for her to visit, "Grandma, I know we talked just last week, but I really miss you and would like for you to come to Pittsford for Mother's Day. I don't want you to be alone, and I guarantee you'll feel special. Besides, I really want you to meet my siblings," Jada told her.

"It's a short notice, but I'd like to come," Ms. Emma Jean said.

"I'm so happy you're coming, but, Grandma, I need you to understand something. I've matured and have been able to forgive you. I've avoided having this conversation with you about my mother, but I no longer can, so I want to get it off my chest. Grandma, you really hurt me by denying me a relationship with my mother. I miss her so much even though I realize that she didn't shield me from harm and had to go to prison. I forgave her even when you couldn't. She's my mother! How *dare* you keep me from attending her funeral? I'm still in disbelief, and I'm shocked that you would hurt me like that. Did you even consider the pain I would endure? I'm a grown woman now with my own ideas, goals, and beliefs, so it's necessary for me to find my own way in the world. I forgive you, but if you want to be a part of my life, I need you to let me live it with the people of my choosing. With that said, if you come out here, please keep in mind that Victoria is my siblings' mother, and the Reverend was all of our father. I don't want to hear you making any disrespectful comments about them or doing anything that would cause me harm or unnecessary stress," Jada demanded.

"Baby, I'm sorry! I never meant to cause you any harm, but your mom took me through so much and I wanted her to do things different with you.

I know I'm old school and that can't continue to be an excuse, but it tore me apart when she ran off with you and you got violated. I know she believed that she was doing the right thing, but she couldn't seem to make good decisions. Your mother loved you so much, so don't ever forget that. I love you too, and I promise not to say anything negative about your family," Ms. Emma Jean promised.

"Thank you, Grandma. I really appreciate it. I plan on purchasing your ticket and sending it in the mail. I can't wait to see you," Jada told her.

After hanging up, Jada got on her laptop to look at the different websites and to compare prices. She was thrilled to find that the airfare was more economical for her grandma to stay a few extra days. She realized that it could also be a risky proposition, since Ms. Emma Jean spoke her mind often and at times when it wasn't necessary. It seemed as if her mouth always got her in trouble and her words ended up hurting somebody's feelings. Jada booked a roundtrip ticket and said a prayer asking God to put her grandma in time-out during her visit. Jada wanted to talk things over with Victoria so she would know what to expect.

Jada told Victoria that her grandma was going to stay a few extra days, "Hi, Mom. I called my grandma back, and I want you to know it will be cheaper for her to stay a few extra days," Jada informed her.

"Jada, Ms. Emma Jean is welcome for however long you would like," Victoria replied.

"Thanks, Mom. I really gave her a good talking to, and I think she realizes that she hasn't always been the easiest person to get along with," Jada acknowledged.

Jada excused herself, as she wanted to consider taking advantage of some of the speaking engagements she had been offered when she was on her book tour, but she needed more information from Amanda. She wanted to confirm them over the next few months. When she called Amanda, she got her answering machine and decided to leave a message. She then checked her emails to see if anyone needed her immediate attention. She was speechless after noticing an email with the subject line: 'Invitation — Guest Relations'. The sender was Harpo Productions and she could tell the email was valid. Her eyes widened from her excitement and her heart was beating rapidly. She clicked on it and began reading the contents. Her mouth dropped wide open as she read, 'You are invited to the *Dr. Phil Show.*'

The producer emphasized that she needed to reach out to him as soon as possible. Jada knew that she needed to proceed with caution and go over the details with Amanda who was responsible for making sure everything was legitimate since offers like these were junk mail the majority of the time. Jada took a shower and went to bed, sensing that it was a good idea since her emotions were all over the place.

Jada woke up the next morning earlier than usual and got dressed. Breakfast was a bowl of oatmeal and a large glass of orange juice. She then walked over to the church to share her exciting news with Keisha. She also wanted to get some clarity about the projects Keisha expected her to be a part of. While she waited for Keisha to get off the phone, she texted Amanda again and was happy when she answered. Her text said that she was tied up with another client and would call her back as soon as she could. When Keisha got off the phone, she looked as if she'd received some bad news and her eyes had started to water.

"Hey, sis, is everything okay?" Jada inquired.

"Yes, Jada, I'm okay. I was reminiscing with an old friend about Daddy. Boy, could that man preach! I wish he was still here to see all of us working together. I miss him so much," Keisha said.

"Aw, sis, I'm sure he's watching over us, and he will always be the glue that keeps this family together. I bet he wouldn't be as shocked as we think he would, knowing that Terrance has returned home and is working in the ministry," Jada said.

Keisha felt comfort from Jada's words before Jada told her about her good news and the breakthrough she had received after telling her grandma the truth, "My grandma will be here for Mother's Day," Jada gleamed before bragging about her invitation to be a guest on the *Dr. Phil show*. Keisha was excited about her baby sister's good fortune. She grabbed Jada's hands and they began jumping up and down and screaming like elementary school girls. There was something so sweet and innocent about the two whenever they spent time together.

"OMG! Jada, you've hit the jackpot! That's awesome! When will they be taping your episode?" Keisha asked.

"I don't know. We still need to talk to the producer. I'm expecting a call from Amanda and she'll advise me on how to proceed. Oh yeah, I forgot to mention that my book has finally made the New York best sellers list. I think that's what prompted the invitation to the show," Jada declared.

Keisha gave Jada a sisterly hug before telling her that she had some pressing business to attend to. They both felt blessed beyond measure and knew the Reverend would be proud of them.

# Chapter 6
# Wayward Tribulations
## (Megan's Trials)

Megan was on cloud nine after being invited out to dinner with Cory again, and she couldn't wait to complete her work day so she could get dolled up for her date. Cory was taking her to the Sogo Sushi and Hibachi Restaurant in town. She loved the food and boasted about the fact that their menu listed California Eel Rolls and Pineapple Martini. She said they were to die for. Cory loved dinner dates and wining and dining his lady friends, and Megan was enjoying the opportunity to try out expensive restaurants around the city, as Cory didn't hesitate to pull out hundreds of dollars to treat her to full-course meals. She loved the fact that he was a perfect gentleman, although she still had some red flags about dating him. She couldn't get past the fact that Keisha had confirmed that his daughter Rhonda was a piece of work, and his infrequent church attendance really bothered her. He hadn't stepped into Victory Baptist Church prior to the night they met since the Reverend had died. Megan wondered why he hadn't followed up with meeting David since his return from vacation.

When the clock struck five, Megan powered down her laptop, collected her personal belongings, and ran out of the office without taking the time to turn off the lights. She had made an appointment earlier to get her eyebrows arched so that she would look flawless. She waited a few minutes when she arrived at the salon for Stephanie, her aesthetician, to escort her to the back room where she'd be instructed to sit in the large black chair where the work would be performed.

Stephanie began threading her eyebrows, which took twenty minutes, and after receiving Megan's approval, she was given a generous tip. On the ride home, Megan thought about Cory and how good-looking he was. She kicked off her pumps as soon as she got home and took a quick shower. She considered washing her hair but realized that she wouldn't have enough time. If she washed it, she would be late and Cory would have to date a wet-headed woman still in her bathrobe. She giggled when she considered the fact that he was a man and probably wouldn't mind being seen in public with such a beautiful woman — even with wet hair. She recalled all those awkward conversations she'd had with Keisha about why Black women don't wash their hair every day. She quickly lathered her body with her favorite scented body wash and then rinsed off the soapy residue before grabbing a towel to dry off.

She wore a matching bra and thong set that made her butt look larger than it was, since Keisha had teased her about her having a flat butt. She had considered taking part in the new fad by getting butt implants, but after seeing a few women parading around town with butts that looked like someone had taken a knife and carved out two lopsided basketballs, she concluded that her butt was perfect just the way it was.

She slipped into her sexy, little, black, off-the-shoulder lace dress, knowing it would garner Cory's full attention. She used some hair gel to slick her hair back. She wanted to give herself a sexier look by highlighting her distinctive facial features. After applying some light make-up, she looked like she had just walked off the runway. She poured herself a glass of red wine and sipped it while waiting for Cory to arrive. When she heard his car pull up, she grabbed her clutch and opened the door after he knocked.

"My, don't you look beautiful tonight," he said.

"Thank you, and you look nice too. I'm starving," she said while attempting to change the subject.

Cory walked Megan to the passenger side of his Jaguar to open the door for her and made small talk with her as they drove to the restaurant. He talked about his day before bragging about what a good dad he was. Megan listened, but she was annoyed that he had brought up his daughter and his job so early in the date. She tried to focus on what she liked about him, which was his good looks and muscular body. Cory was the first Black man that she'd taken seriously when he asked her out. She thought most Black men were good looking, but since she had worked in cooperate America for years, she didn't move in the same circles as they did. She was left to date White men who thought their shit didn't stink, making her unlucky in love.

When they arrived at the Sogo Sushi and Hibachi Restaurant, Cory parked and quickly came around to let her out. He grabbed her hand and they walked inside. The hostess acknowledged that Cory had a reservation for two, which was good because the restaurant seemed to be busier than usual. They were led to a nice table for two in the corner. After the waitress took their order, Cory asked Megan about her interests. She talked mostly about the work she did at the church.

"I had no idea that you were related to Keisha. I was telling her about you, and she mentioned that you're her cousin and told me that your real name is Derwin. I can't believe your name hasn't come up in our conversations, since we've been best friends for years. I'm glad we got a chance to meet each other. The Williams family has always held a special place in my heart. Keisha and I went to high school together, and we have remained best friends ever since. Actually, were more like sisters," Megan explained.

"Yep, we're first cousins, but our families aren't that close. My mother and the Reverend had a falling out nearly ten years ago, and she still holds a grudge, but it hasn't stopped her from attending church every Sunday. That's church folk and family for you. My mother forbids me to have a relationship with David and Terrance. We used to sneak to the park to play basketball when we were teens. We loved the competition, and, boy oh boy, could those Williams brothers hoop, especially Terrance," Cory told her.

"I get it. My family is that way too. We've all got a lot of dysfunction going on, but now that you're all grown up, you can choose who to have a relationship with, without worrying about your mother's opinion," Megan offered.

After they finished dinner, Cory asked Megan if she wanted to go on a carriage ride around Pittsford Park. The night air was still warm, making the thought so enticing. Pittsford Park was the perfect place for couples to spend time in because of its romantic atmosphere. She accepted his offer and noticed that there were a few carriages to choose from, but Megan was drawn to the one with the draft horse. He was beautiful and a gentle giant of sorts who looked as if he weighed at least 2,000 pounds. There was a sweet little man sitting on top of the carriage with the red velvet seat waiting for his next customer. Megan marveled at the Cinderella Horse Carriage they took a ride in.

"It's a nice night for a romantic ride," the driver said as he walked toward them. "This horse's name is Whitfield, and he's a great horse," he added.

"He's beautiful," Megan said as she stroked his mane.

"Hop in. I'm offering a special tonight only. Instead of the standard thirty-minute ride around the park, I'm offering a full hour for the same price," he told them.

Cory looked at Megan for her approval before assisting her into the carriage. She was blown away by his ability to come up with romantic dates worthy of a princess. She smiled as they passed the embankment. A flood of memories filled her mind. She thought about all the tribulations she and Keisha and Natalia had gone through over the years, one of which was the nasty fight where she and Natalia had argued about her-then husband Carlos and her brief affair with him. They argued, fussed, and things had become physical, causing them to fall into the freezing, murky water near the embankment.

Things had really changed since those early days when their friendship was being tested in every direction. Pittsford Park had become their place of reckoning. When the ride was over, they walked slowly to Cory's car while still enjoying the evening. He opened the door for Megan, but before she could get inside, he planted a sensual kiss on her lips. She thought her knees were going to buckle. She hoped there would be at least one more kiss, but Cory surprised her when they arrived back at her condo by not even asking her to come inside for a nightcap. He simply walked her to the door like a gentleman and said goodnight.

Megan plopped down on the couch to reflected on her memories of a great evening. She couldn't believe that she had finally met a man worthy of her time and attention. She thought to herself that Juan's prayers were working on her behalf and she had found a promising suitor. She wanted to get married someday, especially after being single for so long. Her younger siblings, Matthew and Mattie, had beat her to the alter and had children of their own. Her parents had also rekindled their marriage, and things had been great between them. She called Keisha to brag about Cory being the perfect gentleman.

"Keisha, I just got home from the most fabulous date with your cousin. Girl, the man took me to dinner and for a romantic carriage ride through Pittsford Park afterwards. We strolled past the embankment too, and it's so beautiful this time of year. Now tell me that's not faith!" Megan bragged.

"Megan, we do have some gentlemen in our family, you know," Keisha teased.

"I hope Cory continues with his good behavior, because so far he has an 'A'. Girl, he hasn't even tried to sleep with me, but he did steal a peck on the lips," Megan told her.

"Girl, if you don't respect yourself, no one else will. You definitely deserve a good man, but don't get too ahead of yourself. I don't want you to get hurt," Keisha added.

After hanging up, Megan made some entries in her favorite journal. She realized that she had come a long way spiritually and emotionally over the past few years. She thanked God for the life she was currently living and for her church family that Keisha helped introduce her to. Her thoughts covered the pages as she wrote about her feelings about the important people who were part of her journey. It felt great to fill the pages with praise and love instead of dark thoughts. Megan was on the right track, and the "Old Megan" whose life was on a wayward path was slowly disappearing.

# Chapter 7

# Wayward Dilemma
## (Family Business)

D avid called an impromptu board meeting to discuss the mission and the long-term goals for the church. Some of the more pressing issues they needed to discuss were the financials, membership, and the expansion of the church. The congregation had grown since the Reverend's passing. David summoned the elders, Sister Earnestine, Uncle Milton, Brother Mark, Jada, Terrance, Megan, Natalia, and Keisha. They sensed that there were some major changes coming. Board meetings usually took place four times a year unless there was an emergency. Once everyone was seated, David didn't waste time bringing the meeting to order.

"Good afternoon, I've called this meeting because we have some pressing business that we need to discuss, and I didn't think it could wait. First, I want to credit all of you for driving up our membership over the past few months. I can't believe that we have grown thirty percent since Dad's death. In fact, we've grown so fast that we barely have enough seating for our new members. I'm proposing that we expand our church, and the time is now. We need to consider adding on to our current building, or we can vote to begin construction on a second location. I figure that between our six talented ministers currently available we could split off with senior staff assuming pastoral roles at both locations with no problem. I believe our members deserve it, and it's the direction that Dad wanted to eventually see the church go in someday. I had a preliminary meeting with the banker to see if we met the qualifications and to go over the financials to see if it's feasible. The bank is willing to support us in whatever option we chose. I've put a lot of thought into this, and it is time to introduce the idea to you to gain your valuable input. Should we decided to build a second location, a pastoral team could be built around Keisha, Terrance, and Natalia, and the other built around Jada, Megan, and myself, and we could remain in this building if everyone is in agreement."

Terrance said, "Bro, look, I'm glad that membership has grown, but if we're going to move ahead with a second location, how do you think I would be able to assist Keisha and Natalia with the pastoring? I see myself as a youth minister, not an assistant pastor or senior pastor," Terrance admitted.

Brother Mark barked, "I'm not sure about all of this so-called talk about making the church bigger. The Reverend put his blood, sweat, and tears into this church, and he ain't even been dead long, and here you young folk go wanting to make changes. I don't like all this crazy talk, David."

"Look, I hear you both, but it's really not about any of us; it's about the success of this family ministry. Terrance, you're going to have to dig a little deeper, man. You've been called home for a purpose that's bigger than yourself. Take a look at this," David said and pulled out a leather binder that housed some important documents.

"Dad always knew you'd come home and would serve our family ministry in a large capacity. It's not the time for self-doubt, and, Brother Mark, if we're not willing to grow, we will lose all our new members who can barely find a seat on Sundays. Do you really want that to happen?" David asked.

Terrance took a few minutes to review the legal documents, and he read a transcript that had been written by the Reverend for his final invocation but had never gotten the opportunity to share with anyone, not even Victoria. Terrance paraphrased as he read the contents out loud, trying to get to the heart of the matter. When he was finished, he summarized what he had read, "Our father's prayer was that if he were to leave this earth untimely, his children, David, Keisha, and I would join together as one to become ordained ministers with the intent of keeping the Victory Baptist Church legacy burning strong. His hope was for the church to thrive well into the future. His desire was to make peace with Keisha and me despite his initial resistance toward her becoming a minister and his disappointment in me for not living the life he had planned."

Jada handed Terrance a few tissues after noticing that he was getting emotional. He continued to share the rest of what was written, and by the time he finished, it was difficult for Terrance not to change his previous perspective and conclude that his father had been a remarkable man. The Reverend never gave up on his family or his children who meant the world to him. Terrance felt blessed, knowing that his father never gave up on his dreams of him coming home to assist his siblings in the family ministry someday. Terrance began to feel guilty for not talking to his father for all those years. He wished he could turn back the hands of time, and he realized that he really wasn't that different from the Reverend. *The apple didn't fall too far from the tree*, he thought to himself. There wasn't a dry eye in the room after Terrance finished reading the document. Megan and Natalia couldn't believe that David had included them in the long-term plans for the church. Victoria came into the room while Terrance was reading the document, and she could barely hold herself together. The Reverend had shared his wishes with her a time or two, but to hear her son reading her late husband's wishes out loud was eerie.

Keisha and Jada rushed over to her to provide comfort, but it seemed like Keisha was affected the most. It was surreal. She had worked so hard to bring everyone together, and to actually receive confirmation from her deceased father that she hadn't acted on her own accord to keep the siblings together caused her to praise God. "Hallelujah," she shouted.

David suggested that the board members take some time to pray about the proposal he had presented to them. He asked that a date and time be scheduled so they could reconvene to vote later. In the past, whenever there were talks of expanding the church, the idea was quickly shot down, but it seemed possible that everyone would seriously consider the options. It was time for Victory Baptist Church to make some changes.

Victoria attempted to lighten their mood by announcing that she had made her scrumptious chicken and dumplings along with a carrot cake. She insisted that there was plenty of food and encouraged them to come over to the house to eat.

David called Loretta and asked her to head over with the girls, "Hey, baby, grab the girls and come over to Mom's. We've just ended the meeting, and the leadership team is still in a good mood of sorts. Mom invited us over for chicken and dumplings. Hurry! I'll hang out here at the church for a little while to wrap up some business but will meet you there. By the way, do you think we should reveal our good news tonight, or are you still stewing over the fact that we didn't have a gender reveal party? It might be better to announce it now while everyone who we care about is in the same place," David said.

"I've gotten over not having a gender reveal party, David, so if you think the time is right, then let's tell them. We will be there in fifteen minutes," Loretta replied.

David remained at the church and privately praised the Lord as he waited for his family. He thanked God for how well the meeting had gone.

Natalia walked with Keisha over to the house and told her that she was concerned about how her relationship with Terrance would impact the ministry and their ability to date. She said she was in disbelief that they were actually considering her for one of the pastoral roles. She recalled how many hoops she and Megan were made to jump through when they initially applied to be staff members at Victory Baptist Church. It was a grueling process by all accounts, and she had fought hard to prove her worth. She admitted that her relationship with Terrance could be merely a fantasy on her part, since it seemed to be dead on arrival after being stood up for dinner.

Keisha couldn't contain her joy and told Natalia not to worry and that everything would work itself out. She showered her family with hugs as she walked around their spacious living room talking to everyone and telling them that she loved them dearly. Victoria was busy in the kitchen, warming up the food and putting together a couple of trays of hors d'oeuvres. Making her family and friends comfortable by filling their stomachs was her forte, and it was rare to find anyone willing to turn her down when invited to eat her meals.

David was nervous as he walked to the house to wait for Loretta and his girls. He couldn't wait to spill the beans, knowing that their news would bring joy to his family. Terrance noticed that David seemed a little distant when he walked into the house, and he wanted to find out why. David told him that he was okay and took another opportunity to tell Terrance how happy he was that he was home and out of imminent danger in Albuquerque.

Since his return, over forty Black young men had lost their lives battling the police, and a few were friends of his. He was happy to be in a more stable environment. David apologized for putting him on the spot during the meeting but told him it was necessary to get his point across. Terrance assured David that even though he was completely caught off guard, it was nice to know that he had his vote of confidence. They engaged in a bear hug.

"Oh, I didn't realize that you are that strong," David teased.

"I love you, man," Terrance replied.

David walked over to look out of the oversized window in the living room to see if Loretta had pulled into the driveway. A huge smile covered his face as he walked outside to escort his family into the house. He kissed Loretta and promised her that she would get the baby shower she deserved. Still feeing anxious, David opened the door and announced their presence.

"The gang's here," David announced, and he didn't waste time letting everyone know that he would like their attention, "Can I have everyone's attention please? Loretta and I have some great news," he reported as he studied their faces. He nodded at Loretta to signal that it was time to announce their news.

"Hello, family. As you know, David and I have been trying to become pregnant for a long time. We have prayed for a baby boy, and David believes that it's the right time to share our news with you. Were pregnant! And it's a boy and we will name him Calvin," Loretta reported.

Everyone burst into cheers and words of congratulations for David and Loretta who were happy that the cat was finally out of the bag. It was good news, and they couldn't stop talking about it. Naming the baby Calvin after the Reverend was icing on the cake.

"We're going to be the best big sisters in the whole wide world," Aleyah and Asia bragged in unison.

Victoria was taken aback. She had no idea that she was going to be a grandmother again and needed to excuse herself for a few minutes to gather her composure. The thought that her third grandchild would be a boy who would have his grandfather's name reminded her of the goodness of God. The announcement was better than unwrapping a present on Christmas day.

David explained how he and Loretta had wanted to wait until she was in her second trimester to tell them, but they couldn't keep the good news to themselves. David beamed with pride as he repeated that his unborn son would keep his father's legacy going. As a child, he was grateful that his parents allowed him and Terrance to have their own identity by not naming them after the Reverend. However, his view had changed since his father's death. He found it fitting for any of the siblings to name the first male child after the Reverend, but he and Loretta were the only ones with children.

Loretta couldn't stop smiling as she was flooded with affection and congratulations. She told the family that Aleyah and Asia would have a hard time sharing the spotlight with their baby brother. Up until that point, they were the only grandchildren and were spoiled. They got lots of attention on their birthdays and especially Christmas.

"Don't you two worry; your Aunt Jada will always spoil you. I've got to make up for all your missed birthdays," Jada told the girls.

"Sis, don't get them started," David warned.

After the large pot of chicken and dumplings was eaten, Victoria began serving the carrot cake paired with a dessert wine. It was delicious and every bite melted in their mouths. David went into the closet to pull out the karaoke machine and told them that he was getting ready to set things off with his rendition of Prince's "Purple Rain". He began belting out the lyrics with vigor, and everyone laughed as he attempted to hit the high parts with his falsetto.

"Not too bad!" Keisha said.

"You know I got skills, sis," he teased.

Jada grabbed the mic from David and told him to play the Pointer Sister's popular hit "We Are Family". She asked Megan, Natalia, Keisha, and Loretta to join her in singing it. It was the perfect song to celebrate their closeness and commitment to one another on such an emotional day. After a few more songs were played, David ended the night with prayer. He prayed for their church and his unborn child. Uncle Milton took over to pray for the Reverend's legacy to remain on good footing. While all heads were still bowed and eyes closed, David told them how blessed he was to have had the Reverend as his earthly father and how happy it made him that so many others loved him too. He prayed for Victory Baptist Church to continue to flourish and for their family to continue receiving the many blessings for doing the will of God. David prayed for everyone's safe travels home and reminded them to pray about their role in the church and how they would vote on the expansion.

Everyone was exhausted by the time the house cleared out. Keisha and Jada joined Victoria in the kitchen to share their individual accounts of the evening. There were so many great memories that were made, and overall the night was a beautiful expression of love shared by family and friends. The news of the new baby was by far the best news of the night. Keisha vowed to spend more time with her nieces Asia and Aleyah, since she only saw them at church or at Sunday dinners. She realized that life is short and they would be young ladies before she knew it.

Knowing that Loretta was having her third child and that she didn't have any children was a harsh reminder that her biological clock was ticking. She wondered if there was really any substance to Juan's prayers and the chance for her to meet a significant other, but only time would tell.

# Chapter 8

# Wayward Agony
## (Jada's Contemplations)

The constant ringing of Jada's cell phone had gotten on her nerves because she was awakening out of a dead sleep. She rolled over to see who was calling, and it was Amanda. She had been expecting her call and quickly answered it.

"Good morning Jada. I'm sorry it's taken me so long to return your call. I had a death in the family, and one of my other clients was having a major crisis that needed my attention. I was able to review the email from Harpo Productions and must say that I'm so happy that they have invited you to be a guest on the *Dr. Phil Show*. I forwarded the contract to legal for their review, as we need to make sure everything is legit before we agree to book the show for you," Amanda warned.

"Amanda, I nearly had a heart attack after seeing that email. I love Dr. Phil and used to watch his show all the time. I'd love to be a guest, especially since they're talking about a subject I'm familiar with. Did you notice that 'Surviving Molestation' is the topic? It's a pretty heavy topic, but I'm confident I will be able to hold my own with the audience. Let me know once you hear back from legal. I've been wanting to talk to you about the possibility of my slowing things down with the touring stuff. My family has asked me to join the ministry full-time, so I plan to cut back on the amount of engagements I commit to. Part of me believes that the ministry is my purpose, and my siblings are also considering expanding our church. It would be a great opportunity for me to impact the lives of others from all different walks of life. I've been doing some soul searching lately and will let you know my intent soon," Jada told her.

"Jada, you have to do what's best for you and your family. Take your time and make a sound decision, as your career could take off in a new direction. It sounds as if God has a great plan for you, and I think you're lucky to have such a strong and supportive family," Amanda told her.

Jada was relieved to have shared her thoughts with Amanda, and she always wanted to let her know her intentions so that she could advocate for her positively regarding the business decisions she made. There were numerous speaking engagements and book tours that she needed to reschedule if she decided to become more involved in the ministry. Jada decided to talk to David to gain more clarity of his vision for her and wanted to ask him some qualifying questions. Her decision would be life altering either way, and she desperately wanted to make the right one. Jada found herself thinking about her grandma's trip to Pittsford again, and she couldn't help but feel some anxiety the closer her arrival came. She called her grandma again just to make sure they were on the same page, since Ms. Emma Jean had a reputation for hearing what she wanted to hear.

"Hi, Grandma! I'm calling to ask you to bring that pretty yellow dress with the bright flowers on the collar that you have, and you should also consider bringing your fancy cambric church hat that makes you look like royalty. You might as well put them both in your suitcase tonight so you don't forget them. I would really love to see you in that outfit," Jada told her.

"Jada, are you sure that Victoria and your siblings want me to come? I'm going to feel like a duck out of water while I'm there. Victoria is a nice lady, but I'm sure she remembers all those dreadful things I've said and done to her over the years. Honey, I don't want to interfere with your happiness, especially since you are in the early stages of establishing a bond with them. It might be too soon for me to come," Ms. Emma Jean said.

"Grandma, my stepmother and siblings are gracious people who accept everyone. I haven't known them to treat anyone badly, and the fact that you're a part of me guarantees that they'll be good to you too," Jada proclaimed.

"Okay, baby! Have you sent my ticket yet? I'm gonna start packing tonight, and I can't wait to see you. I've missed you, Jada," Ms. Emma Jean reported.

After sharing their, "I love yuzs," Jada hung up to get dressed. She had a lot on her plate that needed attention, but first she wanted to go over the plans with Victoria for what they could do while her grandma visited.

Jada looked for her and found Victoria outside in the front yard planting flowers underneath their large oversized living room window. She enjoyed soaking up the sun while tending to her garden.

"Mom, I called my grandma again to help ease both of our anxieties about her visit. She's flying out tomorrow, and I realize that you two haven't met in person and that things have been contentious over the years. I know you've tolerated her bad behavior, and I don't expect you to forget about all of her dirt, but I'm hoping everyone can get along, at least while she's here," Jada told her.

"Jada, I forgave Ms. Emma Jean a long time ago; besides, we have something far more important and worth getting along for, and honey that's you. I would never hurt you and don't want to be at odds with your grandma either, sweetheart," Victoria told her.

"I'm so excited for her to experience our Mother's Day celebration and to be able to participate in all of the festivities afterwards. Those women are still bragging about last year's celebration," Jada reported.

"Honey, we all pride ourselves on making things special for the ladies. We work hard but still welcome new ideas. Keisha thinks she's going to take over the planning this year, but I've got news for her; I'm in charge, and things will still need to be run by me first," Victoria declared.

Jada laughed at Victoria, knowing that she had no idea that things were being planned behind her back. She needed to talk to David so she could make a sound decision about whether or not to place her speaking engagements and book tours on hold. She had the potential to make lots of money but realized that money wasn't everything. There were souls that needed saving, and there wasn't a price that could be put on work like that.

David was in his office working on his sermon for the week when she walked in. He worked hard just like the Reverend did, spending a lot of time perfecting his message.

"Hello, big brother. I've been talking to my agent and considering your proposal to go into the ministry full-time a lot, and it's a great opportunity but I would like more details. You mentioned that Megan and I would share the pastoral duties with you, so what exactly did you have in mind?" Jada asked.

"Girl, you need to stop playing! You've graced the pulpit on more than one occasion, and in the words of Bruno Mars, 'It's like 24K magic in the air,' every time you do. Sis, you've got an anointing, and I have to give you props for considering putting family over fame and money. You have helped to grow our membership too, and we will make the perfect pastoral team. I would never ask you to stop pursuing your dreams, but what I can tell you is that God will make room for all of them. I'm asking you to share a piece of yourself every other Sunday in the pulpit if we are able to get approval for the second location. No pressure from me, but just be ready for the vote when the time comes, and by the way, we need to sit down with Keisha and Terrance to discuss the part of the document where Dad noted his wishes of how to divide the church's assets. He left you out, but I don't think it was to be meanspirited; I believe he just never expected you to live in Pittsford or to have a relationship with your siblings. Nevertheless, I'm willing to divide the assets four ways, but Keisha and Terrance will need to agree. No worries; we will talk to them soon," David assured her.

"Thanks, David. You've really cleared things up for me. I've still got some soul searching to do, and I truly appreciate your generosity. I love you for that, and I did wonder why Dad left me out, but I understood where he was coming from. I'll be ready for the vote when the time comes," Jada said.

Jada felt relieved after talking to David. There was something special about him and his ability to make people feel like he'd walk to the ends of the earth for them. God had Jada in the palm of His hands, and her footsteps were being ordered. She checked her calendar to see what she had planned so far. She noticed that the revenue from her book sales was gaining steam and on target to make her a best-selling author. As Jada sat quietly, she heard the Holy Spirit whisper in her ear, "You're right where I would have you."

A flood of tears rolled down her beautiful face, and she was happy to receive confirmation once again from God that He wanted her to become fully engaged in her family's ministry. She couldn't wait to reveal her intent to vote favorably for the expansion. She walked into the house to prepare the guest room for her grandma and made the bed with the beautiful green comforter she ordered from Amazon. Ms. Emma Jean's favorite color was green, so she also picked up some beautiful plastic flowers from Hobby Lobby with matching vases to make things special.

Jada then went shopping for a new dress, knowing that she would be asked to make some kind of tribute or to even deliver a special message during the lantern celebration. She shopped at Lord & Taylor, an upscale department store, and found a dress right away. It was a lovely lace bell-sleeve white dress. She went into the dressing room to try it on, and it fit perfectly. She already had shoes and accessories to complement her look. In her mind, she began a countdown to the start of the Mother's Day celebration. She was fully aware that she might have an outfit change with such fashionable women in the house trying to shape her thoughts about fashion. She was open to learning as much she could about fashion from the Wayward Sisters.

# Chapter 9

# Wayward Miracles

## (Natalia's Dreams Come True)

atalia was still stewing from Terrance's rudeness and the fact that he never called to tell her that he wasn't coming to dinner. However, she realized that her anger was unwarranted, as it wasn't his fault since David called the impromptu meeting to go over church business. Terrance felt bad too, as he was eager to come over and had intended to after the meeting, but his mother invited the board members over to eat, knowing they wouldn't turn down such an invitation. The talks of expanding the church and the announcement that David and Loretta were having another baby made his no call/no show excusable. Natalia believed that getting involved with Terrance could be complicated since the expectation was that they would be paired together and working side by side as a pastoral team. It made her question if she and Terrance were ready for a serious relationship. Lately, Terrance had been complaining a lot about Sarah and her bad behavior. They were equally concerned since Sarah refused to leave him alone and pleaded with him almost every day to take her back. Sarah's goal was to make him miserable and regretful for leaving her. Natalia realized that she was treading on shaky ground with their breakup being so fresh. She decided that it was necessary for her to pull back a little so that she didn't look desperate for a man in the eyes of Terrance.

Natalia felt encouraged after receiving a text message from Terrance asking if he could come over. He wanted to apologize in person for standing her up. She wanted to see him too but still had a few things she wanted to get off her chest. He could sense that she was annoyed but decided to keep his cool. It wasn't his fault that their dinner date had been interrupted. After getting her okay, Terrance went to Trader Joe's to pick up some flowers and to grab a bottle of wine with a hope that the items would help him pick up where they had left off. Natalia's face lit up when she opened the door and found Terrance standing there looking strong and sexy. She didn't hesitate to ask him to come in.

"These are for you," he said.

"What have I done to deserve flowers — and wine?" Natalia asked.

Terrance gave her a mischievous grin as he attempted to change the subject by talking about David's unborn baby, "I can't believe my big bro is finally having a son," he boasted.

Natalia seemed to be satisfied with his apology. He started rubbing the small of her back while he shared his thoughts.

"Natalia, I'm going to get straight to the point. We've been flirting a lot, and I know you're feeling me. I just got out of a long-term relationship as you know, but I must admit that I'm feeling you too. I don't want to compromise our relationship in the ministry by muddying the waters, and not to mention having Keisha killing us if things were ever to get messy. The church and my family's reputation are the things that are most important to me, and I will never compromise them. However, if we're going to do this relationship thing, we have to be careful and take things slow. You could be a psycho or something," he joked.

"Terrance, I have been known to put a man in his place a time or two, but I can assure you that I don't have the time or desire to be involved in any drama. My boys are my life, and I want to set a great example for them. I am crushing on you and realize that we could be playing with fire. I agree that we should keep things on the down low for now to see if we're even compatible. For the record, I believe that you could be my Prince Charming," Natalia admitted.

Natalia could barely finish her sentence before she found herself in Terrance's arms being passionately kissed by him, a kiss that seemed to last forever. He began to explore her sexy body with his hands, and they were everywhere. Natalia couldn't contain herself, as she moaned loudly, knowing that she couldn't resist him. Terrance paused long enough to ask her if Juan and Marco were at home, and when she shook her head to indicate they weren't, he pulled her closer. She could feel his manhood rising as he placed her hands on it so she could feel its thickness better. He gently pulled her loose-fitting dress over her head to reveal her sexy body that was covered by a matching bra and thong set. Terrance didn't waste time removing them and lifting her up so that she could straddled her legs around his body.

He carried her into her bedroom and laid her down on the bed before exploring her private parts with his fingers. She moaned as he pleasured her clitoris until she exploded with multiple climaxes. Feeling satisfied, she opened her legs wider to invited him to insert his manhood into her and was surprised how much of it she could handle since he was well hung. He gently went deeper as her inner parts continued to erupt with climax after climax. It took Terrance forever to cum. He was an experienced lover who had self-control, and he wanted to make sure that she was pleased first. Knowing that he had satisfied her, he allowed himself to cum and he love the way she felt. After he finished, he rolled over next to her and gently stroked her hair. He told her that she was beautiful repeatedly. She led him to the shower where they continued to enjoy each other prior to getting dressed. They wanted to make sure they were back in the living room just in case Juan and Marco came home early. They couldn't afford to get caught being naughty by them.

Natalia felt slightly embarrassed for letting her guard down and having sex so soon, but she couldn't stop thinking about Terrance's skills in the bedroom. *OMG!* she thought, *The man is so romantic.*

She started cooking, and Terrance waited while watching the Sports Channel. She smiled as she prepared the food and anticipated Juan and Marco's arrival. During the commercials, Terrance flirted with her by pressing his muscular body against hers to distract her.

"You better stop, or Loretta won't be the only one who's pregnant," she joked.

When Juan and Marco walked through the front door, they were surprised to see Terrance sitting in the living room looking too comfortable to be a guest. However, they had no idea that their mother had a crush on him and that his feelings were mutual. It was Juan who had prayed that she would fall in love with someone special and get married. Natalia played things off by explaining that Terrance was there to deliver a proposal regarding church business that needed her consideration and she had invited him to stay for dinner. She finished setting the table and plating the food. Terrance complimented her on her cooking and said that the pork chops, veggies, and loaded baked potatoes were delicious.

Juan and Marco asked Terrance to play a quick game of basketball, and he hurried outside to accommodate their request. Natalia cleaned the kitchen, and, as she cleaned, she thought about how much Juan and Marco could use a good male role model in their lives. She considered how their father's life had been cut short, causing them to become fatherless. Her emotions were all over the place as she admitted that she felt a deep connection to Terrance. She realized that there were no guarantees when it came to relationships and hoped that having sex with him didn't make things awkward. When Terrance and the boys came back inside, they were all sweaty. Juan and Marco bragged about being better players and having the ability to get up and down the court quicker. They invited Terrance to come back over, and he told them that he promised to come back soon.

"Mom, I hope you can find a man that's just as cool as Terrance. We like hanging out with him, and he told us that he wants to take us to see the Nets at Barclays Center in Brooklyn one day. I can't wait," Juan said.

"Well... I'm sure there are plenty of other cool men out there besides Terrance," she joked.

Natalia tried hard not to let on that she had feelings for Terrance. She wanted to be truthful, but she thought it was best to keep it to herself for now. Natalia excused herself to get ready for bed. She took a long, hot shower and wanted to call Keisha afterwards. She wanted to ask her to set up one of their familiar meetings at the embankment like old times. She had gained some confidence and was feeling bold enough to let the Wayward Sisters in on her little secret about dating Terrance.

"Hey, Keisha, it's been an exhausting week for me, and I bet everyone else feels the same way too, and to tell you the truth, my mind has been all over the place. I was hoping we could meet at the park tomorrow to talk, and there's no better place to let off steam than the embankment," Natalia told her.

"Natalia, I was sitting here with a glass of wine in one hand and my journal in the other. It's like my mind wants to download all of my emotions at once. I think it's a great idea for us to get together, and I'm hoping for a breakthrough for at least one of us since there is so much on our plates right now. I know the Holy Spirit is going to meet us there," Keisha replied.

"Could you call Megan? Perhaps we can go to the Village Coal Restaurant for lunch afterwards," Natalia suggested.

"No problem; I'll tell Jada tonight and Megan the first thing in the morning. She's always down for an encounter at Pittsford Park," Keisha said.

As Natalia laid in her bed, she couldn't help but to reminisce about her earlier encounter with Terrance. Her thoughts were vivid as she fantasized about the two of them making love in different positions and her giving herself freely to him mind, body, and soul. The image of his naked body would forever be etched in her mind. She thought that even if their relationship didn't last, she would still have the benefit of those sexy images of his body to fantasize about on lonely nights. Natalia had flashbacks of Terrance holding her with his strong hands wrapped around her body. She fell asleep after pleasuring herself for several minutes with her vibrator that she kept in her dresser drawer next to her bed. In her opinion, Terrance was the perfect package — gorgeous, pearly white teeth, and a full neatly groomed beard. His naked muscular body was so amazing that any woman would blush. Natalia was hopping that Terrance thought her body was sexy too and that he wanted to keep her around for a long time.

Natalia felt invigorated when she woke up the next morning. She dressed herself in leggings, a razorback sports bra, and her favorite Nike running shoes. She pulled her hair back into a ponytail before heading over to the church.

Keisha and Jada woke up earlier than usual, and after getting dressed, they prepared their favorite protein shakes with almond butter and chia seeds. Keisha swore by them, especially after she learned that they boost antioxidants and omega-3s. She received tips on healthy living from her friends who were experts in nutrition and also from reading various medical journals. She had a willingness to share information with everyone and bragged about the benefits the shakes provided when they exercised. Keisha texted Megan to tell her to come to work ready to jog and asked her to meet them at the church in fifteen minutes. The Wayward Sisters had an awareness that meetings in Pittsford Park would bring both positive and negative outcomes. As individuals, the embankment was a special place for them, but as sisters it was the place where they assembled to lift their burdens and to have an encounter with the Holy Spirit. They always left better than when they came. Years of wayward secrets had been buried throughout the open landscape of the beautiful park.

"Good Morning," Natalia said as she walked into the kitchen.

"Girl, I hope you have good news to share. We've all been through it lately, and I could use some positive vibes," Keisha reported.

"That's right! You better," Megan chimed in.

"I suggest you finish drinking those shakes, because you're going to need all the energy you can muster to process the news I have to share," Natalia teased.

They followed Natalia out to the parking lot and piled into her Acadia. When they arrived at Pittsford Park, the Wayward Sisters didn't hesitate to make their way to the embankment. The brisk morning air gave room to a beautiful skyline. They loved listening to the birds chirping and the smell of nature. Keisha asked them to join hands before requesting that Jada lead them in prayer.

"Dear God, thank You for my sisters and the love and respect we have for one another. I ask that You build a hedge of protection around us, as we vow to always give You the praise, glory, and the honor. We are in the palms of Your hands, and You have led us here in this moment for a purpose. We are thankful that You continue to allow us to use our gifts in ways that edify others. We ask that You reveal the things we need to know and the things that are unpleasing to You. I pray for these things and more in Your precious name, Amen," Jada prayed.

Natalia couldn't wait to reveal the reason she had brought them together, "Do you guys remember when Juan said he wanted me to fall in love and get married someday? Well, I think I've found 'Mr. Right'. Things are happening so fast between us that I was totally caught off guard, but I can't help myself; the man is so sexy," Natalia reported.

Keisha told her, "Girl, there's no way you could've kept that a secret. Are you saying that you've fallen in love in a matter of weeks? Natalia, we're all thirsty for a man, but there's no need to act desperate. I mean, you can't afford to go through another heartbreak, and you need to consider my godsons; that's all I'm saying."

"I can't believe it either. Who is this guy?" Megan demanded.

"He's a good man and was raised by awesome parents, and his siblings aren't too bad either. We've decided to slow things down, although I'm head over heels with Terrance," Natalia blurted out.

"Terrance who?" Keisha demanded.

"Duh, the one you grew up with," Natalia asserted.

"What on earth were you thinking, and when did this happen?" Keisha inquired.

"Claim down, sis. You must be blind or something. The two of them have been flirting with each other ever since Terrance came home. I thought something was up but figured it was just innocent flirting, so I left it alone. It wasn't any of my business," Jada admitted.

"Keisha, I would've thrown my hat in the ring too. Terrance is too damn fine! Please excuse my language," Megan said.

"I would have never thought you'd go sneaking behind my back to get with Terrance. He's still my baby brother you know, and what part of him just getting out of a relationship don't you understand? Just for the record, I don't approve, but I'm not going to be a hater and stand in your way, Natalia, but I will say this; if your relationship interferes with your responsibilities in the church, I'll will personally call an emergency meeting and have you fired," Keisha warned.

"Keisha, you know me well enough to know that I would never do anything to compromise the church's mission, especially since I had to jump through hoops to be accepted around here. I'm not willing to throw that away just to be with Terrance," Natalia replied.

"Girl, I'll be okay. The two of you mean so much to me, so just relax. Let's get this run out of the way. I think our hips have spread a little since our trip to New York. The 'Three Ps' — pizza, pastry, and pasta were so tempting, and none of us could resist them," Keisha asserted.

The Wayward Sister breathed a sigh of relief, knowing how protective Keisha was when it came to her brothers, especially Terrance. Natalia had assumed that Keisha was going to rip her head off and was surprised when she didn't.

Jada was very happy for Natalia and couldn't stop telling her how cute she and Terrance were as a couple. Jada wanted Terrance to be happy, especially after leaving New Mexico to move back home. With that out of the way, the Wayward Sisters anticipated an experience with the Holy Spirit as they jogged. They all started out together, and then Keisha sped up ahead of them with Megan following closely behind. Jada and Natalia stayed back, but all of sudden Natalia picked up her speed too.

As Megan jogged, she thought about Cory and the direction her life had taken over the past few years. She wanted to be in a serious relationship too but had been burned a few times in the past whenever she failed to listen to her inner voice cautioning her to slow down. She was finally happy knowing that she was making a difference with her contributions in leadership at the church. She wasn't willing to let anything interfere and was hoping to take on more responsibility, which always made her feel empowered. There wasn't any room for heartbreak in her life. She prayed that God would give her a sign to let her know if Cory was worth her attention, but so far God had been silent. The only thing she'd heard was His confirmation that she would be receiving an even bigger leadership role and that her territory was going to be expanded.

As Keisha jogged, she recalled her near fatal accident in Pittsford Park when she was hit by a car and it had nearly cost her everything. She thanked God for sparing her life and for answering her prayers, especially the ones concerning her siblings. She had prayed that they would enjoy a harmonious relationship. As she ran past the embankment, she felt a quickening in her spirit and heard an audible voice that said the words, "Matrimony and longevity," and she assumed that the Lord was confirming Terrance and Natalia's relationship and their future marriage, so she mumbled under her breath, "Yes, Lord," and continued to run the course.

Jada caught up with Megan and then ran past her without incident. She kept a steady pace while thinking about her grandma. It wouldn't be too long before she arrived, and she began to feel guilty, knowing that deep down inside she was afraid of the 'What-ifs' with Ms. Emma Jean. *What if she says this; what if she does that?* The what-ifs were a little scary. Although Jada loved her grandma dearly, she knew that she had issues with keeping her mouth shut. She didn't want her grandma to upset anyone with her bluntness, especially Victoria. She recalled overhearing her grandma starting shit with her dad when she was growing up. Ms. Emma Jean swore that Victoria was guilty of hating Jada for being the Reverend's illegitimate daughter. It *was* possible that Ms. Emma Jean could set things off and cause a lot of tension, even though she had promised not to. Tears ran down Jada's face as she considered everything that could go wrong. Then, all of a sudden, she felt a warm sensation throughout her body that gave her comfort and a sense of peace, knowing that God would fix it — whatever *it* was.

Natalia continued to jog behind the others, as she wanted to thank God for His goodness and for covering her and her sons. She was in a good place emotionally and financially, and the thought of finally having a loving interest with a person whose family she respected and loved caused her to feel blessed. *What a merciful God we serve, and His promises are the same today as they were yesterday and forever*, she thought and praised Him, knowing that He was well pleased with her life, her choices, and, most of all, her obedience. She was reaping the benefits of love that she'd thought she would never find.

The Wayward Sisters met back at the embankment after finishing their route. They looked as though they'd been through a metamorphosis but knew it was part of the process and also well worth it. Pittsford Park would forever be their place of reckoning.

They headed back to the church, knowing there was plenty of work to do considering that they all had a role in the church. The Wayward Sisters exchanged, "I love yuzs," and Natalia reminded them that she planned for them to grab some lunch at the Village Coal Restaurant, but no one had an appetite or wanted to go. Keisha brought up the upcoming Mother's Day event to make sure they were all participating in some way, and they took a few minutes to bask in the fullness of the Lord before going their separate ways.

Keisha went to her office to meditate on the word she had received from God and asked Him to provided her with a confirmation. She, too, desired to be in a committed relationship and asked for forgiveness for her past failures, as she had forgiven herself for her failed marriage to Sean. Things simply hadn't worked out between them, but she realized that it was because they were too young and weren't ready for such an important commitment. She wanted to find a man like David or the Reverend who loved the Lord, went to church, and had a heart for helping others just as much as she did.

She imagined herself being married to a mighty man of God and having children. Being in her mid-thirties caused her to think about her biological clock, but she also knew that it could be dangerous getting out ahead of God when it came to matters of the heart, so she decided to wait for His instructions and turn her attention back to the business that needed her immediate attention.

Natalia felt on top of the world, knowing that she could depend on the Wayward Sisters no matter what. They'd always had each other's back, even after some of their biggest disagreements. She looked forward to what the future would bring privately and professionally. She was the happiest she had been in a long time. As a young girl, she had been constantly doted over by her parents, and they had cultivated her gifts and talents by taking her on family vacations to Puerto Rico and making sure she participated in activities. As a woman, she hoped she and Terrance could make some amazing memories together, but of course the jury was still out.

# Chapter 10

## Wayward Losses

### (Megan Yields to Love)

Megan had some time to spare before going back to work, so she decided to take a hot shower, thinking it might help to get her energized. When she walked into her condo and checked her cell phone that she had left behind on the charger, there were three missed calls from Cory displayed. She wondered why he hadn't followed up with a text message, which was his preferred method of communication since it was quick and he believed he was more likely to reach someone. After showering, Megan got dressed and returned Cory's call. He seemed out of breath when he answered the phone.

"Hey, Cory, what's up? Why are you out of breath?" she inquired.

"It's Rhonda. She's stolen my wallet, and I think she has run away this time. I've been searching for her all morning without any luck. She has been hanging out with the wrong crowd, and I'm afraid she could be in some kind of trouble," he reported.

"Have you considered calling the police?" Megan asked.

"No! They wouldn't do anything anyway since she's not considered a missing person until she's been gone for at least twenty-four hours. The last time she ran away, she came home after a couple of hours. She has never stolen anything from me, and she knows I don't play when it comes to my money. One of those friends of hers probably put her up to it. I don't usually keep a lot of cash around the house, but I just happened to withdraw some cash to make down payments on the home projects I've been working on. I left my wallet on my dresser, but I'm not worried about the money, as it can be replaced. However, I am worried about Rhonda," Cory reported.

"That's awful, Cory. I don't know what to say. Is there anything I can do to help?" Megan asked.

"Megan, thanks for calling me back, and yes, I need someone to talk to so I can let off some steam. You're never judgmental. I can't go to my family because they're so damn negative, and they always talk shit about my parenting skills. Rhonda has taken our family through the ringer, but I don't need people judging me, or her, for that matter," Cory reported.

Megan recalled her conversation with Keisha about Cory's daughter, and she was right; Rhonda was a troubled teen. She didn't have the time or the desire to deal with a troubled teenager, and just thinking about all the stress that came with it made Megan anxious. Cory asked her to come over to help him figure a plan of action to find her. Megan agreed to help and left right away. When she arrived at Cory house, he suggested they go door to door looking for Rhonda. He told her that he had just got off the phone arguing with Sister Alexander over Rhonda. They walked over to his neighbor to the left. Mr. Howard was a nice man who loved planting flowers in his meticulous yard and spending time outdoors.

"Excuse me, Mr. Howard; have you have seen my daughter?" Cory asked.

"Yes, I saw her last night around 10:00 P.M. She was standing in front of your house arguing with some older man who looked disheveled. I thought he was drunk, or high on something. I've seen him once or twice before. I believe he's one of those druggies who lives downtown underneath the bridge," Mr. Howard reported.

"Druggie! My Rhonda might be a lot of things, but a druggie isn't one of them. What are you trying to insinuate? Where exactly downtown is this bridge where bums hang out?" Cory inquired.

"Mr. Alexander, I'm not insinuating anything. Heck! I don't even know Rhonda, and frankly, this is none of my business. Just check the bridge over on Monroe Avenue," Mr. Howard barked.

"Look, Mr. Howard, I need to find Rhonda, and I have a bad feeling that something is wrong. Thanks for your help," Cory told him.

Cory and Megan hurried back to get in his vehicle to head downtown. Meghan could tell that Cory was upset, knowing that his daughter was in danger. She grabbed his right hand to pray for Rhonda's safety.

They arrived at Monroe Avenue not knowing what to expect. It was a familiar street to anyone who lived in the city. Cory hadn't been downtown in a long time and wasn't aware of the destitute men and women, young and old, living tainted lives and destroying the otherwise family-friendly reputation of Pittsford.

He parked on a side street, and they began searching for Rhonda. Cory saw several young men loitering and asked if they knew or had seen his daughter while pulling up a picture of her on his iPhone. He was disappointed after they said they didn't recognize her. He and Megan kept searching and questioning whoever they came in contact with. As Megan combed the streets, she noticed an older man who fit the description that Mr. Howard had given them. The man looked as if he had been bingeing all night, making Cory reluctant to approach him, but it was a matter of life and death for his daughter's survival.

"Excuse me, sir; I'm looking for this young lady. Have you seen her?" Cory asked.

"Ugh, who wants to know?" the man questioned in a sour tone.

"I'm her father, so if you know anything about her whereabouts, you better tell me, and for the record, I'll be the one asking the questions," Cory snapped.

"Okay, okay. I know her. She likes to hang around here looking for Meth and any other drugs she can get her hands on," the man told him.

Cory grabbed the old man by his collar and demanded that he take him to her. Megan followed closely behind as the man led them to some tents underneath the bridge. When Cory got closer, he noticed a figure lying in the darkness halfway out of one of the tents. He ran toward the tent, hoping it wasn't Rhonda, and tried to force his way into the small opening, but instead, he ripped a bigger hole in the opening to fit inside.

He was horrified and sick to his stomach. His worst nightmare had come true. It *was* Rhonda, and her immobile body was in an unconscious state. He yelled her name repeatedly, but she didn't move or respond.

"Call 911," Cory yelled while attempting to wake her.

Megan nervously rambled through her purse to find her cell phone, and she pulled it out to call 911. It was difficult for her to watch Cory attempting to wake up his lifeless daughter. Her eyes produced a stream of tears that rolled down her face.

She could hear the ambulance getting closer, and soon two EMTs rushed over to work on Rhonda. They injected her with a dose of Naloxone in her leg, and it started working immediately. Her lifeless body was placed on the stretcher, and she was rushed to the nearest emergency room.

"Is my daughter going to be okay?" Cory yelled.

Megan told him, "Come on, honey. Give me your keys. We have to follow them to the hospital."

Megan did her best to keep up with the ambulance driver who was frantically weaving in and out of traffic before arriving at Highland Hospital. She and Cory waited in the emergency room for the ER doctor to give them an update. The doctor reported that Rhonda was going to survive, but the levels of Meth that showed up on her toxicology report were dangerously high, and if they had not found her when they did, she would've died on the street.

"We're going to have to keep Rhonda overnight so she can go through detoxification. We also recommend that she be admitted into our substance abuse program, as it's the best in the city. Our staff will talk to her about being admitted. We hope that she will be willing to go," the doctor explained.

"No worries. I will make sure she gets admitted. I'm so thankful that we didn't lose her," Cory said.

The search for Rhonda had been emotional for Megan too, making her relieved that things had ended the way they did. She realized that Cory and Rhonda would have a long road ahead of them and that professionals would be needed to turn things around. Although she felt sorry for their plight, she reminded herself that their challenges were theirs to bear. Being in a serious relationship with a man whose daughter was addict to drugs proved to be taxing. Besides, she needed to stay focused on her role in the ministry. Fighting to be a part of something bigger than herself was a thing she couldn't allow anyone to interfere with, especially a man.

She considered all the trauma she had gone through and how it had nearly destroyed her. She prayed for God to give her the courage to tell Cory that she was no longer interested in being in a committed relationship with him. It was important to her to let him down easy. She believed that she and Cory needed more time to get to know themselves as individuals before throwing all caution to the wind to be in a relationship.

Cory and Megan left the hospital, knowing that Rhonda was out of the woods and in good hands. On the drive back to his house, Cory couldn't stop thanking Megan for being there when he needed her. He told her that he didn't know what he would have done had she not come over to help him. Her mind wandered as he talked, and in the midst of it all, she felt a quickening in her spirit. The Holy Spirit was giving her a vision. She saw Cory walking through the doors of Victory Baptist Church.

*That's it!* she thought. She realized that God was using her to turn Cory's heart back to Him.

"Cory, I'm so happy that you trusted me enough to ask for my help. I thank God for His favor and for saving Rhonda's life. It's going to be a long road to recovery, but God is faithful. It's difficult for me to tell you this, but I've enjoyed the time we've spent together, but right now we're at difference places in our lives, and I don't want to be in a romantic relationship right now. It has nothing to do with you, because I think you're a good man. My commitment is to the church, and that's where my heart is. Rhonda really needs you right now. By the way, I recall you telling me how close you and the Williams men were growing up. They're amazing ministers, and both are so anointed that I believe they can help you and Rhonda strengthen your relationship with the Lord. David and Keisha preach a good word every Sunday. The congregation has grown since the Reverend's passing, and you never know; perhaps all of this is part of God's plan, and maybe He used me to turn your attention back toward Him and to help deliver Rhonda from her addiction," Megan reported.

"You might be onto something. Ever since I stepped foot back into Victory Baptist, I've been having a strong desire to attend church even though many Sunday's have passed, and I still haven't had the courage to walk through the doors. It's because I don't want to deal with the condemnation from my mother and the other members who can't seem to practice what they preach when it comes to Rhonda and me. They'd rather gossip about me being divorced and that I'm a single parent," Cory told her.

"I understand, but what you should focus on is God's ability to turn things around. It's by His grace that we're here. If you trust in Him, I know He will surprise you," Megan boasted.

Cory and Megan said their goodbyes and agreed to remain friends. Megan was proud of herself for having had the courage to be speak her truth. She thanked The Holy Spirit for helping her to find the right words to let Cory down easy. She felt blessed that she was able to use her influence to have him reconsider his relationship with God. Megan realized that God has a funny way of getting our attention no matter the circumstance. He's always there and His faithfulness is everlasting.

By the time she got home, she crawled into bed and didn't call Keisha to tell her about the details of her day. She figured that one way or another she would hear about it. She secretly hoped that it would be a future testimony for Rhonda and envisioned Cory praising God in front of the packed congregation about Rhonda's deliverance from disobedience and drug use, and then she fell fast asleep without incident.

Megan realized that she had really changed over the years and that her relationship with God was stronger for it. She learned that although the people she loved didn't always rise to the occasion, God's grace and mercy was always available. She had a deeper sense of self that only a special man could appreciate, and God would bless her with him one day, but for now she needed to trust HIM more.

# Chapter 11

# Wayward Blessings

## (Dreams Realized)

**K**eisha sat in her office meditating on God's word, and she couldn't help but consider everything that was happening to her family. *What an awesome God we serve*, she thought. So many of her prayers had been answered, and even the ones she didn't utter were coming true. "God knows everything," is something the Reverend said whenever anybody questioned God's will. He was blessing her family beyond measure, for example, allowing David and Loretta to become pregnant with their first son who would become the namesake of her father, along with the growing of the membership that was requiring a second location. Keisha was happier than she had been in a long time, knowing that she was the glue that kept her family together. She prayed that nothing or no one would ever be able to interfere with the many blessings God had for them.

With Mother's Day approaching quickly, Keisha wanted to ensure that things were going according to schedule. She hadn't heard back from Valerie regarding Mrs. Jakes' willingness to accept the invitation to be her guest speaker. She decided to reserve a couple of rooms at the Hilton Garden Inn just in case. Afterwards, Jada crossed her mind, so she prayed that things would go smoothly when her grandma arrived. She realized that it was a big gamble to have her visit, but if Ms. Emma Jean wasn't allowed to visit or any drama occurred while she was in town, both scenarios could cause

Jada to leave Pittsford and return to Dallas, never to be seen again. If Jada left, it would break their hearts, so she decided to call her to see how Jada was doing.

"Hey, sis, did you talk to your grandma again?" Keisha asked.

"Yes! I've been worrying about how she and Mom would get along, but we had a heart to heart talk and I don't think she'll do anything to compromise my relationship with y'all, but I've seen her act a fool a time or two when it wasn't necessary. She knows how important her promise to avoid any drama is to me," Jada reported.

"Girl, I'm glad you have the courage to address your concerns before she comes all the way out here. You don't have to worry about Mom; she'll go out of her way to make things comfortable for your grandma. Mom understands the power of forgiveness and will overlook any grievances quickly. She never ceases to amaze me when it comes to forgiveness. Let me know if there is anything else I can do to help while she's here," Keisha told her.

"Thanks, sis. I love you so much, and don't you ever forget it."

With that conversation out of the way, Keisha went back to work. She was proud of the direction she and David had taken the church. They had really made a difference in the community and with the congregation. She was excited about being given the opportunity to work with Terrance and Natalia at the new location if it came to that. She recalled Natalia's proposal for the new robes for the choir and had shoved the requisition to the bottom of the pile, so she pulled it out to review it. She agreed that they needed new robes for the choir known for their soulful renditions of hymns and top Gospel tunes sung with conviction. Natalia made praise and worship a great experience for everyone in attendance.

The cost of the robes would be a few hundred dollars, and Keisha signed the requisition and then forwarded it to David for final approval. Keisha called Sister Earnestine to get an update on her efforts to keep her mother in the dark about things.

"Hello, Sister Earnestine. How are things going? Mom hasn't let on that she knows anything about our plans, has she? If not, I owe you ladies a lot of credit, as she hasn't said anything to me. Good job! I'm wondering about the plans for the food?" Keisha said.

"Keisha, your mama doesn't know a thing. She too busy focusing on making sure Jada's grandma is comfortable. Hold on, baby. Let me grab a copy of the menu," Sister Earnestine told her.

When Sister Earnestine returned, she read the menu, "Chicken 'n Waffles Casserole, Mimi-Bagel Breakfast Sliders, Ham & Cheese Breakfast Roll-Ups, Jalapeno Popper Egg Cups, Mimosa Fruit Salad, Cheese Bacon Quiche, Watermelon and Raspberry Salad with Mimosas, and Starbucks Coffee."

"Oh, my goodness, Sister Earnestine, the ladies are going to love it! I'm getting hungry just thinking about that chicken and waffle casserole. Please make sure you all keep Mom distracted as time gets closer, because it will get harder to do. Oh, and by the way, the color scheme this year is purple and green. I wanted to get some of those tinted mason jars or some sort of country-style vessels to place the fresh cut flowers in. I think I know a place where I can buy some. I will check it out and try to confirm delivery this week," Keisha reported.

"We can meet on Thursday to finish decorating, and I will call you tomorrow with more updates," Sister Earnestine replied.

Keisha was satisfied after talking things over with Sister Earnestine. She decided to call Valerie again to follow up but didn't get an answer. After feeling discouraged, she considered Plan B in case Mrs. Jakes couldn't attend. "Go away, Devil," she declared.

No sooner than she said those words, her cell phone rang and it was Valerie.

"Keisha, I have some great news for you. I spoke to Sister Jakes' daughter Sarah, and she talked to First Lady Jakes. She has agreed to be your guest speaker and is ready to sign the contract. She also asked about accommodations. I told her that you will email her the rest of the information. God really does move mountains. I'm going to check my schedule to see if I can come too," Valerie said.

Keisha let out a shout of praise, "Thank you, God, for your mercy! Valerie, I'm so happy that you want to come too. I can't wait to see you, and thanks again for coordinating this for me," Keisha replied.

Keisha continued to tie up the rest of the details for the Mother's Day celebration, and before she could get to the next task, she heard a knock on the door. It was Megan and Natalia, and they had come to talk about the collaboration of "Oh Happy Day".

Natalia had been working hard on the arrangement. Keisha examined their faces and wondered what they were up to. Megan broke the ice by asking if they remembered the good ole days when they used to compete for everything. She brought up all of the auditions they had attended and how competitive they were for the limited roles in Mr. York's class, "Keisha, I can still hear your voice the time you auditioned with that Maya Angelou piece. It was the first time I heard 'Phenomenal Woman', and, girl, you killed it. You got a standing ovation. You have always been so brave; it's one of the many things I admire about you. I was anxious, knowing that I was going to have to follow you, but you guys know I've always had a flair for the dramatics, so when it was my turn, I gave it my all on that monologue from *West Side Story*. I couldn't believe that after all of that drama we all made his roster. I really miss those days. That was how our beautiful friendship began, and it's still resilient to this day," Megan told them.

"Girl, you're right about that," Keisha agreed.

"Well, Keisha, I've been thinking about the Mother's Day celebration and how the choir needs to do something over the top. I tested my idea on Megan first, and now we're here to get your buy-in. I want to do a special rendition of 'Oh Happy Day'. It's a song that everyone is familiar with and can sing along. It's time for us to showcase our voices just like we did in high school. The choir has never heard us sing together, so it would be fitting for this special occasion. They've heard me sing since I'm our choir director, but they will be in for a real treat once we start to harmonize because we sound so good together," Natalia reported. "You guys think you know me, but I'm going to surprise you with my answer. *I love it!* It fits in perfectly with the program and spirit of the day. By the way, I just signed the requisition for the new choir robes and forwarded it to David. He will approve it soon. This is going to be a great time. Are you sure the company has enough robes? Did you check to see if you can place a special order this late?" Keisha inquired.

"Yes! We only need fifty robes, but I ordered a few extras just in case we get some new members or someone leaves and doesn't return their robe. I'm so happy that you trust me. Ladies, I really hate to bust your bubble, but you'll have to take a back seat when I sing my part," Natalia teased.

"Well, just for the record, I'm not even in the running. The competition has always been between you and Megan. You're the divas with the vocals that command attention," Keisha added.

"Natalia, we shall see who the congregation likes the best. They haven't heard me sing, so I suggest you go home and brush up," Megan asserted.

The Wayward Sisters could barely contain themselves. It felt good to allow some playfulness in their day whenever possible and not be so serious all the time. It was the one thing that they had loved most while in high school. Being carefree and lighthearted made them feel good. They had spent a lot of time hanging out in Pittsford Park, although there were times when they had faced some real crisis that had drained them emotionally.

Natalia excused herself to work on the arrangement with the musicians before choir practice started. She was feeling on top of the world. Being the choir director meant that she was able to meet the needs of the choir based on her ideas and experiences without always having to justify her decisions at every turn.

 She was able to impact the congregation with her music ministry and was thrilled that Megan and Keisha were on board. She couldn't wait for Mother's Day. Natalia told the choir that their robes were being purchased and they would be wearing them soon.

"Are you guys ready to work hard? Today we'll start with vocal exercises, with the sopranos and altos taking the lead. Tenors and baritones follow me. I need your help rearranging our instruments."

She pointed out what they needed to do and asked them to return to practice when they finished, "I need you to really concentrate on your parts, as we need to be flawless. Our rendition of 'Oh Happy Day' will be worthy of a Dove Award," Natalia joked.

Choir practice lasted for a few hours with the choir's voices and the instruments needing to be tuned. Natalia became distracted when Terrance walked into the room. She hadn't seen him since their rendezvous and prayed things wouldn't be awkward between them. To her surprise, Terrance rushed over with a sense of urgency and planted a juicy kiss on her lips in front of everyone.

"This is my lady, and if you think you've seen a lot of me lately, you will be seeing me a lot more," Terrance announced, not realizing that Juan was there helping out in the back room. He came running out to see what was going on. Terrance felt a little embarrassed and uncomfortable.

"Man, did you just say you and my mom are dating? No wonder she's been acting like a teenager. Sorry, Mom, but you're the one who told Marco and me that this is the way you acted when you first met our dad," Juan teased.

"Yes, Juan, your mom and I are dating. Don't worry, son; I will treat your Mom with the respect she deserves," Terrance told him.

The choir was shocked. Terrance's bold declaration of their relationship was refreshing and a sign that good things were coming. Natalia wondered if he had told his family about them but decided to ask him at another time. With all the excitement, Natalia thought it was a good idea to end choir practice. Juan gave Terrance high fives before he pulled out his cell phone to call Marco, "Hey, bro, I know why Terrance has been hanging around and Mom has been acting so weird. They've been sneaking around behind our backs to date. Terrance is cool, and Mom has finally found a good man," Juan bragged.

"For real? I can't wait to give Mom a hard time. She's always teasing us and stays up in our business when she thinks she knows something and then says our girlfriends aren't good enough," Marco laughed.

"You got that right," Juan agreed.

Natalia blushed as she was being congratulated by the choir members. She found it difficult to look Juan in the eye or anyone else for that matter. Terrance told her that he planned to take them out to dinner, but Natalia said she wanted Marco to be there too.

"I got you, man. I've already alerted Marco, and he's changing clothes right now," Juan announced, but Marco didn't get in the shower or change his clothes. He decided to wait until they came to the house first and then he would get moving. He had played basketball and was tired and wanted to relax for a bit.

Natalia said, "I apologize if we embarrassed you, Juan. We wanted to keep our relationship hidden for a little while longer, but Terrance is so spontaneous. I hope you and your brother aren't disappointed in me. I never expected to be linked romantically to Terrance, but this is proof that things can happen when you least expect it."

"Mom, we really like Terrance. He's a good dude. I find him to be easy to relate with, plus he's so dope on the basketball court. Did you run this relationship stuff though my godmother or anyone else who could oppose it? Juan asked.

"Well, son, your godmother and Megan are aware, and... oh yeah, Jada too. The only people that Terrance hasn't told are David and Victoria, and I'm a little nervous about how they will react. I don't want Victoria to think I have bad intentions since Terrance is younger than me, has no children, and just got out of a bad relationship," Natalia admitted.

Natalia attempted to change the subject on the drive home. She told Juan that she was proud of him for helping out at the church lately and that his generosity and caring spirit would take him far in life. Juan smiled and thanked her for taking good care of him and his brother under dire circumstances.

"I've been thinking about my dad a lot lately. He was my hero, but there were other times when I couldn't stand to be around him. I wish he could've been around a lot longer to see Marco and I grow up. I know he would've been so proud of us," Juan said.

"Oh, my sweet Juan, you changed your father's life the day you were born. He loved you and your brother dearly. Unfortunately, he was young and wanted to live life his way, but things didn't work out favorably for him. I want you to remember that people don't always get things right the first time in life, and most of us need a 'Do-over' before we succeed. It makes me sad, too, that your dad had to lose his life so early, but I promise that he'll always be in your heart and that his memory will live on if you allow it to," Natalia told him.

Natalia became emotional after hearing how much Juan missed his father. She prayed that her boys didn't think she was trying to replace him with Terrance. She believed that she deserved to be happy and have a romantic partner who showered her with the desires of her heart. She and Carlos had gotten pregnant, married, and lived a life of chaos. Getting married at such an early age caused her to lose the opportunity to follow her dreams and to go to college. Her parents, Javier and Rosemarie Sanchez, loved their daughter, and she was the apple of their eye. They were disappointed that her being with

Carlos meant that she would lose out on everything promised to a young, middle-class, intelligent, and talented girl.

Natalia, now in her mid-thirties, vowed to do things differently. She had prayed that God would make her life better and would send her a man who would encourage her to be her best self. She believed that Terrance was that man. She recalled how Keisha prayed at the embankment when they were in high school that they would have men worthy of them someday. She credited her for her current situation, since knowing Keisha had allowed her to meet Terrance.

Natalia walked inside the house and noticed that Terrance had beat her there and was already inside talking to Marco who still looked like he had played a laborious game of one-on-one. However, he didn't waste time chastising his mom and Terrance for their deception.

"Mom, I know you didn't think all that flirting you've been doing with Terrance has gone unnoticed. I knew you were crushing on him. You were always staring at him whenever he came over. Terrance, I hope you'll be good to my mom. I like you too, but my mom's feelings and care come first," Marco declared.

"Man, I wanted to tell you guys, but we thought it was best to keep it quiet. We didn't want our relationship to interfere with our commitment to the church, but with your permission, I would like to date your mom and to spend more time with the two of you. You've got my promise that I won't break your beautiful mom's heart," Terrance reported.

"Terrance, I was the one who prayed for Mom to find a good man and to fall in love. Mom was acting like an old maid after our dad died. Marco and I just want her to be happy. You can date her, but don't hurt her," Juan said.

"I hear you both, and actions speak louder than words, so I will show you," Terrance said.

Terrance was happy that Juan and Marco felt comfortable enough to speak their minds. He attempted to change the subject by suggesting they order pizza from Pontillo's Pizzeria instead of going out to eat. He wanted to share his vacation plans with them. Initially, he wanted to take Natalia to Puerto Rico after hearing how much she loved vacationing there, but he changed his mind, knowing that the island had been hit by Hurricane

Maria. When they first met, they spent hours on the phone talking about her summers there as a teenager and how her cousin taught her how to surf. She hadn't seen her cousins and friends in years.

Terrance wanted to meet the people she spoke highly of, but after he noticed that it was starting to upset her whenever he mentioned going there, he didn't think it was a good idea. Her relatives were going through a rough time since many parts of the island were deemed unsafe. Terrance called a travel agent to get information about all-inclusive trips to the Grand Cayman Islands. He planned to take Natalia, her boys, Leroy, and Natalia's parents.

When the pizza arrived, Juan and Marco slapped each other high fives, knowing that their favorite pizza would be devoured within minutes. Terrance paid and tipped the driver, and Natalia placed paper plates on the kitchen table and made a pitcher of strawberry lemonade. The pizza was dripping with gooey, fresh mozzarella cheese and was topped with scrumptious pepperoni. While they ate, Terrance asked Natalia if she could picture herself laying on a beautiful sunny beach with pure white sand, and then he asked Juan and Marco if they knew how to snorkel. They all talked over each as they tried to answer Terrance.

"I've never tried snorkeling, but it sounds fun," Marco reported.

"Of course I can imagine myself on a beautiful beach, since I love beaches, especially the ones with crystal-clear blue water," Natalia replied.

"Mom, can you teach us how to surf?" Juan asked.

Terrance told them about his plans to take them to the Grand Cayman Islands. He said it would be a lot of fun, and he was hoping they wanted to go. He also said it would be a good way for them to get to know each other better. He told them that he wanted to bring Leroy too, since he had a lot in common with Juan and Marco and he wanted to do something special for him too. He cautioned them not to start packing their suitcases since he needed to wait to see how the board members would vote. He said that if they voted to build a second location, it would be possible for them to squeeze in a weeks' vacation. He asked Natalia how she felt about her parents tagging along.

"Terrance, you haven't even met my parents yet. Don't you think it would be awkward trying to get to know them this way?" Natalia asked.

"Not really, as I'm pretty sure your mom will love me and that your dad will think I'm the perfect man for you," Terrance said with confidence.

"True dat!" Marco blurted out.

"Grandma Rosemarie and Grandpa Javier love to travel, and it will be just like old times," Juan said.

Natalia believed that Terrance was a good choice and the best man she'd dated. God was blessing her with a man who her sons adored, which was important to her. Terrance had great qualities, such as being kind, considerate, handsome, trustworthy, and he came from a great family. Those things made him marrying material. A trip to the Grand Cayman Islands sounded enticing, but she thought it would be difficult to convince her parents to tag along since they hadn't spent much time together lately.

"I'll check with Mom to see if she and Dad can go. They are pretty selfish when it comes to me. After all, I'm their only baby girl. It will take a confident, respectful, and established man to win them over," Natalia bragged.

"Sounds like your describing me, baby. I figured we can leave around the Fourth of July. You can get back to your work on the tribute you've been working on, and I can keep the boys company. You have a few days to get an answer from them," Terrance said as he planted a kiss on her forehead.

Terrance challenged Juan and Marco to a few one-on-one basketball games. In their excitement, they failed to clean up after themselves, which was something that irritated Natalia. "There's a cost to having three men under one roof," she said to herself as she cleaned up their mess. She peeked out of the kitchen window to admire Terrance. His ability to engage with Juan and Marco was impressive. Her heart was full of joy, and she believed that God had planned a bright future for her and her sexy boo.

# Chapter 12

## Wayward Memories

### (Family Flashback)

Megan couldn't resist the urge to refrain from being so hard on herself. She thought she had fallen in love with Cory for the right reasons but admitted that her dreams of winning in love with him hadn't lined up the way she wished they had. Cory couldn't be that special man because of the baggage he brought to the table, but she was willing to hold out hope that he and his daughter would develop an imitate relationship with God in the near future. Megan had become obsessed with her position at the church and worked hard to strengthen her relationship with God over the past few years. She was impacting the world through her contributions and was committed to spending a lot more time with her parents and siblings. Their once strained relationship was now on good footing. Mental illness and substance abuse ran in her family and had nearly claimed the life of her and her mother.

Megan was grateful that her mother had overcome her substance abuse dependency. She was a completely different person than she once was, and they had become the best of friends while spending time going on mother and daughter outings. While in high school, Megan felt unworthy, and her self-esteem plummeted shortly after her parents' divorce. She hated her life and the fact that she didn't have pretty clothes and all the latest gadgets like her peers. Going to Pittsford Sutherland High School added to her frustration. Her peers enjoyed great middle-class lives and were spoiled brats who got everything they wanted. Her father Stephen, a district attorney, allowed his family to experience the good life and made sure they remained in their suburban home when he moved out. Megan was forced to take on more responsibilities than most girls her age. She saw firsthand the emotional breakdown of her mother. Janice wasn't able to control her emotions and would burst into tears at the slightest irritation. She didn't realize how manipulative and controlling her mother was, and her poor example caused Megan to become just like her later in life. Janice dated a lot of men, who she paraded around the house like trophies with no regard to the impressionable eyes of her daughter.

Megan's mother had cursed her by forcing her to take on motherly duties that didn't belong to her. Life with Janice robbed Megan of her childhood and the attention she desperately sought from both her parents. Janice neglected her children by avoiding her responsibilities and hiding in her room. She became disconnected and selfish and only cared about the men she was interested in. It was a miracle that Megan and her siblings made it through those dark times. Megan recalled her mother's boyfriend, Andrew, a pervert who lurked around their house waiting for an opportunity to violated her. He knew their routine and would show up every morning to get a glimpse of her as she came out of the bathroom after her shower. Her blonde, shoulder-length hair would still be wet, making her look irresistible to him. When she told her mother about Andrew's creepy behavior, she blew her off, claiming that she was exaggerating and that Andrew was harmless. She chastised her for not being nicer to him, and she continued to allow him to visit.

Megan credited her sister Mattie for stopping the would-be rapist the morning he cornered her as she tried to leave the house to catch the school bus. Mattie had returned home to tell Megan that the bus was coming, and her loud voice had distracted him so Megan could break free when he had pinned her down and almost had her underwear off. She decided to keep the ugly details to herself, but the ordeal had cost her a lot, including the inability to refrain from being promiscuous once she entered high school.

Keisha became Megan's saving grace after introducing her to Jesus. She thanked God for Keisha being a great friend and sticking with her through the good and bad times. As an adult, Megan learned to forgive her mother for not protecting her and for chasing every rabbit hole for a man to make her feel loved and to help numb her pain. Megan mirrored her mother's low self-esteem and devalued her body too. She didn't think she was beautiful, but Keisha and Natalia made sure she knew she was beautiful at every opportunity.

Shortly after graduating from St. John Fisher College, Megan worked in corporate America in a predominantly male environment and couldn't seem to avoid her wayward ways. She lusted for the attention of men who didn't deserve her attention. She recalled her failed relationship with a debonair Italian man named Vinnie who dressed impeccably from head to toe. He smelled like a million bucks and wined and dined her and spent money on luxury weekend outings. However, after seducing her and making sure she was strung out on cocaine, he disappeared.

She lived a dysfunctional life dependent on prescription drugs and alcohol. She never thought that she would fall victim to such a loser, but God delivered her and placed her on the other side of freedom to live an abundant life. Stephen and Janice eventually remarried and were showering her with the love and support she deserved.

Megan learned to spend time with people who supported her in positive ways. She learned to cope by alternating from the Williams house and her parents for support. She also started a ritual on Sundays by having dinner with her parents and siblings Matthew and Mattie who were now married with children of their own. Her parents taught them to believe in the American Dream and the institution of marriage, but her father fell short when he cheated on her mother. Megan was amazed by God's mercies and by the work He was doing in her family.

Megan spent a lot of time praying about the upcoming vote to expand the church, and the idea of being able to utilize her degree in theology intrigued her. She wanted to share her power life story and to use it as her platform by highlighting the good parts of her middle-class life as well as the dark periods of her life. She believed that people were better off married than choosing to be single all their lives. Keisha and Natalia had both been previously married, although their marriages didn't last. Megan wanted to be lucky enough to have someone want to put a ring on it. She prayed for future matrimony and a life of bliss.

# Chapter 13

# Wayward Courage

## (Jada's Liberation)

By the time Friday rolled around, Jada was anxious about her grandma's visit. Ms. Emma Jean was flying into the Rochester Airport and would need to be picked up, so she asked Keisha and David to ride along for extra support. She couldn't wait for her grandma to meet her family and to show her around Pittsford, a city she'd become fond of. Pittsford was vastly different from Dallas, and her grandma hadn't visited too many places, so she wanted her to see as much as possible. Ms. Emma Jean was a stubborn woman who once she made up her mind it was difficult for anyone to change it. Growing up, Jada recalled how her mother and grandma constantly backstabbed the Reverend and Victoria. Most of their rants were about her father being a womanizer who got another woman pregnant behind Victoria's back. They believed the Reverend was a hypocrite who preached the opposite to many. They claimed he treated Jada differently and blamed Victoria for tolerating his bad behavior. Ms. Emma Jean said Victoria was bitchy and that she thought she was better than everyone else. When Jada became a teenager, she realized her mother and grandma were wrong about them. They were "hating" on them, and it angered her whenever she overheard them making negative comments. Her grandma did her best to keep her away from her dad and her siblings, but despite her efforts, the Reverend found a way for them remain in contact. They'd talk on the phone and exchange letters. They enjoyed a relationship where forgiveness and love were unconditional between them.

Prior to picking up Ms. Emma Jean, Jada wanted to relieve some stress so she asked Keisha to accompany her on a run in Pittsford Park. Jada was convinced that Pittsford Park was a place where you could experience an encounter with God at the embankment, and jogging there had become part of her regular routine. It was her spiritual oasis and place of reckoning. Keisha was thrilled that Jada had asked her and decided to join her to make sure she was okay.

"Sis, why are you so anxious? I thought you had a good talk with your grandma and that you told her your expectations. You said she would be on her best behavior."

"Keisha, you don't know my grandma, and to be honest, she might be bipolar. One minute she's the sweetest lady in the world, and the next she acts like a vicious spider who will attack with deadly venom. I'm afraid that she'll show her vicious side, and that's the last thing I want to happen because that could damage our relationship," Jada told her.

Keisha replied, "Sis, don't worry; we'll be respectful. But I can't say that Mom will hold her tongue if Ms. Emma Jean starts attacking her unfairly. Mom is sophisticated, reserved, nice, and a lot of other adjectives, but when it comes to being disrespected, she doesn't play."

After taking a few minutes to get ready, Keisha and Jada jumped into Keisha's vehicle and headed to Pittsford Park, and like on all other occasions, Keisha led Jada to the embankment to pray prior to taking a brisk jog. The air was cool. Keisha grabbed Jada's hands and started to pray so they could get done faster.

"Dear Lord, we thank You for this beautiful day and for the many blessings that You have bestowed upon our family, and we praise Your mighty name. Thank You for covering us. We come boldly in Your presence to ask that You watch over us in the coming day and guard our tongues and hearts. Give us peace and harmony. We thank You in advance. Amen," Keisha prayed.

Keisha gave Jada a loving hug before taking off on the trail, with Jada following closely behind. Keisha kept a steady pace. Running was her forte, and it kept her in good shape. She wanted to run a marathon someday, but up to this point her responsibilities at the church kept her plate full.

They ran the usual route, but Jada continued to feel anxious about her grandma's visit. She attempted to think about something else, but her mind kept replaying thoughts of Ms. Emma Jean disrespecting her father. She prayed for peace, and then, suddenly, she felt a quickening in her spirit. Her palms became sweaty, and she felt weak, which caused her to stop in her tracks. She heard a small whisper and was in disbelief; it was her father. The word, "*Liberation,*" rang out loud and clear.

She took a moment to meditate on his word and could feel her body regaining strength. She was in a peaceful state, and in the moment she realized that his word was meant to encourage her to live her life without fear or regrets. She was in agreement and believed that she needed to be free of anxiety and was no longer obligated to be under her grandma's control. Feeling as if a huge weight had been lifted, she ran a little faster to catch up with Keisha so they could finish their run.

During the ride home, Jada couldn't help but share her experienced with Keisha, "Today was amazing. I heard from Dad, and he encouraged me to take back my power from my grandma," she bragged.

Keisha assured her that she was equipped with good advice and was responsible for her own happiness. When they pulled into the garage, they noticed that David was there and hurried to get showered and change clothes. Victoria fixed them a delicious breakfast, consisting of bacon, eggs, French toast, hash browns, and coffee. Once dressed, Keisha and Jada joined them in the kitchen.

"Mom, you know I only come over when I smell food," David joked.

"I know! I figured I would make you all a hot breakfast since you have a long day ahead of you. They say breakfast is the most important meal of the day," Victoria reported.

"Thanks, Mom. I'm going to need all the energy that I can muster. Everything tastes delicious," Jada replied.

"Jada, I'm glad your grandma has decided to come see you. We heard a lot about her when we were growing up, especially when Mom and Dad argued. Those were trying times for everyone. I think it's a good idea that you asked her to come during the Mother's Day weekend. There will be a lot going on that should keep everyone busy and in a good mood," Keisha told her.

Victoria said, "Keisha, I'm so glad you brought that up. Your dad and I used to have some spirited disagreements. I want to apologize for causing you and your brothers so much stress. We knew better, and trust me; we tried to keep things out of earshot. Jada, I'm sure you can understand that your dad and I had some problems in our marriage that stemmed from your mom and grandma's meddling. I forgave them a long time ago. I love you, sweetheart, and I've always advocated for you. I've worked hard to make things special for your grandma, and we will have a great time. I don't want you to worry about anything while she's here."

"Thanks, Mom! I appreciate everything that you've done for me and my grandma. I feel a lot better now and look forward to her meeting you all," Jada replied.

David told Jada and Keisha that it was time to get moving since they were likely to run into traffic near the airport. He gave Jada a brotherly hug and before getting into the vehicle assured her that her grandma would be treated with kindness and respect.

When they arrived at the terminal, they waited patiently at the curbside to pick Ms. Emma Jean up. In the meantime, she was waiting for an airport employee to escort her to the baggage claim area. When Jada finally saw her, she jumped out of the car and ran toward the American Airlines entry door to greet her. She gave her one of the biggest hugs that she could muster. David and Keisha exited the vehicle too, but they waited for Jada's lead for introductions. Jada relieved the airport employee and wheeled Ms. Emma Jean over to the car to meet them.

Ms. Emma Jean was a strong African-American woman with a lot of wisdom. Her beautiful, dark complexion, head full of gray hair, and distinguished Afro demanded respect. She looked like she was in her early seventies with a standoffish attitude. The woman didn't mix words and would bite your head off if you got sideways with her or were in her personal space. You could tell that she had lived a life that had ebbed and flowed through good and bad times, but she had survived.

Jada held her grandma's hand as she introduced Keisha and David. She felt confident and proud, "Grandma, this is David, my oldest brother, and Keisha, my big sister. I'm so happy to be here with them. They make me feel special," she reported.

"I'm happy to meet you both. Thank you for all the love you've shown my dearest Jada," Ms. Emma Jean told them.

"Thank you, Ma'am. I'm happy to call Jada my sister," David said.

"Ms. Emma Jean, Jada is a smart and beautiful young woman. I have grown to adore her not only as a sister but as a friend. I appreciate the wonderful job you and her mother have done raising her," Keisha added.

The ride home to Pittsford was mostly quiet. They were in their own bubble thinking about how the next few days would go. When David pulled into the family's driveway, everyone started talking nervously.

David grabbed Ms. Emma Jean's suitcase and escorted her up the walkway leading to the front door. Victoria was standing there ready to greet them. She was dressed comfortably in a pair of slacks and a T-shirt but looked beautiful and didn't waste time introducing herself.

"Ms. Emma Jean, it's so good to finally meet you in person. Jada has missed you, and she is always talking about you. Please come in and make yourself comfortable. We've tried to make things relaxing for your stay," Victoria said.

"I appreciate it! By the way, your home is lovely, and Jada tells me that you're a good cook, so I can't wait to see for myself," Ms. Emma Jean asserted.

Jada gave her grandma a tour of their beautiful home before escorting her to the guest bedroom. She told Ms. Emma Jean about the city of Pittsford, their family church, and gave her an update about her business ventures.

Jada talked her grandma's ear off. She was happy that her doctor had given her a clean bill of health. A few years earlier, she had faced a health scare with cancer, but by the grace of God she had beat the dreadful disease.

Keisha excused herself to go over to the church. She needed to ensure things were in order for the Mother's Day celebration and to make a few calls. She called Northwest Lantern Company to verify that the five hundred lanterns she had ordered would be delivered on time. She verified that the delivery address was to the Faith and Hope Church located down the street, as their pastor had agreed to join in the celebration in exchange for the use of his space. She called Valerie and confirmed that Sister Jakes and her daughter Sarah were arriving on Saturday evening. Then she called Sister Earnestine to see how things were going behind the scenes and was pleased with all the updates she received. The last person she needed to talk to was her mother, but she had avoided her. Now it was necessary so she could make sure the tasks she was responsible for were completed.

Keisha walked back over to the house and went into the kitchen where she found Victoria sitting at the kitchen table with Jada and Ms. Emma Jean.

She joined the conversation right away, "Sorry for my absence, but I had some really important calls to make. Mom, we need to go over some details. Do you need my help with the menu or decorations?" Keisha asked.

"No, Keisha. The ladies have been prepping all week, and we have everything ready to go. I was wondering what you plan to do about the floral arrangements. I've been meaning to ask you, but you've been so busy," Victoria said.

"No worries, Mom; I have taken care of the flowers. The colors are purple and green this year. I can't wait, and the menu is outstanding, so everything is going to be delicious," Keisha bragged.

Keisha stayed in the kitchen to support Jada and to make sure her grandma felt welcome in their home. Victoria announced that dinner was ready. She'd cooked some Sweet and Smoky Cedar-Planked Salmon that she served with roasted potatoes and steamed green beans. She figured that she couldn't go wrong with that option. After they washed their hands, Victoria led them to the dining room.

Ms. Emma Jean complimented Victoria on how good the food smelled, "Everything smells wonderful," Ms. Emma Jean said.

"Thank you. I hope you enjoy your meal," Victoria replied.

Jada pulled out a chair at the opposite end of the table for her grandma before volunteering to say grace. Terrance walked into the dining room. He had been in meetings all day and hadn't had the opportunity to meet Ms. Emma Jean.

"Grandma, this is Terrance. He's the youngest. He and I were the last to agree to join the family ministry. It's been great to work together, and we have so much to offer the congregation. I know our dad would be very proud of how we've kept his legacy moving forward so far," Jada reported.

While Jada was talking, she heard her grandma purposely clear her throat, and when Jada gave her that look, Ms. Emma Jean rolled her eyes. Jada couldn't believe that she was starting her antics already, but she hoped that no one else had heard or seen her acting a fool.

"Hello, Ma'am. Jada has told us a lot about you, and speaking for myself, I couldn't wait to meet you. We love Jada, and she has changed our lives for the better in such a short time. You have done a really good job of raising her," Terrance told her.

Ms. Emma Jean nodded her head in agreement but chose not to engage any further. Although everyone sitting at the table found her lack of response to be rude, they ignored her and continued to eat. After dinner, Keisha cleared away their plates and helped to tidy the kitchen before excusing herself again. She was ready to go to bed, knowing that there were going to be a lot of challenges in the coming days. Victoria and Jada remained in the kitchen with Ms. Emma Jean, but they were careful not to bring up the Reverend's name again to avoid any more of her snarky responses.

# Chapter 14

# Wayward Excellence

## (Keisha's Influence)

Keisha felt on top of the world and was so proud of herself for keeping such a big secret from her mother. She knew that Victoria would be ecstatic when she found out that she was being honored on Mother's Day in front of all of her children. Keisha used the event as a good excuse to go shopping. Lately, she hadn't had a lot of time to go shopping, which is her favorite pastime. She decided to invite Megan and Natalia so they could spend some much-needed girl time.

She called Megan first, "Megan, I feel like spending some money, so are you free to go shopping and do lunch tomorrow?" Keisha asked.

"Keisha, you're talking my language. I'm ready to spend," Megan said.

Before calling Natalia, Keisha told Megan that she was going to invite Natalia too, and it would be just like old times, especially when they used to have lunch at the Village Coal Restaurant.

"Hello, Keisha. What did I do to earn the honor of receiving a telephone call from you?" Natalia joked.

Keisha told her about their plans, and Natalia was willing to tag along with her besties. Keisha went back into the kitchen for a cup of tea. Jada and her grandma were still sitting at the kitchen table sharing laughs and talking about the sightseeing they did earlier. Jada had taken her for a long drive to show off some of the landmarks in Pittsford.

Jada asked Keisha if she would remain in the kitchen to sip her tea, something Keisha didn't want to do, but supporting Jada was more important than allowing a grumpy old woman to intimidate her.

"I hope you are enjoying your stay. Pittsford is one of those places you'll either fall in love with or won't care too much for. It's worlds apart from Dallas, but I hope you like it enough to come back someday for another visit," Keisha said.

"So far so good. It's pretty out here, but I couldn't deal with this cold weather all the time. I've lived in Dallas for so long that I've forgotten what it feels like to shiver, and I'm not interested. I'll stick with the heat!" Ms. Emma Jean told her.

Keisha gave Ms. Emma Jean a hug before excusing herself for the night. Once on the other side of her bedroom door, she got undressed and took a much-needed, long, hot shower.

Jada remained in the kitchen for a bit longer to brag about her opportunity to get to know her siblings and the many ways God was blessing her. She wanted her grandma to be happy for her.

"Jada, your folks seem nice, but the jury is still out on Victoria. I think she's a phony who doesn't really want me here, but I'm hoping that I'm wrong. I told you that I will be on my best behavior, and I plan to keep my word," Ms. Emma Jean reported.

"Thanks, Grandma. I realize that you and Victoria have some bad blood, and it's hard to change the way you feel about someone who you think has wronged you, but I believe that God has the power to lead you both to forgiveness. Working in the ministry has been an eye-opening experience, and I have witnessed so many people turn their lives around, and those of their families. I can't wait for you to see how God's anointing works in our church. I've never seen anything so beautiful," Jada told her.

"Like I said, Jada, I'm not going to do anything to rock the boat, but I'm entitled to my opinion and shouldn't have to apologize for it," Ms. Emma Jean reported.

Jada suggested they go to bed since it had gotten late. She planned for them to spend the majority of their Saturday helping the women at the church to ensure that everything was in order for the Mother's Day celebration.

She escorted Ms. Emma Jean to her bedroom and reminded her of where the extra towels and toiletries were if she needed them. When Jada walked into her bedroom, she felt relieved to finally have some time to herself. She immediately fell down to her knees to pray for her family. Once satisfied, she prepared for bed by removing her make-up, washing and moisturizing her face, and then she took a shower. Jada went to bed with high expectations for the weekend and hoped to make some awesome memories with her family.

The smell of bacon was in the air, causing Jada to wake up to it. She loved bacon and wanted to make sure she got a few pieces, so she hurried to get dressed. She slipped into a pair of jeans and a T-shirt. Jada wasn't surprised that her grandma was already up. She was an early riser who could be found strolling the neighborhood back in Dallas, and it was how she stayed in shape.

"Good morning, Grandma. I hope you slept well. Are you ready for a hearty breakfast? Mom is cooking, and I must say she hasn't made anything that I don't like," Jada said.

"Oh yes, Jada. I slept like a baby, and I'm kinda hungry too," Ms. Emma Jean replied.

Jada took her grandma's hand and escorted her into the kitchen where the rest of the family had already congregated. Victoria greeted Ms. Emma Jean and offered her something to eat. Keisha and Terrance said hello too. There wasn't a lot of chit chat going on during breakfast, with the exception of Keisha informing Ms. Emma Jean of the agenda for the day before asking Jada what she had planned.

Keisha inquired of Jada, "I'm getting ready to hit the mall with my girls. I haven't had the time to do any shopping lately, and my wallet is bursting at the seams and waiting for me to empty it. We're also having lunch at the Village Coal Restaurant. Would you and your grandma like to join us?"

"Sis, I've made plans for Mom and my grandma already. We're heading over to the church to help the women decorate and to put the finishing touches in place. Afterwards, I'm treating them to a tea at the Oak Hill Country Club. They're hosting a Mother's Day Tea along with a Kentucky Derby style hat contest. My grandma has the secret weapon to win the grand prize. It's a beautiful, yellow, wide-brim Kentucky Derby Church Hat with several beautiful colors mixed throughout. It's pretty fashionable. She found it at a local thrift shop," Jada bragged.

"It does sounds like a winner. Mom, which one of your lovely hats that you have tucked away in your closet do you plan to wear?" Keisha inquired.

"I'm going with my feather cocktail-style hat since I'll be wearing a bigger one on Sunday," Victoria said.

Keisha excused herself and wished Ms. Emma Jean good luck. Terrance gave Victoria a kiss on her cheek and excused himself too. He planned to hang out with Juan and Marco while Natalia was shopping. He figured they could enjoy a noneventful day of bonding and eating the food Natalia had prepared for them along with watching sports on television. She had made chili and cheese dip, nachos, mini-pizzas, and chicken wings that were guaranteed to keep them out of trouble during her absence.

Ms. Emma Jean told Jada that she was ready to start the day. As they walked over to the church, Jada made small talk and was excited to show off the family's famous church. When Ms. Emma Jean walked inside, she was in awe of the beautiful sanctuary and could be heard gasping as she took in all of its beauty.

"Jada, it's beautiful and looks just the way I imagined it would. Your father had a flair for the nicer things in life, and by the size and contents of this church, I can see where he spent his money. No wonder he always claimed to be poor and would never send any extra money when your mama asked for it," Ms. Emma Jean said matter-of-factly.

"Grandma, stop it! That's nonsense! The congregation financed this beautiful building and all of its contents. I wish you would stop all of this nonsense and your claim that he didn't take care of me, because it's not true. I will have you know, my father showed me proof of all the money he sent to my mama to take care of me, and it was more than enough. It's really a damn shame that you and Mom told lies to try to turn me against my father and siblings," Jada reported.

Ms. Emma Jean slapped Jada and said, "Watch your mouth, child. Your damn father was never a 'Daddy' to you. We were the ones who raised your ass. Your mama received the money he sent, but she needed a lot more for other shit that included me. I get so tired of you sticking up for him. Child, you're so gullible."

Jada could feel her blood boiling, but she decided it was better to hold her tongue. It was too early for her to allow her grandma to get under her skin, so she ignored her rudeness and acted like nothing happened. When Victoria walked into the sanctuary, she could sense that Jada was agitated, but she thought it was better to ask her what was wrong later when Ms. Emma Jean wasn't around.

"Follow me, ladies. The women are ready to get started. The flowers were delivered earlier this morning, and, oh, my gosh, they're gorgeous freshly cut purple Hydrangeas with green foliage. They will look amazing in the mason jars sprayed with gold paint we purchased. The goal is to place the centerpieces on the tables along with the tablecloths and then to strategically place all of the small lanterns in various places around the event center. While you ladies are working on that, I will be in the kitchen going over the menu with the caterers. I need to make sure they're ready. It should take a few hours to complete all the work necessary, and then we can head over to the country club," Victoria told them.

Ms. Emma Jean said, "Well, there's been a change in plans. I'm not going to the country club. I need to take a nap when we're done, and I will find my way back to the house. One of you can wear my lucky hat to win the contest."

Victoria knew something was up when Jada didn't console her grandma and didn't volunteer to walk her back to the house. Jada stormed off, leaving Victoria standing there with Ms. Emma Jean.

"Ms. Emma Jean, I'm so sorry that you don't feel well. Is there something I can do to help? We need to get you feeling your best for tomorrow," Victoria said.

"I'll be okay, Victoria. I'm just a little exhausted," Ms. Emma Jean declared.

Victoria excused herself, as there were so many other things that need her attention than focusing on any disagreements between Jada and her grandma. After checking in with the caterer, Victoria called Keisha to see when she would be back. She also needed to warn her about the drama then happening.

"Keisha, how much longer will you be shopping? I thought you were expecting a delivery. The ladies were almost finished decorating the Family Event Center when Jada and her grandma became at odds. Ms. Emma Jean got an attitude and said she wasn't going to the country club. It's such a shame, since Jada took all that time to plan something special for her. She claims she's not feeling well, but Jada told her we're going without her. I refuse to allow that toxic woman to mess up my weekend," Victoria declared.

"OMG! Ms. Emma Jean is a damn fool. Excuse my language, Mom, but it's true. We are finishing up with lunch, and I should be back in about an hour. If that lady snaps at you, I'll have her tucking her tail between her legs and headed back to Dallas on the first thing moving. I'm not having it! Besides, Lady Jakes will be here at 5:00 P.M., and I will need to focus all my attention on her. Have fun with Jada, Mom. I will see you guys soon," Keisha said.

Keisha was still fuming after she hung up, but she didn't want to burden Megan and Natalia with the nasty details. She couldn't believe that it hadn't even been 24 hours before Ms. Emma Jean showed her ass.

Meanwhile, Victoria continued overseeing the preparations and verified that the decorating was completed and the event center looked impeccable. She asked Jada to see if her grandma was ready to go back to the house to lay down. She needed a reason to get away from her and to blow off some steam. Jada tried to be sweet to her grandma, but she was madder than hell but tried to fake it.

"Thanks, Grandma, for helping out. I know you don't want to go to the country club, but I really would like to go since it's something that I've been planning for a while. I promise we won't be gone too long," Jada told her.

"Jada, I'm not fooling with you! It's only been a few months, and these people have rubbed off on you. You're so snooty, just like them, especially Victoria. Yes, I do want to go lay down, and for the record, I can't wait to leave this place. I should have never come. Don't worry; I can find my own way to the house, so go on — get!" Ms. Emma Jean barked.

In that moment, Jada realized that things had gone off the rails. Ms. Emma Jean was on one of her nasty rants that Jada had witnessed on more than one occasion. The nerve of her, accepting an invitation to Pittsford and then acting the fool over nothing, knowing that she held a grudge against Victoria. Jada tread carefully with her grandma to avoid all the land mines and traps that Ms. Emma Jean had placed from the start.

Jada hurried to Victoria and signaled that she was ready to go. When they got in Victoria's vehicle, Jada burst into tears and couldn't stop apologizing for her grandma's bad behavior. Jada felt guilty for believing that her grandma would extend an olive branch to Victoria. Jada couldn't be consoled, but after a few minutes she was able to pull herself together.

"Honey, I'm so sorry that you're hurting, but this is not your fault. Ms. Emma Jean has always acted this way. It's part of who she is. The woman is set in her ways, and I don't see her changing anytime soon. I remember when your mama found out that she was pregnant by a married pastor. I can't begin to tell you about all the trials and tribulations she has taken us through. I hate to even bring up these things, but, sweetheart, trust me; I wouldn't bring up these things if you were a child, but you're a grown woman now, and I want you to know the degree of drama we went through over the years. The funny thing is, your mama wasn't even the one who caused the majority of the problems. Ms. Emma Jean used your mama's pregnancy to manipulate everyone. Trust me; I've tried my best not to pull out my inner Michelle Obama neck rolling, finger pointing, and all, to put my foot up her butt. She even tried to blackmail the church by telling your father if he didn't send her $50,000 dollars in cash, she would destroy him by telling the congregation that he wasn't the perfect lamb they believed him to be with an illegitimate child on the way. I was plotting to do some bad things to her to get even with her. Those were some very trying times for us, and Ms. Emma Jean's actions nearly destroyed our marriage," Victoria explained.

"Oh, my gosh, Mom! I had no idea. All I know is, my grandma had a million negative things to say about you and my father. I recall her going after you with all the venom she could muster, and I didn't really understand why. I hid under the table in the living room, shaking profusely and waiting for her to go to bed after hearing her rants. Then I would sneak into my bedroom and cry myself to sleep. I'm not surprise that my mama ran away from her when she was a teenager. My grandma used me and my mom as pawns to get what she wanted, including blaming you and my father for her bad behavior," Jada explained.

Victoria's heart was breaking for Jada. She reached across the seat to give her a loving hug. Jada vowed to stand up for herself and Victoria for the duration of her grandma's stay. They made a pact to enjoy their time together at the country club without Ms. Emma Jean. Jada was happy that her father had married such a beautiful, loving woman and felt blessed to be able to have a meaningful relationship with Victoria and her siblings.

They drove to the Oak Hill County Club and were thrilled to see that they had a chance to walk away as the winner of the hat contest. There were some women with head-turning Kentucky Derby hats worthy of compliments, but Ms. Emma Jean's hat was much fancier. The host escorted them to their seats where they were served champagne tea along with warm scones. It was a lovely distraction, and they enjoyed themselves.

Keisha had enjoyed her shopping trip and delicious lunch with Megan and Natalia, but it was time to switch gears to get ready to pull off the best Mother's Day celebration that the church had ever seen. She delegated some work by sending Megan to Envision Graphics to pick up the plaques, and she delegated Natalia to pick up Terrance and the boys to help make sure the chairs were placed in the event center along with ensuring that the choir and the instruments that were being utilized were ready to go. She headed down to Faith and Hope Church to talk to Pastor McKinney. She needed to ensure that the five hundred lanterns had been delivered and that his members knew the scheduled time to start was 9:00 P.M.

Keisha's heart was full of joy after seeing all the beautiful lanterns strategically placed. She chatted with the pastor for a few minutes before rushing back to the church.

Keisha peeked into the Family Life Center, and it looked absolutely breathtaking. She walked into the kitchen where she saw employees of the caterer prepping the food. They had done such a great job and everything sounded tasty: *Chicken 'n Waffles Casserole, Mimi Bagel Breakfast Sliders, Ham & Cheese Breakfast Roll-Ups, Jalapeno Popper Egg Cups, Mimosa Fruit Salad, Cheese Bacon Quiche, Watermelon and Raspberry Salad with Mimosas, and Starbucks Coffee.* Keisha couldn't wait to eat. The next thing on her list was to call David to check on Loretta and to make sure she and the girls were getting prepared.

"Hey, big bro. How's my sister-in-law and that baby boy doing? I can't wait to kiss my nephew and to spoil him. What time will Loretta and the girls be here tomorrow? Check to see if they want to spend the night," Keisha said.

"Slow down, Keisha. You haven't allowed me to answer any of your questions. Loretta is doing well and the baby is fine. That's a good idea, but don't you think it will be too stressful? That's a lot of females and not enough bathrooms," David joked.

"We'll be fine. It's your choice, and please tell my nieces that I love them," Keisha replied.

Keisha still had several things on her list to complete. She took a few minutes to be alone in the presence of God in the sanctuary. She prayed for her family and began working on her message and introductions for First Lady Serita Jakes. It was going to be a wonderful gathering to celebrate and honor the women in the church, including their own First Lady Victoria Williams.

Keisha's thoughts were interrupted by her telephone ringing. It was Valerie, "Keisha, I want to let you know that we'll be arriving on time this evening. Do we need to take an Uber to our hotel, or will you be picking us up? First Lady Jakes would like to stay in for the evening and plans to order room service. She needs to rest and to get ready for tomorrow," Valerie reported.

"My cousin, Lamar, will be picking you ladies up and taking you to the Hilton Garden Inn. I don't blame First Lady Jakes for wanting to enjoy a restful evening. We can't wait to hear her inspirational story. Lamar will also provide transportation to the church in the morning. Sleep well, my friend, and thanks again for making this possible," Keisha said.

Keisha was excited to know that everything was coming together nicely. The last thing she needed to do was practice their rendition of "Oh Happy Day". Keisha called Megan and asked her to bring the plaques to the church so they could also rehearse for about thirty minutes. She walked into the room where choir practice was being held and was reminded that Terrance and Natalia were dating. They were acting like teenagers who couldn't keep their hands off one another. She remembered that her mother and David were not aware that the two were dating.

"Okay, guys, I don't have a lot of time to sit here and watch the two of you flirt. We need to get in a quick practice. It's been a long day, and I'm ready to turn in. By the way, when do you plan to tell Mom and David about your love affair?" Keisha inquired.

"No worries, Keisha; we plan on telling them soon. I gave the choir the night off so the ladies could relax and get themselves ready for tomorrow, but we can still do a few runs," Natalia said.

Natalia sat at the piano and played the melody of "Oh Happy Day". The catchy tune caused Keisha to become excited. She joked around with them for a few minutes before Megan arrived. Megan hadn't lost her finesse and showed she still had the pipes to prove it. Keisha rehearsed her part and felt confident. Then, all of a sudden, Natalia opened her mouth and there was no denying that their rendition was going to be a real crowd pleaser. The Wayward Sisters wanted to bless the congregation in song. With everything checked off her to-do list, Keisha went home.

When Keisha walked into the kitchen, she found Jada and Victoria trying on their fancy hats. Jada was still talking about how Ms. Emma Jeans' church hat helped her to win the contest. They giggled like little school girls but tried hard to keep their voices down since Ms. Emma Jean was still relaxing in her room. They shared their experiences with Keisha before going to bed. Jada decided to check on her grandma to keep the peace.

"Grandma… are you okay?" Jada asked.

"Come in, Jada. I heard all the commotion and figured that my lucky hat must have helped to win, huh? I'm feeling better, and I want to apologize for my actions. I really am excited about being a part of the celebration tomorrow. Will you please except my apology?" Ms. Emma Jean asked.

"Grandma, life is too short to hold a grudge, and besides, you raised me. I accept your apology and will see you in the morning," Jada replied.

Jada had mixed feelings after leaving her grandma's room but realized that she would have to forgive her many times over. If she wanted to remain in God's good graces, she had to forgive, and she prayed that her grandma wouldn't step out of line again in the coming days — but time would tell.

# Chapter 15

## Wayward Terrors

### (Jada's Fears Realized)

nother beautiful sunrise covered the Pittsford skies, and the feeling of excitement was in the air. Mother's Day had finally arrived, and this Sunday would be perfect. The Williams family hurried about, getting dressed and being careful not to get in each other's way since there were more women than bathrooms. Surprisingly, the festive mood had rubbed off on Ms. Emma Jean and she was beaming. She could be heard humming from outside of her bedroom door. Sunday's were special, and the women took a bit more time considering what to wear to church.

Victoria, the fashionable matriarch, knew how to put herself together, and she received a lot of compliments from the congregation on her beautiful wardrobe. Victoria was excited about the Mother's Day Celebration and wanted to look her best. She decided to wear a beautiful, blue Donna Vinci Church Suit with shoulder adornment and ruffled cuffs. She was loved by everyone, and they believed that she was the perfect First Lady because of her elegance and sophisticated nature. She paired her suit with a beautiful, large, matching church hat. She was ready to pamper the women who waited all year to attend the special church service. Hosting galas was her forte! She prepared a light breakfast and coffee for her family.

Loretta and the girls had spent the night. Aleyah and Asia loved any opportunity to be in the presence of the powerful Williams women who were great role models. They were the picture of excellence and exhibited ladylike behavior whenever possible. Being part of the Williams family had been nothing less than a miracle for Loretta. She hadn't had such a great childhood, and those in her family weren't believers, so going to church had been out of the question. Loretta had met David when they were in elementary school, and she had admired his prominent family from afar. They dated in high school, fell in love, and married some years later after she became a member of his church. She joined a group Bible study that met once a week that David taught.

Keisha and Victoria thought that Loretta was a diamond in the rough and took her under their wing and showered her with love. They taught her how to be a role model in ministry, but when it came to being a mother, they couldn't teach her anything. She was a great mom who had developed her mothering skills by babysitting her younger siblings.

When Loretta emerged from her room, she was dressed to the hilt in an elegant pencil dress with a lovely flower print and pink sweater that made it a complete ensemble. Loretta loved getting dolled up and started a make-up line with Zoe, a talented church member who had graduated from the Fashion Institute of Technology in New York City. Zoe arrived early to help the ladies with their hair and make-up. Aleyah and Asia looked pretty in their pink frilly dresses. Zoe fixed their hair in beautiful loose curls, and they couldn't wait to show off and receive all the compliments available to them. They ran into the kitchen to be spoiled by their grandmother.

Jada was nervous and excited at the same time. Being in Pittsford with her siblings and Victoria to celebrate Mother's Day was something she'd dreamt about, and having her grandma in town too was icing on the cake. Jada had gone all-out to look her best, as she was instrumental to the success of the event too. She had grown to love Victoria more than her own mother. Jada switched gears and decided to wear a perfect black, high-flare sleeve, skinny dress that hugged her figure perfectly.

After she was satisfied with her appearance, she knocked on her grandma's door to let her know it was time to walk over to the church. Jada couldn't believe how beautiful her grandma looked in her yellow Carmela jacket dress along with the prize-winning beautiful Derby hat. For the first time, Jada noticed her beautiful features and wondered how she could be so vicious and nasty. However, she vowed to have a great day and couldn't wait to honor and praise the women she loved.

Keisha started her morning on her knees, praying to God for a peaceful celebration. It would be a day to honor the women in the church who had made a difference in the lives of others. Keisha looked in her oversized closet and pulled out the beautiful outfit she'd purchased. She had a flair for the dramatics and loved making a bold entrance. She had purchased a beautiful skirt set with a gold jacket lined in red. It was stunning! She hoped she didn't overshadow First Lady Jakes. Keisha took a shower and got dressed before calling Valerie to check on her and First Lady Jakes. Valerie assured Keisha that they'd slept well and were eager to get to the church. Keisha gathered her notes and joined her family in the kitchen where they exchanged compliments. They joined hands in prayer and walked over to the church as a unified family.

Megan and Natalia arrived early and were both dressed impeccably too. They exchanged hugs and "I love yuz" before each ran around the church like chickens with their heads cut off, making sure that everything was ready to go. Sister Earnestine reassured them that she and the women of the church had things under control. Terrance called Keisha to wish her good luck and to let her know that Lamar had already gone to the hotel to pick up Valerie and First Lady Jakes. After thanking him, she verified that the waiting room being used to host pastoral guests was stocked with necessities such as coffee, water, and snacks. She then ran over to her office to grab her lucky Bible that had once belonged to the Reverend. She also put on her beautiful pastoral robe that her father had given her after he had changed his mind about her becoming a minister.

Her eyes began to water as she reflected on the contentious times they'd shared and how their relationship had evolved prior to his death. She thanked God for giving her an earthy father who had made her a better person. She checked her make-up and felt proud of her accomplishments as she pumped herself up prior to addressing the congregation.

Natalia took roll call to make sure all of the musicians and choir members were in the building so they could have a brief practice. Terrance, Juan, and Marco helped pass out the new choir robes to the members. Natalia summoned Megan and Keisha to run through their rendition and couldn't stop smiling at the thought of seeing the congregation's reaction. After their vocal tune-up, Megan and Keisha did a final check to make sure there were no loose ends that needed attention. First Lady Jakes, her daughter Sarah, and Valerie were escorted to their seats in the front pew. Keisha greeted them and was humbled to be in their presence. These mighty women of God had come to make an impact in the lives of others, and they looked amazing.

"First Lady Jakes, Happy Mother's Day. It's such an honor to meet you, and thank you very much for your willingness to leave your congregation to be here with us today. I can't tell you how grateful I am for your sacrifice. Please let me know if there is anything you need to make your stay more comfortable," Keisha told her.

"Keisha, thank you. It's my pleasure. I followed your father's career over the years, and he was such a fine man and preacher too. Some people have compared him to my husband. I love the way you've taken the lead to represent women in ministry, and you are excellent! I personally thank you for the work you do. I can't wait to deliver my message, as it will be a good word for the ladies," she boasted.

Keisha thanked her and gave her a hug before excusing herself, as it was getting close to the celebration service's start. She looked for Jada and found her sitting next to Victoria and Ms. Emma Jean in the pew. She signaled to her know that it was "Go time". The pews were packed, and the women of the congregation were eager for the celebration to begin. Jada took her place at the pulpit, but before she could even say a word, she received a rousing applause.

Jada proclaimed, "Welcome, ladies! Y'all are looking good today. Go ahead and give yourself some applause for that. I will be talking about the essence of a woman, and, ladies, let's be clear, the true essence of a woman lies in her attributes. It's who she is, what she has to offer, and how she treats the people around her. It's difficult for some of us to appreciate who we are, because we don't know 'whose' we are. That's the crux; we belong to God, and HE is our father, and we are made in HIS amazing image, and that alone makes us women of many talents. Those of us who have been blessed with beautiful facial features and shapely figures often put all our eggs in one basket, thus relying on our physical beauty to get us where we want to go in life. That's where I caution you, as we have to remember that our inner beauty supersedes our outer beauty, because outer beauty will eventually fade away. If you don't believe me, take a moment to consider how cute you were as a baby, and then think about how you look right now. Don't worry; some of y'all are still cute! But I encourage you to get to know 'whose' you are and get to know God in an intimate way. He will never leave or forsake you, and in your time of trouble, He will always be there."

When Jada finished, Keisha addressed the congregation, "Thank you, Jada. Boy! My baby sister sure can preach; don't you agree? I'm so happy that each and every one of you loves yourself enough to have gotten up this morning and put on your best for this Mother's Day celebration. Whether you're a mother or not, I'm sure you can think of at least one woman who has poured love into your life and deserves to be honored today. This world is full of great mothers; God planned it that way, so with that said, boy have we got a treat for you. Our special guest comes to us all the way from Dallas, Texas. Many of you are familiar with the great preaching and teaching of her husband, the Reverend T. D Jakes. However, this woman is phenomenal in her own right. I'm not going to attempt to tell her story, because she is the only person who can do that. Ladies, please get up on your feet and give a warm Victory Baptist welcome to First Lady Serita Jakes from the Potters House," Keisha told them.

The congregation jumped to their feet as First Lady Jakes took the podium. She looked lovely and was such a classy lady and well-respected woman. All eyes were on her as she got ready to deliver her impactful message. She thanked Keisha for giving her the opportunity to speak and to tell the ladies about the power of a woman and what is required of her as a first lady.

"Being a leader and a first lady requires being truthful and authentic. You have to know that your pain and joy is on display. First ladies are ordinary people who go through trying times while smiling in public to elevate the agendas of their pastor husbands. To make it through, we strengthen our relationship with God, and we grow stronger as our Christianity forces us to remain grounded. Inside every woman is a little girl, and inside every little girl there is a woman asking the world to pay attention to her. As we mature, we have to get rid of those petty things we hold on to, like bitterness and jealously. Ladies, we know better! My beginnings were humble. I'm a coal miner's daughters who has gone through trials and tribulations just like you. For example, my brother Ricky was murdered, followed by my seeking a relationship with a young man to avenge my brother's death. However, being revengeful cost me a lot, and I was subjected to violent tendencies while being exposed to bouts of domestic violence. When you do the Devil's work, the tables will eventually turn on you; life is that way. The next devastating chapter of my life turned out to be a blessing, as I learned that my fourteen-year-old daughter was pregnant, and I can tell you that was something that me and the pastor weren't ready to hear. Heartbreak is always lurking around the corner, so we have to be happy in every chapter of our life, knowing that God is in control. Run to Him and not away from Him, and I promise that your life will get better. Happy Mother's Day, ladies. I salute you all and challenge you to follow your dreams," First Lady Jakes told them.

When First Lady Jakes exited the stage, the congregation stood up on their feet cheering. Keisha thanked the Lord for His grace and for how beautiful the day was going so far. She walked to the podium and introduced the choir that was known for their riveting sounds. Natalia led them through a few traditional Gospel songs, and they looked great belting out the lyrics in their new robes. They were ready to showcase their rendition of "Oh Happy Day", and with the musicians playing the melody, the choir sang the lyrics, "Oh Happy Day, Oh Happy Day, When Jesus Washed, He Washed My Sins Away."

The sopranos, altos, and tenors sang a few bars to showcase their talents before the Wayward Sisters took over. Megan and Keisha joined Natalia at the piano, and when they started singing, they brought the house down. It was just like old times, and when it was Megan's turn, she didn't hold anything back. Keisha believed that she was the least talented of the three but received a standing ovation. Natalia's angelic voice had always been a crowd pleaser, and she sounded more beautiful than most could remember. She sang effortlessly while hitting notes that were unimaginable for most. Their rendition of "Oh Happy Day" was a hit, and combining their talents was something they planned to do more of in the near future.

Keisha presented awards to some amazing women who had made sacrifices to help others in the community. Her final presentation was to no other than her lovely mother. She called David, Terrance, and Jada to the stage. Victoria was taken aback after being given the beautiful plaque and a dozen red roses. She couldn't believe that her children had pulled off such a meaningful tribute in her honor. Each shared their favorite memory of her while growing up, and by the time they were done, there wasn't a dry eye in the building.

Other family and board members were called to the podium and showered Victoria with affection. A flood of tears ran down her beautiful honey-brown face, but her salt and pepper hair showed off her elegance and beauty.

Keisha announced the conclusion of the service and asked everyone to join her in a final prayer, and then Sister Earnestine and the ushers quickly led the women into the Event Life Center for brunch. The caterers did an excellent job serving, and after they finished eating, Keisha grabbed a microphone and explained how the evening activities would work. She told them to meet at the Faith and Hope Church a few short blocks down the road at 6:00 P.M. She said it was important to be on time and encouraged them to change clothes so they would be comfortable. She limited her instructions to eliminate any speculation about what was going to happen, as she wanted to keep the special lantern tribute secret so Victoria wouldn't realize she was being honored a second time. The event center cleared out within minutes, leaving the staff and caterers with plenty to clean up.

Keisha invited Valerie and First Lady Jakes to the house to relax before they flew back home to Dallas. They weren't able to stay for the special tribute since First Lady Jakes wanted to spend time with her family on Mother's Day too. The house was crowded with close friends and members of the church who were engaged in side conversations. First Lady Jakes took a few minutes to pray for anyone who needed it. Victoria put on a pot of coffee and played some of her favorite jazz. It was her way of making everyone feel welcome and comfortable.

Ms. Emma Jean was moved by First Lady Jakes' prayer and happy to get the opportunity to meet her. She was also impressed with the catered brunch but wasn't surprised that they could afford to serve such an expensive meal since she believed that the Williams family was affluent. Try as she might, she couldn't shake her disdain for Victoria and was forced to fake it. She didn't want to be accused of ruining the day, so she excused herself to take a quick nap.

Jada was thrilled that she wouldn't have to put up with her grandma's negativity and bad behavior, and she spent the afternoon loving on Victoria, her siblings, and her nieces. It was an awesome day!

Keisha pulled David and Terrance off to the side to tell them about the lantern celebration. After spilling the beans, they believed it was a perfect idea and a great way to end the evening. They were ecstatic and couldn't wait to participate, as they needed an outlet to cast their burdens to the wind.

"Mom is going to be so excited, and she doesn't even have a clue that she's being honored again. I always wanted to light up the sky with a large group of people willing to surrender their burdens to the atmosphere. God is going to show up and show out this evening," Keisha reported.

"Sis, your right. This evening is going to be special. Is there anything that still needs to be done? I want to make sure things are perfect," David said.

"Nope! I've hired a lantern team who will assist us. The last thing we need is for someone to accidentally burn up the field, or worse, themselves. We have plenty of helpers on hand," Keisha assured him.

"Keisha, you're so awesome! Your compassion and thoughtfulness never cease to amaze me," Terrance told her.

The three reflected on more childhood memories and the impact their mom had in their lives. Victoria had placed her own goals aside to ensure that they were clothed, fed, clean, homework completed, and sports practices were attended. They credited her for her relentless work behind the scenes, helping the Reverend birth their family ministry. They hugged each before walking away to mingle with the friends and family in their home. Keisha slipped away to run down the street to ensure things were set up and to make the final payment to the lantern company. She reminded Pastor McKinney again of the time and other information needed for the women in his congregation who were going to participate in the ceremony.

"Hey, pastor, I don't know about you, but I can't wait. It's getting close to 'Go time'. Please remind the ladies of the time. I rented a few security guards to direct traffic so everyone knows where to park and things will be seamless as possible," Keisha said.

"Yes, the ladies are so excited. Thank you, Keisha, for bringing your fantastic idea to reality and doing it on Mother's Day. It's going to be perfect," Pastor McKinney reported.

"Okay, I'll see you back here soon," Keisha said.

Keisha went over a few particulars with the crew before rushing back home to see First Lady Jakes off. When she walked in, she noticed that Lamar was there. She said her goodbyes and couldn't stop thanking First Lady Jakes for blessing the congregation. She told her about future events and agreed to visit the Potter's House before the end of the year. With goodbyes out of the way, she excused herself to change her clothes before getting everyone pumped about heading to the church for the activities.

Jada decided to spend some time with her grandma and knocked on her door. Ms. Emma Jean opened it and said she was still tired and wanted to rest. Although Jada was caught off guard once again by her grandma's antics, she made up her mind that she wasn't going to feed into her nonsense and told her that it was probably best for her to stay behind to rest. Jada wasn't willing to allow her grandma to highjack the evening, and her attention seeking tactics were getting old.

Jada went into the family room to join Victoria, who looked beautiful in her casual jeans and blouse. Jada steered clear of bringing up the incident she'd had with her grandma. She figured Victoria wouldn't even notice that Ms. Emma Jean wasn't at the lantern celebration with all the excitement going on and with so many people there.

Victoria rode with Keisha and Jada to the church. When they pulled into the parking lot of Faith and Hope Church, Victoria's eyes widened with excited. She had never seen a lantern celebration and wasn't sure how it worked. Keisha told her to be patient, as everyone would receive directions soon. Jada and Victoria mingled with the over four hundred women gathered there standing by the lantern of their choice. It was a beautiful sight! Women from all walks of life and different ethnic backgrounds and beliefs were gathered there. A wooden platform that served as a stage was set-up with a microphone for the host and the Faith and Hope Choir. Keisha walked up on the platform to welcome the ladies before asking David to open up the celebration with a prayer that was followed by Jada reading of an inspiration poem.

"Welcome, ladies, and Happy Mother's Day to you all. We are here to celebrate one another and to release our burdens at the finale. Lantern festivals are an Asian tradition designed to release lanterns as a way of honoring loved ones, bringing about good fortune, and symbolizing new beginnings. I want each and every one of you to experience this too. But first we need to go over a few safety precautions. There are fire safety professionals on hand to make sure things remain safe and beautiful. We need everyone to listen and follow all of the instructions you receive. The lanterns are fire retardant, biodegradable, and will be released to the atmosphere, but at some point, 99% of them return to the earth. Those of you concerned about them being bad for our atmosphere, don't worry; there will be lantern chasers who will remove them when they land and will dispose of them. Now that we have covered safety, are you ready to have a meaningful evening?" Keisha asked.

The women cheered and were overly excited after David and Jada finished. They were ready to receive instructions on how to release their lanterns. The Faith and Hope choir provided excellent praise and worship, singing songs like "Amazing Grace", and "What A Friend We Have in Jesus". Their beautiful voices filled the air.

Keisha returned to the platform with a representative from the lantern company who explained how to release the lanterns with step-by-step instructions needed to enjoy the evening. Keisha invited her beautiful mother Victoria and her siblings to the platform. Victoria was perplexed and caught off guard again, but she followed her daughters anyway. Keisha told Victoria that she was being honored for her acts of kindness, great parenting, and unconditional love. She explained that the hundreds of people were there to celebrate her life and their own. She was handed a lantern and was assisted in releasing it. Keisha asked her to verbalize the things she was letting go and assured her that she was being supported. Victoria found herself in tears the second time in one day, which was rare since she hardly ever showed her raw emotions in the presence of others.

"Wow! I don't know what to say. Today, I'm full of joy and can't control my emotions. I would like to thank my children. You have all made me so happy today, and I'm honored to be your mother. For me, this is a celebration of life, and the thing I would like to be celebrating the most is the life of my husband. Calvin Williams was a great man and the love of my life, and he gave me four beautiful children. It's Mother's Day, and I wouldn't be a mother without him. Thank you all for honoring me tonight," Victoria told them.

Victoria's lantern was lit in front of many, and her life was celebrated by all of them. Keisha was thrilled that things had come together so beautifully. It was now time for the women to light up the sky with their lanterns, giving them clean hearts by doing so. They all basked in the beauty of the evening and praised God for the opportunity.

# Chapter 16

# Wayward Blessings
## (Natalia's Good Fortune)

After returning home, it was difficult for Natalia, Juan, and Marco to settle down. Terrance joined them to unwind and to share their thoughts about the day. It was perfect, and there was so much to talk about. He couldn't keep his hands off Natalia, who was glowing. His flirtatious, yet "child friendly" ways caused her to blush. The day was one for the record books. It was Natalia's best Mother's Day by far, and she was showered with fresh cut flowers, and Juan and Marco gave her a beautiful card. Natalia honored her mother Rosemarie with a beautiful mother's ring and spa day. Natalia credited Victoria and her mother for their positive influence in her life. They were the reason why she was so strong, and their examples of being good wives were something she planned to model someday. Rosemarie was proud of Natalia and believed she had come a long way since her dysfunctional days when she was married. After Carlos' murder, she had returned to her strong values, and she had surpassed her mother's expectations when she told her that she was going into ministry and now was being considered as a member of the ministry team at Victory Baptist. Rosemarie and Natalia's father gave her an expensive tennis bracelet, which made her happy because it was the one she had hinted about for some time.

Natalia was happy too that Terrance and the boys said that her rendition of "Oh Happy Day" was the highlight of their day. It gave them goosebumps!

Terrance surprised Natalia by giving her a beautifully wrapped box. She tried to guess what was inside by shaking it before taking time to open it. There was a lot of newspaper packed tightly inside, so she pulled it out to reveal its contents. There was a small ring box inside, and she couldn't wait to open it.

"OMG! What is this?" Natalia yelled.

"Wait a minute. It's not what I think it is; is it?" Juan said.

When Natalia opened the box, she was blinded by the glare coming from the beautiful, one-carat, princess-cut diamond on a white-gold engagement ring. It felt like a dream, and before Natalia could gain her composure, Terrance got down on one knee to propose to her. Besides the birth of her children, who had made her a mother in the first place, this was the best Mother's Day.

"Natalia, will you marry me? Girl, I'm not talking about today either! I realize that we need to learn a lot more about one another, and I won't just be marrying you; I'm getting a three-pack," Terrance joked.

Juan and Marco burst out laughing, along with Natalia, after being referred to as a "three-pack". She jumped to her feet and planted a big kiss on Terrance's lips. "Yes," she cried out.

Terrance warned Natalia that he hadn't told David or his mother yet, but he wanted to make sure she didn't get away. Terrance said he planned to tell them soon. He told her they were going on a relaxing honeymoon, which was part of the vacation he had asked her and the boys to go on.

"Terrance, of course I will marry you! I agree that we need to take things slow, but you have made me the happiest girl in the world. I can't believe you didn't tell your mom or brother about us. I hope they see it as a good thing and that your mom doesn't feel like I'm rushing you into a relationship. We might still have to worry about Keisha, because even though she gave us her blessing today, she may not approve of us getting married," Natalia said.

"We know how hard it can be to win over our godmother, so, Mom, I sure hope she's okay with it because we really like Terrance," Juan said.

Terrance was relieved that Natalia had said yes, and he wasn't worried about getting his family's approval. They loved Natalia, and she had been a cherished friend of the family for years. Terrance and Natalia seemed to balance one another, and he believed their love could stand the test of time. Terrance admitted that when he was a teen he'd had a crush on her, but he never believed he stood a chance since she was older.

Terrance asked Natalia to take a romantic stroll around the neighborhood with him. He held her hand and stopped every now and then to enjoy a sensual kiss. They talked about how their lives would be once they got married, and Terrance brought up the idea of having a child since he didn't have any of his own. Having another baby wasn't something Natalia had considered, being in her mid-thirties, she was curious about whether she could have a baby. With Juan and Marco in their teens, it would be challenging, but she'd dreamt of having a daughter someday. Terrance mentioned that he wasn't against adopting and wanted to adopt Leroy, and Natalia wasn't opposed to the idea.

Terrance told Natalia that he was considering taking Leroy on vacation with them. Natalia knew how deeply he cared about Leroy, and because of the hard life he'd lived, he wanted to give him opportunities that he might not get.

They shared their thoughts about their wedding day, and Natalia said she wanted a small, intimate wedding since she had been married before. Terrance agreed and thought that spending thousands of dollars on a single day wasn't necessary. The money could be better spent on things such as vacations or on a down payment on a house. Natalia had never owned her own home and wanted to be a homeowner someday.

Terrance asked to spend the night on the couch, claiming that he wanted to be near Natalia since his house was full with family spending the night. Meanwhile, Keisha, Jada, and Victoria stayed up into the wee hours of the morning talking about the day. Jada thought it was a beautiful celebration and felt blessed that things had gone so smoothly, especially during the lantern release. She told them that after she released hers, she had nearly fainted from the emotional baggage she was letting go. The load she had been carrying was stressful, and she had been lugging it around for months.

"OMG! It was so beautiful to share such an intimate evening with the women of Faith and Hope. I kept thinking about what it was that I wanted to release, and my goal was to feel free afterwards from the shame I've been carrying around for years from being molested. As I let my lantern go and it ascended into the atmosphere, my knees buckled, and if it weren't for the fact that David and Mom were standing next to me, I would have fallen," Jada told them.

"Jada, that's crazy. The best part of my day was seeing Mom's face after she realized that she was being honored twice in one day. I sure hope someone recorded it. Having First Lady Jakes in the building made my day too. She's so down to earth, and so is her daughter Sarah. They both have such strong, relatable testimonies. I know that her message freed somebody, and I can't wait to hear the fruits of God's labor in their testimonies. I know there will be some amazing breakthroughs," Keisha said matter-of-factly.

Victoria couldn't stop thanking Jada and Keisha for celebrating her in such a meaningful way. She told them that besides the obvious of what she had expected to happened, she really enjoyed their rendition of "Oh Happy Day". She asked Keisha to consider singing more often and said it would be a shame to keep her beautiful voice all to herself.

The three shared stories and the beauty of the day in such a lively fashion that they woke up Ms. Emma Jean. She stormed into the kitchen and stood in the doorway with her arms folded. Her body language caused her to look like Medea after finding out that she was going to jail. Ms. Emma Jean didn't say a word, but if looks could kill, they would have all been dead. She rolled her eyes at them before storming back to her bedroom.

Jada jumped up from her chair and ran after her grandma. She tried to apologize, but Ms. Emma Jean didn't want to hear whatever she had to say. She told Jada, "Get the hell out of my way, and get back to your people."

Jada was beginning to think that her grandma was nuts. She was ready for her to go home before she crossed the line and all hell broke loose. Jada was annoyed for the third time in less than 24 hours. She went back into the kitchen with Keisha and her mom.

Keisha assured Jada, "Sis, we're not going to allow your grandma to be a distraction. I have never met such a hateful and jealous woman. We are gonna have to pray for her, and it's really all we can do. Before we were rudely interrupted, Mom, I was going to say that it felt awesome to sing in such a freeing way with Natalia and Megan by my side. Boy, we really had some great times back in high school, singing in all those plays. I'm going to tell Natalia that I'm ready to get back on the horse by committing to sing more."

Victoria suggested that they go to bed, as she was exhausted after being up for nearly twenty-four hours, but she wanted to clean the kitchen first. After that was done and still full of joy, she walked into her bedroom but was annoyed when she smelled an unexpected strong stench. She wondered if it was someone's cheap perfume and hoped that no one had been in her room, but she dismissed the notion since the house had been full of guests and family earlier that afternoon.

She opened her window to air out the room and then got ready for bed. When she got into bed, it didn't take long for her to fall asleep. In about an hour's time, she was awakened abruptly by a shadow hovering over her. The perpetrator wore black gloves and was wielding a large butcher knife. The attacker tried to suffocate her, but it was difficult because Victoria fought back. She attempted to scream, but more pressure was applied to her mouth as her pillow was forcefully pushed down on her face with great strength. She struggled to break free at first but could see the perpetrator. Surprisingly, it was no other than Ms. Emma Jean, who believed that assailing Victoria was vital to her survival.

Ms. Emma Jean felt like she had nothing to lose. She had become depressed after Jada had moved across the country to be with her "new" family. Victoria, being someone who had never been in a physical altercation, found herself fighting for her life against a foe who had caused her a lot of years of heartache. Victoria's adrenaline consumed her entire body as she fought Ms. Emma Jean, who continued to stumbled while aggressively lunging forward toward Victoria. However, in the process, she stabbed herself in the left arm. Victoria saw this as a vital moment and the time to take advantage of her.

She kicked Ms. Emma Jean in her stomach as hard as she could, and she fell to the ground and blacked out for a few seconds. When she regained her composure, she looked like a woman full of rage with the goal of taking Victoria out. Ms. Emma Jean stood up on wobbly legs with the bloody butcher knife in her hand, but Victoria's survival instincts kicked in when she realized that Ms. Emma Jean was trying to kill her. She grabbed the knife from her, and in self-defense forcefully stabbed Ms. Emma Jean in her chest.

Ms. Emma Jean let out a screeching scream before falling backwards onto the carpet.

"Call 911!" Victoria yelled. She collapsed next to her and attempted to administer CPR while crying profusely. She tried to make sense of what had happened.

Jada was the first one to enter Victoria's room. She was devastated by what she saw. Her grandma was lying in a pool of her own blood. Jada frantically urged Keisha to call for help.

"Mom, what happened?" Keisha cried out as she entered the room.

The Pittsford Police and ambulance were dispatched. Victoria was in a state of shock and didn't answer her, but she lay there, listening to the sirens as they got closer. Loud screams of horror could be heard, and when the EMTs arrived, they were directed to Victoria's room where Ms. Emma Jean was lying on the carpet with a life-threatening injury.

The police began a preliminary investigation to find out what had happened. Ms. Emma Jean had started bleeding out, but the EMTs worked quickly to stabilize her. They carefully placed her motionless body on the stretcher, and she was taken to the nearest hospital. Still in her pajamas, Jada grabbed her jacket and followed the ambulance to the hospital in her vehicle. She believed that her duty was to her grandma and that it was more important than waiting to find out how the altercation had started in the first place.

Keisha tried to comfort Victoria, while Loretta shielded Aleyah and Asia from the circus by taking them into the back room. David and Terrance were notified by Loretta of the chaos and were asked to hurry to the house.

The police officers instructed the family to leave the home, as Victoria's bedroom was now a crime scene. Detective De'Luca gathered details from Victoria, but after noticing her emotional state, he suggested that she come to the police station in the morning.

The Williams family checked into the Hilton Garden Inn. Victoria was shaking as she tried to provide her children with details of what had happened. She told them that she had been accosted by Ms. Emma Jean who had hidden in her closet, waiting to attack her after she went to bed. David, Keisha, and Terrance were shocked, and their temperament went from jovial to a state of rage. The wanted to get even with Ms. Emma Jean for the unnecessary pain she was causing their family. Although they were upset, they couldn't help but worry about Jada.

Terrance volunteered to head over to the hospital to check on Jada and Ms. Emma Jean. David encouraged him to go, and to hurry. However, after Terrance left the room, David wondered why he needed to pick up Natalia first. Although the suggestion seemed odd, he had more urgent matters to worry about, such as his mom's disposition. He did what he knew to do, which was to pray. David realized that it was going to take a lot of faith in God to overcome the chaos that was theirs to endure.

Ms. Emma Jean was rushed into surgery upon arriving at the hospital. Her doctor explained to Jada that she was in critical condition stemming from penetrating chest trauma.

When Terrance and Natalia arrived, they rushed to the waiting room, looking for Jada. They found her pacing the floor, and she couldn't be consoled. Terrance approached her and gave her a hug. He told her that they were sorry about her grandma, but his words were met with a barrage of accusations.

Jada yelled, "This is all your fault! Keisha begged me to come to Pittsford, and now my grandma is laying on a gurney waiting to have emergency surgery. If she doesn't pull through this, her blood will be on the Williams' hands, and I will not forgive any of you."

"Sis, you don't mean that. This is none of our fault. We still don't even know what happened," Terrance reminded her.

Terrance was taken aback by Jada's rebuke of them. He couldn't imagine how such a beautiful day of celebrating could turn into such a nightmare. He realized that people could say and do things that they don't mean in the heat of the moment. He didn't want to leave Jada by herself at the hospital, but he thought it might be best since he didn't want to continue to upset her. She needed to remain strong and available for Ms. Emma Jean once she came out of surgery. He and Natalia hurried back to the hotel to comfort Victoria. By now, Terrance wanted an explanation of what had actually happened.

Victoria was distraught but hoped for the best. Never in a million years did she believe that things between her and Ms. Emma Jean would become so volatile. As she was being attacked, she realized that either of them might lose their life, so she had to fight for hers with all the energy she could muster.

Terrance provided them with an update on Jada's mental state and described what he perceived to be a riff in the loving relationship they had cultivated with Jada. Keisha attempted to change the subject so she wouldn't make Victoria upset or cause her to feel guilty.

"Mom, don't worry; everything is going to be alright. We're a strong family, and we can make it through this," Keisha assured her.

As the news spread around the city of Pittsford, friends and church members began to congregate in the lobby of the hotel because they wanted to check on Victoria and the family. Many of them had been aware of the pitfalls of having Ms. Emma Jean visit. Hospital security had to be called to contain the area. Keisha believed it was best to keep her mom shielded. Victoria told Keisha that she wanted to talk to Jada. Keisha encouraged her but hoped that Jada didn't answer her phone. Victoria dialed her number, and Jada's phone rang — and rang, for what seemed like forever. However, the 9th ring was when she finally answered.

"Mom, the doctor just told me that my grandma has died. I'm devastated, and I can't stay here in Pittsford. I know my grandma was nuts, but you didn't have to kill her. How do you think I can ever forgive you?" Jada asserted.

"Honey, you can't mean that. I've done everything possible to be candid with you since you've been here. I told you that your grandma hated me and how manipulative she was. I know how much you loved her, honey, but she tried to kill me, and she's the one who hid in my room waiting for me to go to sleep and then popped out of nowhere wielding a butcher knife. I had to defend myself, Jada. I know things will be chaotic, but I'm begging for your forgiveness. I love you as my own daughter," Victoria explained.

Jada hung up on Victoria without saying a word, causing Victoria to begin weeping uncontrollably. She felt guilty that Ms. Emma Jean had died and blamed herself. Keisha tried to comfort her and was curious about what Jada may have said to upset her, but without notice, Victoria blurted out, "Ms. Emma Jean has died."

"Who told you that? Did Jada specifically say that?" Keisha demanded.

Victoria's cell phone rang, so Keisha gently removed it from her mother's hand to see who was calling. Keisha answered it and found Detective De'Luca on the other end. He was calling to inform Victoria that Ms. Emma Jean had been pronounce dead. He recommended that Victoria stay at the hotel until the investigation was completed, and he hinted that things were looking like a case of self-defense. Keisha was numb and thought her family didn't need the negative implications. Keisha confirmed with Victoria that Ms. Emma Jean was dead. It was going to be a long night, but the family had weathered storms before and had come out better on the other side with God's favor.

# Chapter 17

# Wayward Changes
## (Jada's Metamorphosis)

he Pittsford Police Department cleared Victoria in the death of Ms. Emma Jean, coming to the conclusion that she had acted in self-defense. The Williams family tried to get things back to normal, including Sunday church services. Natalia and Megan stepped into the gap to keep things going by taking turns preaching to the congregation.

Jada was livid that no one was going to be charged in the death of her grandma. She took refuge, and no one could get in touch with her. It was almost as if she had disappeared from the face of the earth. Her siblings were beside themselves, and the thought of losing her was upsetting, but they realized that their hands were tied. They would have to pray that she would eventually reopen the lines of communication.

Throughout her childhood, the Reverend and Victoria had tried to stay in contact with her by asking her mom and Ms. Emma Jean to allow her to spend summers and Christmas breaks with them, but they wouldn't allow it. When the Reverend found out that her mom had gone to prison, he tried to do what any good father would do by trying to get his daughter. However, Ms. Emma Jean went to the courts and used her manipulating ways to beat him to the punch and was granted legal custody of Jada. When asked, she swore that she had no idea who Jada's father was and told them that her mother had slept with multiple men. Her mom hadn't named him as the father and had never attempted to get child support from the Reverend. In fact, Ms. Emma Jean had convinced her mom to blackmail him instead to make sure that Jada would be well taken care of.

Their ploy didn't work, since Jada had heard many conversations where her mom and Ms. Emma Jean admitted that the Reverend was her father, so she always knew that the Reverend was her dad. They were able to establish a close relationship by writing secret letters to one another. Being with her family was something Jada dreamt of, but she now needed some personal space to process the loss of her grandma.

The community embraced Victoria by sending her personal letters, flowers, and they made telephone calls to show their support after Ms. Emma Jean's death made the front page news in the *Pittsford Post*. The town's most provocative newspaper, responsible for satisfying its reader's thirst for captivating stories and gossip, splattered the horrifying details of the innocent first lady killing a helpless grandma for all to salivate over, but those who knew Victoria realized that the newspaper's goal was to sell papers.

It backfired, since church attendance for Victory Baptist Church increased. Many wanted to support the church to show their solidarity to Victoria in that way. David was perplexed, and he wanted to respect Jada's boundaries, but he needed to know her plans about being part of the family's ministry, and she would need to make her decision known through her vote.

He decided to move forward by contacting the board for the meeting to reconvene to vote. He informed them that they needed to meet at the church at 7:00 P.M. David realized that the family being under duress wasn't a reason for not keeping church business in order, so he attempted to contact Jada and left several messages after she didn't answer. Some of the board members arrived earlier than expected, as they wanted to share their feelings about the vote and concerns about Jada. They believed more than ever the importance of expanding the church because of the increase in membership. The thought of having two locations was exciting, and knowing that the Reverend was looking down on them, giving his approval, made everyone happy.

The pastoral team for the new location would be Keisha, Natalia, and Terrance, with Megan, Jada, and David remaining at Victory Baptist's original location. They briefly discussed the possibility of bringing in another pastor to the team, as their plan B, should Jada decide not to be part of the family's ministry.

Keisha hurried over to the church to join everyone and to report that she had received a lengthy message from Jada. The contents of the message caused Keisha to be optimistic, as Jada had invited Keisha to the embankment to share a private conversation. They hadn't spoken to one another since the night Ms. Emma Jean had died. Jada said that she had gone to Dallas to bury her grandma and was responsible for planning her home-going service.

Keisha was nearly out of breath as she provided them with the details of the call. Ms. Emma Jean had been cremated, so Jada had come back to Pittsford. She had struggled to forgive the Williams family, and it was anyone's guess how their talk would turn out. Jada had been convinced by the Holy Spirit to reach out to Keisha. She had started to feel lonely and remained confused about the details of her grandma's death. Keisha was the only one who could help Jada find a path to forgiveness.

"Guess what? Jada has finally called, and she asked me to meet her at the embankment this evening. I think this needs to be a Wayward Sister intervention like the ones we had back in the day. I believe God has a plan for our family. David, you might need to push back the starting time of our meeting, or you might even postpone it," Keisha told them.

"Girl, count me in! I believe that we can get Jada's attention. She knows how important the growth of our church is and that it will take all of us to make it happen. She and I talked about it, and she was very excited to work together on crafting a message on molestation that could benefit the young women in our church," Megan asserted.

David encouraged them to hurry over to the park to meet Jada before she changed her mind. He hoped that she wouldn't be upset by Keisha allowing Megan and Natalia to tag along. He asked the other board members there to pray for a miracle. When they arrived, the Wayward Sisters hurried over to the embankment, and once they got closer, they saw Jada sitting on a bench with her back turned toward them.

Keisha cautiously approached her and tapped her on her shoulder. Jada looked disheveled as if she had taken the entire world and its problems on her shoulders. Her eyes were swollen from crying, and she had a migraine.

Jada didn't hesitate to embrace her big sister who had become her greatest supporter. Tears of joy ran down both of their faces.

Megan and Natalia joined them for a group hug and exchanging, "I love, yuz." They held hands to show solidarity, and in unison they turned toward the murky water at the embankment and looked to see their reflections in the water. If they saw them, it was a sign that everything was working according to the perfect will of God. They closed their eyes, and Keisha began the countdown. She counted from one to ten, and when they opened their eyes, four beautiful reflections were staring back at them.

"Hallelujah!" Keisha cried out.

Jada explained to them that she realized her grandma was guilty of going after Victoria and told them that it was difficult for her to shake the guilt she felt for inviting her grandma to visit in the first place. She told them that she believed in forgiveness and the power of it, which was why she couldn't hold a grudge against the people who loved her, and that she appreciated her siblings who had embraced her when they didn't have to. Jada also said that she wanted to start seeing a therapist to help her deal with her grandma's death. She admitted that she couldn't wait to cast her vote for the expansion of the church and wouldn't dare pass up the opportunity to be a part of her father's ministry.

Keisha pulled out her cell phone to call David to let him know that he and the others could relax; things were going to be okay. They would be able to hold the vote on time.

On the way back to the church, Keisha told Jada about Victoria's health so she would be prepared to face her, "Mom is going to be so happy that you have decided to remain part of the family ministry as originally planned. She tried to act like your absence wasn't bothering her, but she hasn't been the same without you. When I first told her that you were coming to Pittsford, there was a light in her eyes that I hadn't seen since we were kids. She and Dad spent a lot of years bickering over you and the situation, and it took her some time to deal with Dad's infidelity, but I think any woman would struggle with something like that. They seemed to argue less as Mom started forgiving him and especially as the two of you got to know each other. She has always accepted you as her own daughter. Mom's a strong woman with Christian values, and she has an incredible ability to forgive others. She never wanted to be at odds with Ms. Emma Jean or to compete with her for your love and attention. We agreed to have Ms. Emma Jean visit way too soon, knowing that she had an unhealed heart full of animosity and hate for Mom. I'm so sad that you had to lose her, but I know deep down in your heart that you know this ordeal wasn't Mom's fault. Sis, we're so sorry for your loss, but please know that we will always be here for you. We love you dearly, and there's nothing you can do about it," Keisha explained.

"Keisha, I know the things you are saying are true, but I was afraid and didn't want to be blamed for my grandma's actions, so I went on the defensive so I wouldn't have to defend myself. I have never been happier than I have been over the last few months being with you all. Thank you for everything, sis," Jada said.

Jada felt as if a huge weight had been lifted from her shoulders. However, there were still a few others she needed to face, but the hardest one was Victoria. She believed it was necessary to get things straight with her before she could vote in good conscience. Her guilt wouldn't leave her, knowing that the Williams family home had been violated in the most intrusive way possible, and it was always going to be a reminder of her grandma's cruelty and her death. The Pittsford Police cleared the family to re-enter the home, but they continued to stay at the hotel for the time being. Victoria had considered selling the house but took into consideration the thousand memories they had shared there, and the fact that it was adjacent to the church made the option of moving unlikely.

When Jada walked into the sanctuary, she found herself face to face with the woman she'd come to accept as her mother. They embraced for what seemed like an eternity before Terrance attempted to lighten the mood by delivering some important news of his own.

"Sis, save some of that affection for your favorite brother," Terrance joked.

They laughed as Jada rushed toward him for a loving hug before they walked into the meeting room to hold the vote. It wasn't surprising that the members voted in favor of expanding to add a second location to Victory Baptist Church with the Reverend's children heading up the pastoral staff. Cheers erupted!

Keisha couldn't believe that her efforts to bring her siblings together had finally paid off. In fact, the outcome had surpassed her expectations. Terrance was nervous but thought that then was as good a time as any to tell David and his mom that he was engaged to Natalia. He pulled her close to him, cleared his throat to get their attention, and made his announcement.

"I know everyone remembers Juan's desire for his mom to meet someone, fall in love, and eventually get married. Well, God has answered his prayer. Natalia and I will be getting married," Terrance told them.

Victoria was taken aback by the news. However, she felt that despite all the controversy, God was continuing to bless her family with a lot of positive news, like David and Loretta having a baby boy, the expansion being approved, her four children in ministry, and now, to top things off, Terrance was getting married, which also meant that Natalia was going to be her daughter-in-law and she was gaining two grandsons. Victoria adored Juan and Marco, and for them the feeling was mutual.

Everyone's lives were coming full circle. David was dumbfounded, but he already loved Natalia like a sister. He teased Terrance about having to give up his "Player's card" so soon after getting rid of his crazy ex-girlfriend and was now being roped in by an older woman. The news had gone over better than expected. David brought the meeting back to order to pray for his family, the board members, and their ministry.

David provided an update regarding the construction schedule for the new location, "I feel so blessed," he said. "Our new location is about thirty minutes from Victory Baptist, and it has the capacity to seat 3,000 members. The construction is scheduled to begin on June 30th with a groundbreaking ceremony scheduled for June 1st."

David told them that the construction would be completed by New Year's Eve. The board was excited and couldn't wait to see their footprint on the location. David explained that the pastoral team needed to work together to build the excitement in the community for the second location, and one suggestion he had was for them to rotate every other month in the pulpit. It would allow the members to choose the location they wanted to worship at.

"David, that's a great idea! I think the members will love the ability to choose which location they will attend. You know that my sermons will always be on point, so don't be offended if they are always at the new location," Keisha boasted.

"Don't start, Keisha. God don't like that. Besides, we all know who they will be flocking to see every Sunday," David joked.

It wasn't unusual for David and Keisha to show their sibling rivalry every now and again. They realized that they were both talented but acknowledge that it was the Reverend's blood running through their veins. Victoria was quick to chime in whenever they went on a rant about who was the better preacher.

"I'll have you kids know that your ability to speak so eloquently comes from me and not your father! When I was in high school, I was chosen to be the captain of the debate team. I won numerous awards and attended a lot of competitions. It baffles me as to why I don't have the nerve to get in the pulpit. Lord knows the Reverend spent years trying to encourage me to do it," Victoria shared.

"Oh snap! Mom, who knew you had the gift for gab? This is the first time you've shared this with us. I guess we should've considered making you part of the pastoral team, but your talent is better used to keep us sane. All that preaching can take a toll on you," Keisha told her.

"Mrs. Williams, I knew you were holding out on something," Megan joked.

Victoria told them that she had considered moving back into the family home and believed it was necessary to keep a strong connection to the Reverend. Keisha assured her that she would not have to live there alone and that Jada would continue to live there too. Terrance made it clear that he only planned to be there for a few more weeks, since he and Natalia were getting married soon and that they weren't having a big ceremony but would be getting married while they were on vacation in the Grand Cayman Islands.

Victoria and Keisha didn't make a fuss about not being there. David ended the meeting, and they vowed never to allow anything or anyone to come between them or to disrupt the family ministry.

# Chapter 18

## Wayward Truths

### (Megan's Epiphany)

Megan felt like she needed a vacation after dealing with so much drama lately. She realized that her life would forever be changed in the coming months with the growth of Victory Baptist Church. She could see herself in the pulpit delivering the messages she had crafted while she was still in seminary school along with the private notes that were written in her journals. She would be able to easily transform them into sermons. She prayed that her words would resonate with men and women who were hungry for hope. Megan was thrilled that she was being considered one of the pastors who would remain at the current location. She believed that she, David, and Jada would make a powerful ministry team and would keep in step with tradition by focusing on the strong vision that the Reverend had for his church. She was delighted to have the opportunity to be under the leadership of David and believed that it was nothing less than a move of God. David had become a power staple in the community, and he and Keisha were nothing less than a chip off the old block when it came to having the anointing.

Lately, Cory had been on Megan's mind, especially after considering Natalia's good fortune with Terrance. She had hoped to be able to cuddle up with someone who could make her feel special. She realized that her flame with Cory had been barely lit before she had decided to cut things off with him the first time. Nonetheless, she remained a hopeless romantic, so she decided that she would call him and would use the excuse that she was checking on Rhonda. She also wanted to boast about the changes in leadership at Victory Baptist Church, but she figured that he already knew since his mother was Sister Alexander, and she had been a member of the church for years and never missed a Sunday. Megan lay on the couch and thought long and hard about the implications of calling Cory, but she decided that he was worth the risk.

"Hey, Cory, I hope things have been going well with you and Ronda. I was thinking about the two of you and wanted to check in," Megan said.

"Megan, I'm so happy that you still care," Cory joked.

"Well, if I'm being honest, the truth is, I actually wanted to see you with no strings attached," she told him.

"My, my, my! You're a woman who knows what she wants," Cory said.

Cory took the reins back and asked Megan out on a date. Although he found her forwardness to be sexy, he was too macho to entertain any ideas of women empowerment when it came to chivalry. He told her that they had a lot of catching up to do. He planned for them to watch Netflix and chill at his house while eating pizza. Megan was happy that she had followed her intuition and called him. Cory had a way of making her laugh, and she could use a good laugh to keep from crying. They agreed to get together over the weekend, which was perfect since she wanted to spend some time with her family too.

Megan planned to take a few days off and needed to get Keisha's approval. She was still in awe of the fact that she would become an equal partner and would no longer have to go through David or Keisha to be cleared for time off.

She called her mother to invite her on a day trip to Niagara Falls. They were overdue for a much-needed spa day. She had been there when she was a young girl with her family and recalled the way her mother bragged about the breathtaking view there.

Janice was in good shape for a woman her age, and she loved to hike. There were miles and miles of hiking and other action-packed adventures at the famous landmark. Megan loved the outdoors and could find solace in beautiful places. Since her becoming an adult, Megan and Janice's relationship had become stronger. Janice had always been a remarkable woman who Megan had come to admire. There were many positive attributes she could learn from her mother by spending time with her. It had taken Megan a long time to receive the approval she sought from her parents, but they were proud of her many accomplishments and the fact that she had been asked to be a co-minister.

Megan planned to travel to Niagara Falls by car, which would take an hour and a half. It would allow them to catch up on gossip about family issues, since Janice loved to hear herself talking. Megan's siblings had been on her mind a lot lately, and because of their busy lives, she hadn't called them as often as she would have like to, but Janice could fill her in on the latest tidbits. Megan assumed that Janice was dying to hear the details that weren't reported on the news or written in the newspapers about Ms. Emma Jean's death.

Megan picked her up, and they stopped at Starbucks for some lattes before driving down I-90 to Niagara Falls. Janice told Megan that Mattie and her husband were planning to move out West to California, and Trevor had landed a prominent position at his firm and would receive a substantial increase. They were excited about living there and seeing all of the famous landmarks in the beautiful state.

Matthew and his wife Tiffany were expecting their second child, a girl, who they planned to name Star Janice Martin. Her mom was thrilled that her granddaughter would have her name as a middle name. She teased Megan about being single without children before changing the subject to talk about herself. Janice explained that she and Stephen were happier than they had ever been and would be celebrating their 40th anniversary. She was planning a dinner party at the country club they belonged to as a celebration. Hearing about all the great news that was happening in her family's lives made Megan's heart melt. By the time they reached the hotel, they were tired and ready to relax by enjoying a quite dinner before retiring for the night.

Megan woke up in a cold sweat and didn't know if it was being caused by something that she had eaten or because of her jaded past that had caused her to have an undiagnosed case of PTSD. She needed to see a doctor soon to be evaluated. It had been years since she had overcome a life of using recreational drugs such as Valium. However, lately she was on edge and felt a lot of anxiety. She promised herself that she would address her self-care issues before allowing things to spiral out of control. The main thing she looked forward to was her ultimate spa day. She decided that it wasn't such a good idea to burden Janice with the details of her rocky morning. Instead, she decided to let her hair down and enjoy her mother's company.

Megan showered and hurried down to the lobby to enjoy a light breakfast before heading to Salon Nouveau Day Spa. They planned to get a Swedish message, pedicure, nails polished, eyelash extensions, and a new haircut and color. The services would take up the entire day. After being pampered, Janice and Megan looked like a million bucks. They couldn't stop looking at themselves in the mirror.

"Oh, my gosh! Megan, you look absolutely gorgeous. I'm so proud of the woman you've grown up to be, and your hair turned out great. You're ready for your breakout moment," Janice bragged.

Megan gave her mother a loving hug and a kiss before showering her with compliments too. Janice could be credited for Megan and Mattie's beauty. She had looked just like them when she was their age. Meagan found it encouraging that her mother was taking such good care of herself lately and was on better footing. They decided to skip their plans to go hiking because they were not about to ruin the results from the glam session.

On the ride home, Megan shared all of the controversial details that the Williams family had faced in recent weeks, but she insisted that Janice keep what was told to her confidential. She told her that she was relieved that things had finally begun to settle down for everyone. The family ministry didn't need to be the subject of any more glaring headlines with the construction of the second location. Megan told her mother that everyone was in a good emotional place and believed that the launch was going to be a success. As soon as they arrived back in Pittsford, Megan dropped her mother off and promised to visit again soon.

When Megan got home, she called Keisha to let her know that she was back, and she wanted know how she was doing. Keisha had always been the rock who made sure everybody was okay, but because she was "so strong," she was often forgotten about and no one checked up on her. Keisha was happy that Megan called and that she and her mom had such a relaxing time. Keisha told Megan that she had been feeling out of sorts lately and had considered going on vacation too.

"Keisha, it wasn't that long ago that we almost lost you. Please take care of yourself. A little therapy never hurt anyone, you know," Megan told her.

"Megan, you know I'm the first to advocate for women to go to therapy. There's no shame in it. In fact, I made an appointment to see someone today. That Ms. Emma Jean episode nearly took me out mentally, physically, and emotionally, especially after I found out that she tried to kill my mama. I thank God that Mom was able to handle her, because you know if I had walked into her room and seen Ms. Emma Jean hovering over her with that knife, I'd be in jail, or worse, dead. Everybody knows my mama is off limits," Keisha declared.

"Keisha, I want to give you a hug right now. I'm relieved too that God spared you and your mom. He covered you both, and I thank Him for that," Megan reported.

They both agreed to take better care of themselves. Megan told Keisha that she was considering chairing a woman's group at the church once they broke off into two locations, and she believed that women need to help each other deal with taboo subjects such as drug addiction, domestic violence, depression, and anxiety.

She thought that she and Jada were the poster children for issues like that, and by teaming up with her to be the advocates who had gone through sexual trauma themselves made them relatable and more equipped to provide the vision for a brighter future. Keisha thought it was a great idea and encouraged Megan to sit down with Jada to put the wheels in motion for the group. They said their goodbyes, and Megan spent the rest of the evening unwinding and focusing on her short and long-term personal goals and ones for the ministry as well.

Megan woke up to the sound of her phone ringing, and when she rolled over to see who was calling, she was excited that it was Cory. She wanted him to see the results from her glam session. She didn't hesitate to answer. Cory invited her over for dinner and gave her the option of having pizza delivered or mentioned that he could cook his famous lasagna along with a salad for her. Italian food was his favorite, so he told Megan that he was fine with whatever option she chose. It was lasagna and the salad, because she wanted to get a glimpse of Cory cooking in his kitchen. A man who could cook was sexy and turned her on. He asked her to wear jeans since they weren't going out.

After hanging up, Megan ran to her closet to find something to wear. She laid several pairs of jeans on her bed that include her "Go to" pair. They were the ones that accentuated her curves the best. She decided to wear a black pair with a beige T-shirt and pumps. It was a causal look but made her feel beautiful and sexy. She spent the better part of the afternoon cuddled up underneath a blanket reading her favorite book, *The Story Keeper* by Lisa Wingate. She couldn't put it down. It was a story with an overarching message about ethics and choices.

She was midway through the book before realizing it was time to get showered and dressed. Megan sang loudly in the shower as she lathered her body with her favorite scented soap. She knew she still had the "It" factor. After drying off, she applied her make-up and put on her clothes, and then she stopped at the grocery store to get something for dessert. She didn't want to show up empty-handed. She purchased a lemon meringue pie, mainly because it was her favorite.

Megan looked flawless! She parked on the street when she arrived at Cory's house and noticed that there were two cars in his driveway. She assumed one of them belonged to Rhonda. She confidently walked up to the front door, knowing that Rhonda would more than likely be the one to answer it. Megan rang the doorbell, and to her surprise, a lovely, radiant young lady greeted her. Rhonda was clean and sober, and her once bad attitude had escaped her.

"Hello, Megan. How are you? Dad's in the kitchen fixing his famous lasagna. Believe me when I tell you that it's delicious. Please, come in," Rhonda invited.

"Rhonda, it's so good to see you. Your dad tells me you're doing well these days. Perhaps we can sit down and talk sometime. I'd love for you to speak to the women about addiction and being an overcomer when you're ready," Megan told her.

"I'd love to talk sometime. Thanks for the invite," Rhonda replied.

Rhonda escorted Megan into the kitchen, and Megan couldn't help but to comment on the wonderful smell that was making her stomach growl. Cory looked up and was happy to see Megan standing there looking beautiful with her new haircut with the radiant colors. Her make-up was applied perfectly, a tip she had learned at the spa, and she could always wear a pair of jeans, rock a T-shirt, and look amazing doing it.

"Wow, Megan! You look great. Are you ready to eat? I'm almost finished cooking," Cory asked.

"Yes, I'm starving!" Megan replied.

Rhonda set the table as Megan stayed in the kitchen making small talk with Cory who she following into the dining room once the food was ready. He asked Megan to bless the food before serving it, so she said a quick prayer before they ate. Cory explained that he and Rhonda had been focused on her recovery and that at first it had been a rough road, but they were dedicated to her achieving sobriety. Rhonda shared how her illness had nearly destroyed her relationship with her father and the details of her darkest hour, a time when she said and did a lot of things she regretted. She apologized to them both for her actions on the day she overdosed and told them how much she appreciated the fact that they had been there for her. Rhonda said she'd had several encounters with God, and He showed her that she had a calling on her life and that it wasn't her time to go.

She recalled that dreadful night she took the handful of Xanax and began hallucinating. In her hazy fog, she saw herself ascending downward into a sweltering pit of Hell, but there was an angel reaching out her hand to pull her up before it was too late. As she hovered above the clouds, she saw herself speaking to thousands of women who were hanging on her every word. Although she didn't know what she was saying to them, it felt great to be used in such a mighty way. She grabbed the angel's hand, and God spared her life, giving her another chance to make a difference on earth.

Megan was happy that God had answered Rhonda's prayers and that Rhonda gave God all the glory. Cory thanked Rhonda for sharing part of her story and believed that it was important that Megan see the better parts of Rhonda. He was hoping that she hadn't negatively judged him the same way others had in his past who believed he was a bad father. He changed the subject by asking if anyone wanted dessert, but they were both full.

Cory invited Rhonda to watch a movie with them, and she eagerly agreed. He picked out *Unbroken*, a true story about survival, resilience, and redemption, something he had faith that his family would experience. When the movie was over, Cory reported that he and Rhonda planned to take Megan up on her offer to get them back in church and would rededicate their lives to God. They would return to Victory Baptist Church and would sit in the front pew with his mother, Sister Alexander. Megan was happy to receive the good news and was proud of Cory and Rhonda.

Rhonda excused herself, knowing that her dad and Megan could use some time alone. Cory confessed that he was sure that Megan was partly responsible for the positive changes he and his daughter were experiencing. He said that his goal was to become abstinent from sex and dating so that he could continue to strengthen his relationship with God. Megan agreed and acknowledged that he had helped her realize that she needed to work on herself by herself. In the past, she had believed that she needed a man in her life, but she had been pleased to learn that God's plans were bigger than her own. She gave Cory a hug and told him that she hoped to see him and Rhonda sitting in the front pew soon. She ended her night, and they vowed to remain in touch with one another. Her wayward ways of being inappropriate with men were no more — to God be the glory.

# Chapter 19

# Wayward Nuptials

## (Natalia's Miracle)

errance and Natalia were relieved that everyone who needed to be in the know about them getting married knew, including David and Victoria. With all the chaos surrounding the Williams family, Terrance believed it was the perfect time for them to move in together. He had been spending a lot of time with her and Juan and Marco lately, and everyone was comfortable with having him around. He was the perfect father figure and had a lot of influence over them. He desired for Juan and Marco to have some of the same opportunities he had growing up in a loving two-parent home. He didn't waste any time introducing them to things like community activism, since he believed that it was important for young men to give back. In the short time he had been in Pittsford, he had become a staple in the community by working on causes that involved the youth and by advocating for funding for after school and tutoring programs.

He also volunteered as a coach for the youth in basketball, which was something most of them welcomed and gravitated to. After all, for a man in his early thirties, Terrance still demonstrated agility on the basketball court, and his legacy at Pittsford Sutherland High School spoke for itself. He was a superb athlete and credited his parents for allowing him the opportunity to enjoy a top-notch higher education where sports and academics were equally important.

Natalia had done a great job as a single parent. She was starting to notice some positive changes in Juan and Marco in the short time they'd known Terrance, and their optimism for the future was evident by the amount of college applications they were submitting. They were also eager to work with Terrance a lot more at the church helping others. Natalia was thrilled to have someone helping her with them and proud of all of their achievements.

Terrance felt on top of the world, being in a relationship with Natalia and her boys. However, there was one unresolved issue that troubled him. Sarah, his ex-girlfriend, was trying to ruin his relationship with Natalia, and he wasn't going to allow that to occur. He thought he had made things clear with her when he left New Mexico that he was serious about things being over, but apparently she didn't get the message. He was receiving threats from her, claiming that she was going to come to Pittsford to cause havoc to get even. Terrance wondered how she was able to find out so much information about him and who he was dating, but then he recalled the fact that she and Jada were friends on Facebook.

He looked at Jada's Facebook page and realized that she had been making posts about her family and the fact that Terrance was in a relationship. She had posted pictures of him and Natalia on Facebook. Jada thought they were adorable together and didn't mean any harm, but Terrance had to do something about the situation immediately before Sarah made good on her promise to come to Pittsford. She claimed that she was lost without him, although she tried to act like she had moved on to make him jealous. He kept all the nasty text messages in his phone that she was sending so that he would have a log of her harassment along with the many times she was calling and hanging up on him. She was acting like an unstable villain, and he was concerned.

Not quite sure how to handle the situation, Terrance involved Keisha, knowing that she would handle it. She could go after you with a vengeance if you messed with her family, especially Terrance, and she had never liked Sarah in the first place. Asking her to make Sarah's life difficult would be like taking candy from a baby. In Keisha's opinion, Sarah had been way too controlling over the years, but of course Terrance had seen things differently. He had been too in love with her to see the forest for the trees, so Keisha had left things alone. Keisha was even tempered, but when it came to family matters, she'd flip out, turning into an eye rolling, finger pointing "Sista girl" with an attitude who came for blood. Terrance called her right away to get her vexed.

"Sis, I need your help. I thought I could get rid of Sarah once I moved home, but she isn't going down without a fight. The girl keeps calling and hanging up on me. It's been intense lately, especially after she found out that I've moved on with Natalia. I don't need no problems," he confessed.

"Don't worry. Text me her number and I'll handle that snob," Keisha demanded.

Terrance knew it was best to leave well enough alone after confiding in Keisha. She was a woman who kept her word, especially if she pledged to remedy a situation.

Keisha knew a lot of people throughout the United States, and when necessary, she could take a walk on the dark side by going underground. It was a wayward trait that she was able to hide, and one only a few people knew she was capable of. However, since she and Terrance were so close, he knew everything about her shady activities, including how she had handled Sean, her ex-husband, years earlier when they were going through a nasty divorce. She had him taken care of, so to speak, and although he never physically abused her, he verbally abused her to the point that her self-esteem was broken. She blamed him for her miscarriage and wanted to get even, so she called on some thugs who were friends of a friend, and she paid them generously to break a few of his limbs. He didn't have a clue who was responsible for his "accident" but was able to make a full recovery.

Keisha took care of Terrance's "little problem" by calling a private investigator she knew and asking him to find out as much information as he could about Sarah. Toby told her that he would at least need to have her telephone number to conduct a limited search that would provide some basic information. Keisha provided him with the telephone number that Terrance had given her, and *Bingo!* Toby gave Keisha not only a home address but a work address too. She thanked him for his quickness and told him that his payment would be on the way. With Sarah's info in hand, she called another associate who lived in New Mexico and asked him to handle the job. He told her that it could take a few days to vet the right person. Keisha gave him the okay and went back to her life as a pastor.

In the meantime, Keisha continued to plan for the upcoming changes that were occurring at Victory Baptist. Although she was able to switch gears seamlessly, she had some regrets about tapping back into her dark side. She believed that it could be a hinderance at this juncture of her life, but she refused to allow anything else to happen to her family. Over the past few years, they had endured enough heartbreak and loss. It was a new season, and she was excited about it. She fell down on her knees to pray to God for His forgiveness and vowed never to be swayed toward evil again, not even for Terrance's sake.

"Precious Lord, Oh, God, keep me and my family in Your perfect will. I ask that You cover my mind, body, and soul. Deliver me from temptation and evil thoughts. Forgive me, Oh, Lord, as I am not a perfect vessel and haven't always been in Your will for my life. Lord, You said that me and my family shall be saved. Lord, You said that You would build a hedge of protection around our comings and goings, and, Lord, You said that we would always be perfect in Your sight, and let us always trust and believe that. Amen," Keisha prayed.

Terrance and Natalia were finalizing the details of their upcoming vacation to the Grand Cayman Islands. Natalia was elated and couldn't wait to spend quality time with Terrance and her family. She knew her parents would approve of her marrying Terrance after getting to know him since he was such a good man and came from a great family. Terrance suggested they plan to go before the Fourth of July as first planned since the board voted favorably to expand the church. Natalia called her mom Rosamarie to ask if she and her father Zavier were willing to tag along with them on such short notice. She told her mother that Terrance had proposed and it was likely that they would get married while they were on vacation and that she would love for them to come along.

"Oh, Natalia, your father is aware that you and Terrance are dating, and surprisingly he's happy for you. The boys told him all about it, but I'm not too sure he'll go along with the idea of you two getting married so soon without knowing each other that long. Sweetheart, don't you think you're moving too fast?" Rosamarie asked.

"*Estamos bien. Papa adora'a Terrance*," Natalia replied.

"Okay, honey, I will tell your dad to get ready, because we're going on vacation," Rosemarie declared.

Natalia told Terrance to include her parents as he worked on the itinerary and suggested they email the details to her mom soon so she could book their trip. Natalia was overjoyed, and she couldn't wait to get away.

Before finalizing their plans and packing, she recalled that Terrance and the boys still needed their passports and that she would need to expedite the necessary paperwork to get a quick turnaround. She had to get Leroy's birth certificate and information too from his foster mother and was hoping that Terrance had already received special permission from the courts to take Leroy out of the country. Terrance had pulled some strings with a judge handling Leroy's welfare case, and the judge had modified his placement, knowing that they were willing to adopt him. Those were the last things she needed to do before landing on the beautiful Grand Cayman Islands, with temperatures that averaged 72-88 degrees, a marine paradise surrounded with coral reefs and sparkling blue water.

Natalia planned to teach the boys how to surf and wanted to spend as much time as she could all cuddled up with Terrance on the white sandy beaches drinking exotic cocktails. Zavier and Rosemarie decided to meet them at the Rochester Airport on the day of the trip. The family boarded an American Airlines flight headed to the Grand Cayman Islands and everyone was overjoyed.

Natalia insisted that her father and Terrance sit next to each other during the flight to allow them more time to get to know one another. Surprisingly, by the time they landed, the two of them were inseparable and realized that they had so much in common, such as being family men and hard workers who both agreed that Natalia was important to them.

When they arrived at the hotel, Terrance and Zavier already had a list of things planned that didn't include the ladies. They dropped off their bags and rushed off on a men's only adventure with Juan, Marco, and Leroy in tow.

Natalia and her mother were left to fend for themselves. Natalia didn't know whether to be upset or happy that Terrance had abandoned them. She decided to focus on the fact that his absence would allow her and her mom more time to shop. The two enjoyed uninterrupted quality time, catching up on things like they did when she was a teenager. Being an only child had its advantages, like receiving all of her parents' attention. It was no surprise that she was so confident and able to allow her bright light to shine bigger and brighter than the State of Texas.

Meanwhile, as Terrance, Zavier, and the boys were being guided through one of the many caves, Terrance received a call from Keisha. She realized that he was on vacation but wanted to assure him that his problem with Sarah had been resolved and that he wouldn't have to put up with her antics any longer. Keisha told him that Sarah didn't have the capacity at the moment to talk, and it could be awhile before she was in the mood to stalk him or anyone else.

It just so happened that she had been accosted by an unknown assailant in the parking lot of New York Bank & Trust where she worked. A plastic bag was placed over her head before her jaw was dislocated. Some bystanders who had witnessed the ordeal called the police, and she was rushed to the nearest hospital. Her attacker left a note behind that appeared to be written by a child. It stated, "The gig is up, bitch."

Sarah was unable to provide the police with any leads about who could've done that to her. Needless to say, the case was closed and her stalking days were over.

With Sarah out of the way, Terrance was free to move forward with his plans to marry Natalia, and he was going to while they were on vacation. He didn't ask Keisha any questions but thanked her for always being there for him. She warned him that moving forward he needed to depend on God and his future wife to help him work through his problems, and the only assistance she would be able to give was sisterly advice and prayer like she had always provided. He agreed that she was right, and they hung up.

Terrance returned to the good time to be had with Zavier and the boys, and they spent the rest of the day exploring the caves before joining the ladies for dinner. Terrance was thrilled when Natalia told him that she had made plans for them to enjoy a romantic evening together. She looked amazing in her sexy, strapless black dress, but they never made it out of the room because Terrance's hands were all over her, and she was out of her dress within minutes.

He made love to her the better part of the evening and then shared intimate talks afterward about their life together. Juan, Marco, and Leroy spent the evening with their grandparents on an excursion where they were able to feed fish. Rosemarie and Zavier were a vital part of Juan and Marco's lives, especially after the death of their father, and the boys loved their grandparents.

When they woke up the next morning, Terrance revealed his plans to take them on a 6-hour catamaran trip to Rum Point Beach, knowing how much Zavier loved to be on the water. The beach was beautiful, and the crystal-clear waters were inviting. A gentleman was waiting to lead them to a grassy hut when they arrived.

Terrance explained that they would witness him and Natalia sharing their wedding vows. Although Natalia had expected it, she was still in awe of the fact that it was really happening. Terrance didn't give her the chance to shop for a nice dress, since he thought that she looked beautiful in anything she wore, including the black halter top with the white Capris she had on. To him, the only thing that mattered in the moment was having her parents' and children's permission for them to get married, and they did.

Terrance held Natalia's hand as the preacher officiated their wedding. Her princess-cut diamond glistened in the sunlight as she said, "I do."

By the time their impromptu ceremony concluded, Terrance and Natalia were in tears. It was official; Natalia Sanchez was now Mrs. Natalia Williams. She was happy to have a second opportunity, and this time around things were going to be different. The best part of being married to Terrance was that she got to work with her husband in the ministry every day, and thing could not have been more perfect. Juan, Marco, and Leroy slapped Terrance high fives.

Terrance informed them that he and Natalia had agreed to allow Leroy to live with them and were planning on adopting him. Leroy was in shock, even though Terrance had promised him that he would always be there for him. Juan and Marco were happy for Leroy. They had known him a long time, way back from their Sunday school class days. Natalia was delighted in the fact that she wouldn't have to go through another pregnancy, as she and Terrance would have an instant family that consisted of three children who were near adulthood. However, she welcomed the opportunity to pour love and support into Leroy's life, the same way she did with Juan and Marco. They continued to celebrate their nuptials by taking full advantage of the activities on the island to create family memories before returning home to Pittsford.

# Chapter 20

## Wayward Outcomes

### (Keisha's Promising Future)

The news of the church's expansion had started to be a benefit in changing the story in the community from the negative press to the positive work of changing hearts and winning souls for the Lord. Whenever the doors of Victory Baptist Church were open, it was difficult to find a seat. It was David's turn that beautiful July Sunday morning to preach. He entered the pulpit and preached what was thought to be his best sermon. His message was about family and about not being perfect. He talked about how it was our responsibility to create the lives we wanted to experience with the families we were given. He also spoke about family being anyone we chose to allow into our heart. That day, several people dedicated their lives to the Lord, including Leroy and Jada, who had decided to rededicate her life as well. She wanted God to provide her a clean heart and new promises. She was ready to embrace wholeheartedly her promising future. Keisha and Victoria were thrilled that Jada had made this choice.

Later that day, Victoria invited everyone over for Sunday Dinner. She was still a bit rattled and uncomfortable being in the family home but realized it was going to take courage to overcome her fears. As she prepared the food, she felt a move of God and heard an audible voice that said, *"You're more than a conquer."*

Tears roll down her beautiful face, knowing that it was the Reverend letting her know that she had done the right thing by remaining in their beautiful home they had created and not allowing anyone to force her out. She had a renewed sense of hope and dedication to being the matriarch of her family. She called Terrance to ask if he would barbeque, believing that it was also time to enjoy their beautiful backyard that they had abandoned in recent years.

Terrance was eager to show off his skills on the grill. This would be his first dinner in the family home as a married man. He also wanted to share their plans to adopt Leroy when the opportunity presented itself. Terrance was a grill master and knew how to prepare the perfect steak. Victoria agreed to make the side dishes, such as macaroni and cheese, coleslaw, baked beans, and banana pudding, if he would grill the meat.

Jada rushed into the kitchen and didn't hesitate to help Victoria out anyway she could and to tell her how grateful she was to reside in the home again where she belonged. Terrance arrived with Natalia and the boys, and everyone was happy to greet her as Terrance's wife.

"Natalia, welcome to the family. I wish you and Terrance the best, and of course you know how I feel about Juan and Marco," Victoria told her.

"Thank you! Victoria, calling you Mom will be easy for me since you have always treated me like a daughter, even during my not so good times. It feels good to be an official member of this family," Natalia said.

The backyard was full of family and friends. The smell of barbeque was enticing, and they couldn't wait to eat. While the meat was grilling to perfection, Terrance asked to have everyone's attention, "As most of you are aware, Natalia and I were just married, so I would like to give a toast to my beautiful wife. Natalia, you have made me the happiest man ever, and I take you and Juan and Marco into my life. Your beauty, intelligence, and acceptance of others are just some of the reasons why I fell in love with you. I thank you for investing in my dreams, and your willingness to create a better life for Leroy is remarkable and your willingness to do it by faith. We will be great parents for all three of our children, and I'm ready to take this journey and to continue my Christian walk with my wife and partner by my side," Terrance told her.

"Terrance, I have waited my entire life to have a man love me the way my father does. You're perfect for me, and I look forward to building a life with you and our three sons. I feel blessed to be their mother and your wife," Natalia admitted.

Keisha added, "Well, you guys could've thought that I wasn't going to weigh in on your marriage. Little brother, besides your coming home for me, your marriage to Natalia is a double blessing. I love you both dearly. Heck, I'm already Juan and Marco's godmother; how convenient is that? Now I get to say that I'm the greatest "Aunt mother" and I embrace Leroy too. The three of them are the most respectful and handsome young men that I know. To God be the glory."

"Wait a minute. I have something to add. Congratulations, Terrance and Natalia. We have been family unofficially for years, and now you two just had to run off and get married. I want you both to know that I will continue to be here for you. I love you guys so much," Megan told them.

Asia and Aleyah ran around the backyard with boxes of tissues, passing them out to whoever needed them. It was time to eat, and everyone piled their plates up with the delicious food. Of course, David grabbed one of the biggest steaks available and devoured it.

After they finished eating, David brought out the karaoke machine. There were too many people to sing in the kitchen like they used to, so they brought the karaoke machine out to the backyard. The Wayward Sisters didn't miss an opportunity to do their rendition of "Oh Happy Day" with everyone singing along. It felt great to be carefree and laugh again. David concluded the evening with a prayer.

Keisha and Jada helped Victoria clean up the backyard and the kitchen. Keisha's phone rang, and it was First Lady Jakes calling to give her condolences and to check on Keisha. She had heard about the mayhem the family had faced. She was also calling to invite Keisha to The Potters House for a weekend retreat for single Kingdom women. She also wanted to tell her that she had someone she wanted her to meet.

Keisha felt humbled to have First Lady Jakes call her personally to check on her and to invite her to their retreat, but she was perplexed about who the person was that she wanted her to meet. However, she agreed to go along with it. *God was right on time,* she thought to herself since she had been considering going on a vacation.

"Hallelujah!" Keisha yelled out.

"Honey, what's all the excitement about?" Victoria inquired.

"Mom, you are not going to believe this, but I'm going to Dallas this weekend to The Potters House for a retreat. Jada, I hope this conversation isn't too awkward for you, being that you just left there, but I'm going to take First Lady Jakes up on her offer. I only have one life to live," Keisha proclaimed.

"Sis, there's no way I would blame you for wanting to experience personal growth, and besides, it's a free country. She might have Mr. Right waiting there for you," Jada said.

Keisha hurried to her room to pack some business and casual clothes. She prayed that she was in God's will, and in that moment she felt a sense of peace and was satisfied that it was meant for her to go on this trip. She pulled out her computer to look for flights so she could purchase a round-trip ticket to Dallas before going to bed.

When Keisha woke up, she called David, Megan, and Natalia to let them know that she would be flying out right away to Dallas to attend a retreat over the weekend. She asked David to coordinate the rotation in the pulpit and provided him with information about the things she had been working on. She asked him to help her out in her absence. She called Megan to ask her to drive her to the airport, and she agreed.

The Kingdom woman's retreat proved to be exactly what the doctor ordered. It felt like a great time to be in the presence of God and manifesting his will. First Lady Jakes introduced Keisha to Pastor T. D. Jakes, and she was blown away after being invited to their home for dinner. Keisha had the opportunity to meet their other children, Cora, and their sons Jamar, Jermaine, and Thomas. She hung out with Sarah the most since she already knew her.

First Lady Jakes told her that they were waiting for another guest to arrive for dinner, and when the doorbell rang, and a tall, dark, and handsome man walked through the foyer, and First Lady Jakes called Keisha over and explained that he was the person she had wanted her to meet. His name was Blair Evans, a motivational speaker. It appeared that First Lady Jakes was playing matchmaker. Blair was charming and had the ability to draw you in, causing everyone to hang on to his every word when he gave presentations.

"It's good to meet you, Keisha. I've heard a lot about you, your family, and your church ministry. I'm glad you came down to Dallas, and I'm hoping that you won't be too hard on our First Lady since I asked her to have you come. If I'm not being to bold, I figured we would hit it off," Blair reported.

"Good to meet you also, Blair, but it's apparent that you all don't know me that well. I'm hard to get to know and haven't hit it off with a person of the opposite sex in a long time," Keisha mouthed off.

"I was told that you were spunky and hard to crack, for lack of a better word, but if you agree to hang out with me while you're here, I promise that you will be surprised to learn that we have a lot in common," Blair told her.

Keisha took a deep breath and paused before she spoke. She wondered if God was playing a practical joke on her. She was somewhat attracted to Blair but tried to play coy. The two joined Pastor T. D. Jakes and his family in their beautiful dining room where dinner was being served. It consisted of a Caesar salad, prime ribs, asparagus, and baked potatoes. The food was delicious, and Keisha ate in silence, taking in the intriguing conversation at the dinner table. Pastor T. D. Jakes talked about the state of religion in our country and the lack of faith of Americans who falter under the chaos caused by the White House. Although she agreed with Pastor T. D. Jakes, she hoped that she wouldn't be asked her opinion about the matter since she had been taught by the Reverend to avoid talking politics with anyone but God, since He was the only one capable of changing things, and He required us to go to Him in prayer in times like this.

"So, Blair, what are you seeing and hearing throughout your travels? We are struggling to rein in our congregation as the world continues to spiral out of control," Pastor Jakes stated.

"Pastor, although I see a lot of propaganda being stirred about, I've used my talents to spread hope and faith in the One who created us," Blair responded.

Keisha was blown away by how eloquent Blair spoke and how he carried himself. She was especially impressed by how he didn't allow anyone to pull him into the fray, even if it was Pastor T. D. Jakes that he was talking to. Men with character are hard to find.

The conversation quickly changed to the retreat and how so many Kingdom women have showed up to strengthen their relationship with God by telling their unique personal stories and to fellowship with women from all over the United States.

First Lady Jakes explained how they had hosted the retreat for the past several years, and she believe it had helped women to jump-start their mission, especially after facing personal defeats. She told them about the phenomenal speakers who were expected to be there, one of whom was Blair, who was recommended and highly sought after. Blair had a unique way of helping men and women turn their hearts back to God.

"Wow! That's amazing! I'm so happy that I was ask to come this year," Keisha said.

"No problem, Keisha. God placed you in my heart. You're a trailblazer, but even they need refueling and encouragement. I wanted you to spend some time around those whose stories you can identify with, and the other reason was for you to meet Blair. I envision the two of you teaming up someday and making an impact in Christian circles," First Lady Jakes told her.

Blair chimed in, "I can honestly say that I appreciate that you took First Lady Jakes' invitation seriously." Feeling on the spot and slightly embarrassed, Keisha told First Lady Jakes that she was ready to relax at her hotel for the rest of the evening so she would be refreshed for the retreat, and she was driven to her hotel by Sarah who teased her about her discomfort around Blair.

Once in her room, Keisha looked in her suitcase and pulled out an outfit. Saturday was going to be a packed-full day of activities, and the participants had been asked to dress comfortably. She decided to wear something trendy and chose a pair of Nike leggings along with a matching lightweight athletic top.

Blair was sent over to the hotel to escort Keisha to the church where the Saturday activities would occur. She felt uncomfortable and a little annoyed that First Lady Jakes was still forcing Blair on her. However, he was smiling from ear to ear as they walked to the parking lot.

"Hello, beautiful! I hope you slept well. Today is going to be a great day. I hope you're willing to roll up your sleeves to be stretched by the activities that we have planned," Blair said.

"Of course I am, but I wasn't expecting you. Where's Sarah?" Keisha inquired.

"First Lady Jakes decided that you needed someone strong and handsome to pick you up and to make sure that you are having a good time, so she sent me instead," Blair reported.

"Well, I appreciate you taking the time to pick me up," Keisha told him.

Blair hurried over to the passenger side of his vehicle to open the door for Keisha. She got inside his Land Rover but didn't have much to say on the drive over to the church. She desperately wished she was at the embankment to discern why Blair was in her personal space at this particular time and place.

When they arrived at the church, he escorted her to the area where breakfast was being served, and then he disappeared. The Kingdom women were escorted to the conference room where the activities would take place. Keisha was impressed by all of the beautiful women of different hues, different walks of life, and different professional standings. They were asked to sit in groups of six at the various tables. The first segment was led by Dr. Tisha Watson, Leadership Development Coach, who opened the retreat with prayer before leading them through several exercises before lunch.

After lunch concluded, the women were led outside to a park-like setting where they were introduced to motivational speaker, Blair Evans. Keisha heard several of the women comment on his good looks. He introduced himself and shared his personal story about the trials and tribulations he had overcome. It was powerful by all accounts. His mother had been murdered by her boyfriend when he was a toddler, forcing him to be raised by his drug dealer father, who later became a prominent pastor who resided in Los Angeles.

The women were then challenged to partake in activities that revealed the false narrative they believed about themselves and to replace that false narrative by tapping into their positive energy as Kingdom women. Keisha couldn't believe how liberated and free she felt after following Blair's instructions. She had a newfound respect for him, but the jury was still out as to whether she was attracted to him in a romantic way.

Keisha hung out with Sarah and Valerie following the Saturday activities. She was later invited by them to go out on the town for dinner and perhaps enjoy a glass of wine. They settled on the Wolfgang Puck

Restaurant where Keisha ordered from the menu a Roasted Cauliflower Salad that was delicious just like she thought it would be. They shared some great conversation about the retreat and how First Lady Jakes was going to have a good word at the closing of the retreat on Sunday. The evening ended early and on a good note, and when Keisha arrived back at her hotel, she was caught off guard when she noticed that there were a dozen red roses in a beautiful vase sitting on the counter in her suite. She read the attached card and smirked when she realized that they were from Blair. He was inviting her out to dinner after the Sunday service before she headed back to Pittsford. She had a lot of nervous energy since it had been awhile since a male suitor had attempted to court her. Deep down inside, she was thrilled to have received the beautiful flowers and decided to call Megan to tell her about her unique situation.

"Hey, Megan, how are things going? You're not going to believe this, but first let me say that I'm having a great time at this retreat, but First Lady Jakes has been up to no good the entire time. She has been trying to play matchmaker with an attractive, professional, and beautiful man. He's been relentless in his pursuit of me, and he even convinced First Lady Jakes to have me fly out here. Girl, he's done his homework and knows all about me. Apparently he knows what he wants in a woman. All the women here are drooling over him because he's gorgeous, I must admit," Keisha told her.

"OMG! Girl, Juan really knows how to pray. That prayer he prayed for us to be married has led the three of us into opportunities, and, boy did Natalia hit the jackpot, and perhaps you will too," Megan said.

"I don't know if that's right, but we will see; you never know," Keisha admitted.

Keisha finished her conversation with Megan and decided to go down to the business office located in the lobby of the hotel. She wanted to get some tasks marked off her list. In her opinion, being on a retreat was no excuse for not working. When she walked into the business center, she couldn't believe that Blair there working too. In fact, she didn't realize that he was even staying at the same hotel, but at this point she couldn't run off.

"Hi, Blair. I didn't know you were staying here," Keisha said.

"Well, Keisha, there are a lot of things you don't know about me, but I'd like to change that," Blair reported.

Keisha realized that Blair was overflowing with charm, and it caused her to blush. She thanked him for the flowers and then sat down at the workstation and tried hard to concentrate with him in the room, but things felt awkward. She sneaked a peep of him and wanted to take in the fullness of his presence, and she wondered if he was someone she could be interested in. He seemed to be the perfect man, if there ever was one, but she realized that everyone has flaws. She asked herself if perhaps her flaws would turn him off, and she would never want him to see her dark side that bubbled up to the surface whenever she felt threatened. Over the years, she had prayed for God to help her overcome this unattractive behavior, but she remained a work in progress.

Blair walked over to her and asked if she had time to take a break. He suggested that they get a cocktail at the bar — if she was willing. Keisha took him up on his offer since she hadn't ordered a drink earlier at the restaurant. They secured their electronic devices and then walked into the crowded bar. Blair located a small table in the back of the bar where they could sit and talk. They engaged in small talk before Blair stepped away to have the bartender pour Keisha a glass of wine and himself a beer, and then he asked Keisha about life in Pittsford before explaining that he had been living in Brooklyn, New York for the past few years but was rarely there because of all the corporate and religious speaking engagement he had scheduled. He told her that he was familiar with the city of Pittsford but had not been there. Keisha was surprised that he lived in the State of New York and told her New York City was his favorite city too.

"Blair, I had no idea that you lived in Brooklyn. That's awesome, since New York is my absolute favorite place. My family and I were there not too long ago. My baby sister is a best-selling author, and we joined her for a book signing, and of course I was able to be their official tour guide since I went to college there. Does your family live in the city too?" Keisha asked.

"Someone is very talkative! If I knew that all I had to do was mention the word 'New York', I would've done so when you were acting all snooty. Yes, I do have family that still lives in Brooklyn. I found out late in life that my father has an illegitimate daughter. In fact, we look a lot alike, and she's also a motivational speaker. You met her on Saturday. Dr. Tisa Watson is my sister, and we're close and usually work together hosting conferences and retreats across the United States. In fact, that's how I became aware of who you are. We come to Dallas to attend church at The Potters House whenever possible. I was there when you and Valerie held your conference. My sister and I have been instrumental in helping Valerie career flourish as a paid motivational speaker," Blair explained.

"Oh my! We do have a lot in common. First Lady Jakes really knows what she's doing. I do seem to show the better side of my personality whenever New York is mentioned. So sorry for my rant. So, Tisa is your sister. I think she's phenomenal, and to tell you the truth, you both are. I learned so much today by fully engaging in all of the activities. My father had an illegitimate daughter too, and my brothers and I have embraced her. To tell the truth, I'm so glad we did because she's really awesome. Family is important to me, and I love them. Valerie is a great person, and we've been good friends for a while, but she has never mentioned anything about you," Keisha said.

"It's probably because she was interested in me but found out that we're distant cousins. Don't worry; we never even went out on a date. I just think it's a story she doesn't like having repeated. So, now that we've gotten all of our personal information on the table, what do you like to do for fun?" Blair asked.

"I haven't had any fun in a long time since my father's death and taking over the ministry. However, I enjoy going to Broadway shows, shopping, and vacationing. I want to plan a trip for my family to travel to Europe next year," Keisha reported.

The two talked so long that they didn't realize that it was almost midnight. They collected their belongings, and said goodnight so they could participate in the last day of the retreat. Keisha felt goosebumps and was full of joy, and that was a feeling that she hadn't felt in a long time. She prayed to God about her circumstances and then took a shower before going to bed. When she got out of the shower, she made sure the dress she planned to wear was pristine. She started removing her make-up, brushed her teeth, and slipped into her comfy pajamas.

Her cell phone rang and it was Victoria calling, "Honey, I hate to bother you while you're away, but I thought you should know that Loretta has gone into labor early and that her doctor needs to perform an emergency C-section to save Calvin's life," Victoria reported.

"Oh, my God, Mom! Is the baby going to be okay? I'm scheduling a flight right now to return home," Keisha said.

"Okay, honey, but be safe. We need you here," Victoria advised.

Keisha was so upset she didn't know what to do. It dawned on her that her father's grandchild and namesake was in danger. Her heart broke for David and Loretta as she packed to get ready to go. She realized that she needed to contact First Lady Jakes to let her know that she had to leave immediately and to thank her for inviting her.

After making the call, she took an Uber to the airport. During the flight home, she was worried about the baby, and the thought of Blair crossed her mind too but she realized that he was someone who had crossed her path for a short time and that the time had come to an end.

# Chapter 21

## Wayward Unity

### (Family Solidarity)

When Keisha arrived at the Rochester Airport, a limousine service was waiting to take her to Rochester Regional Health where the family nervously waited to find out Calvin and Loretta's fate. Although they were happy to see her, it wasn't the time for a family reunion. Family and friends congregated in the waiting room. Victoria brought Keisha up to speed on what had happened to cause Loretta to have to go into the hospital. She reported that the family had gathered at the house for Sunday dinner as usual, and after finishing dinner, Loretta began to complain about having some sharp pains in her abdomen that were increasing. David contacted her obstetrician who urged them to get to the hospital right away. Loretta was twenty-eight weeks pregnant and had entered her third trimester. They hoped she would be able to carry her baby an additional twelve weeks, but life doesn't always go the way we want it to. They were hopeful that she and the baby were going to survive.

David was full of anguish as he tried to keep Asia and Aleyah calm. They were inquisitive and couldn't stop asking questions. Jada attempted to distract them by allowing them to play games on her cell phone. She had become their favorite aunt and according to them was a joy to have around. David did what he knew to do by asking them to join him in prayer. He prayed to God for a healthy baby boy and that his wife would be okay.

"Father God, I thank You today and every day for the many miracles You have and will perform. I come before You with family and friends to ask for favor for my unborn son. I ask for favor for my lovely wife that she be able to pull through as well. You are a good God, and we ask these things according to Your will. Amen," David prayed.

The doctor entered the waiting room, and by the look on his face the news was going to be favorable. He explained that although the baby had been born early and would have to remain in the ICU for weeks, he was going to pull through. He went on to explain that Loretta was a strong woman and that she had gone through a lot of complications to deliver her baby boy, but she should be able to be released in a couple of days. Cheers erupted, and everyone was relieved that there was a new addition to the family. The doctor told David that he could see his lovely wife in a few hours. Terrance suggested that they order pizza since they were starving, and when the pizza arrived, they consumed it quickly.

The thought of having a baby named Calvin running around the house was encouraging, and they couldn't wait to meet him and watch him as he grew up. Plans had already been made for his debut in the pulpit, believing he too would have the call of ministry on his life. Keisha was grateful that she was able to make it back home to support David and Loretta. They had always been there for her no matter what.

Once Loretta was cleared, David, his siblings, and daughters went in to see her. She was exhausted but beyond happy to see them. Tears flowed down her face as she was being showered with love and affection. Then they were off to the ICU to sneak a peek at the baby. They looked through the glass window for him and noticed that baby Calvin was laying in his hospital bassinet hooked up to machines, but he was still beautiful.

Jada agreed to take care of the girls at the house for as long as needed so that David could stay with Loretta until she was discharged if he chose to. Once back at the house, Victoria put on a pot of coffee and sliced some fresh fruit for them to eat. Keisha shared the details with Victoria, Jada, Megan, and Natalia of the time she had spent in Dallas. She told them how awesome the retreat had been and about the great guy she had met named Blair. Although Megan knew about him, she didn't spill the beans. They couldn't believe that Keisha had caught the love bug, but they encouraged her to get in touch with him to explain her sudden departure. However, she tried to act like the whole thing was simply a coincidence and that she wasn't interested. The truth was, she couldn't stop thinking about the man who had come to interrupt her otherwise mundane life.

Behind closed doors, Keisha thought Blair's question about fun was warranted. She realized that fun was something missing in her life, and perhaps having fun with Blair would be fascinating. Although she was aware that he was interested in her, she didn't want to make a fool of herself by asking First Lady Jakes for his contact information. She concluded that it was best for Blair to contact her if he wanted to explore the possibility of them getting to know one another.

She called the hospital to check on Loretta and told David that she was going to check on the construction. He was thrilled and reported that the mother and child were doing well. He was confident that both would go home as scheduled. Keisha was glad to hear the good news but was exhausted and ready to go to bed.

When Keisha woke up the next morning, she leaped out of bed and couldn't wait to take her morning jog in Pittsford Park. It was much needed to help her clear out the clutter in her head. Her mind had been consumed with Blair and he wouldn't escape her thoughts. In the past, she hadn't believed that there was a such thing as love at first sight or even second sight in a hotel bar, for that matter, but something had her yearning to see him again.

As she jogged along on her familiar route, she prayed that God would give her peace and help her to make sense of meeting Blair. While distracted, she continued to jog. Then, all of the sudden, she felt a quickening in her spirit. She heard the voice of God utter the word, *"FUN."*

She couldn't believe that He was on board for her to have some fun with Blair, even though she knew that God was the giver of all good things. She completed her jog and headed back to her vehicle. On the drive to the office, she was bursting from the seams with excitement.

Keisha went directly to her office to work. With David being on maternity leave, he'd left a lot of extra duties that needed to be overseen. Keisha called the construction company to follow up on the status of the church, and she was told that the completion date had been pushed up a month earlier. The crew was working diligently, and they were now ahead of schedule. She couldn't wait to share her good news. While sitting there, she imagined how things were going to be when she started working with Terrance and her now sister-in-law Natalia, but she was excited. A brand-new building and possibly a brand-new life with someone special intrigued her.

Her cell phone rang, and she was thrilled that it was First Lady Jakes. Keisha was encouraged and hoped she would bring up Blair during their conversation.

"Keisha, I hope everything is okay with your brother and his baby. I feel so bad that you had to rush out of here during the middle of the night. The good news is that you can come back next year since we have the Kingdom retreat yearly, and with every passing year the talent pool keeps getting better. I didn't get a chance to find out if you enjoyed yourself. I've talked to Blair and explained your situation. He asked for your number, but I told him that I needed to check with you first. Would it be okay to give it to him?" First Lady Jakes inquired.

"First Lady Jakes, I'd love for you to give him my number. I can't begin to explain to you the way I feel about this man who I've known for such a short time, and I feel kind of silly," Jada explained.

"Well, Keisha, if the truth be told, Blair has been watching you from afar, and he really likes you. I agreed to make the introductions when me asked me too because I knew you two would hit it off. He's an outstanding, kind, respectable, and loving young man who I would introduce to my own daughters. I wish the best for you two, and I've got a feeling but I will keep it to myself," First Lady Jakes joked.

Keisha couldn't wait to receive a call from Blair, and she considered all the possible ways they could have fun together. In a few weeks, it would be Keisha's birthday on July 17th, and she was turning thirty-eight but still feeling a little out of sorts about being single, and the possibility of not having any children bothered her. She wanted to have a party with family and friends and started some of the preliminary planning. She recalled Natalia's '80s-themed birthday party way back in high school and decided to do a do-over. She recalled how much fun it had been to dress up and how Natalia's parents had been so cool and they had dressed up too.

She wanted the Wayward Sisters to come dressed the same as back then. Keisha would dress up as the infamous Janet Jackson, in the costume from the "Control" video where she wore a wig and teased it up as tall as possible along with wearing a black leather jacket. Megan would dress as Cindi Lauper and wear a spiked Mohawk wig, a tutu with leggings, a colorful shirt, and a wide belt. Natalia would dress as Whitney Houston in a form-fitting black dress.

Keisha decided to let everyone in on her plans for her party after Loretta was released from the hospital. She realized that this time around the party would be a blast since the members of her family would be involved. She imagined Asia and Aleyah in their costumes. It was going to be a great party for everyone. In the midst of her planning, her cell phone rang and it was Blair.

"Hi, stranger. How are you doing? I hope everything is okay. You missed our dinner date, so I'm calling to ask for another chance to take you out," Blair explained.

"Everyone is fine. My brother's wife will be coming home tomorrow, and the baby will have to stay in ICU for weeks, but all is well. How is it that you're going to take me to dinner with your busy schedule? I'm in Pittsford, New York, as you know," Keisha reported.

"Keisha, I told you that I have family in New York and that I'm able to travel. I can come see you and take you to dinner in a few weeks, if you will allow me to," Blair explained.

Keisha was taken aback but didn't miss the opportunity to invite Blair to her birthday party and told him that she would go to dinner with him while he was in town.

Blair agreed to travel to New York to visit Keisha for her birthday. She told him it was an '80s-themed costume party and it was optional to dress up. After they hung up, Keisha ran into the kitchen and told Victoria and Jada the good news.

"Mom, there's a good chance that I've found Mr. Right, so we just might get the opportunity for me to wear my Vera Wang wedding dress after all. I have a good feeling about Blair. I think he's the one. I can't wait for you to meet him. He's coming to my birthday party," Keisha reported.

"Keisha, you need to slow down and stay focused. I can't believe you've blindly fallen for this guy," Victoria said.

"I'm with Mom on this one, sis. You just met 'What's his name', and you know it will take longer than a weekend to get to know a man," Jada reported.

"Trust me; I've gone to God in prayer, and He has given me confirmation that Blair is worthy of me," Keisha told them.

They changed the subject to discuss how to share the responsibilities of helping David and Loretta, since she'd had a C-section and would be coming home soon. Victoria suggested that Loretta stay at the family home until she made a full recovery and could establish a routine with the baby. That way they could assist her if needed. Everyone thought it was a great idea and hoped Victoria would accept the help.

David and Victoria left the hospital after talking to the doctors about Calvin. He was almost out of the woods but would need to stay there for at least a few more weeks. It was difficult for Loretta to leave the hospital without her baby, but she realized that her girls needed her too.

David told Loretta that she and the girls could stay at his mom's so that everyone could pitch in to take care of them.

Loretta thought it was an awesome idea, "Victoria is so kind, and I feel so blessed that she's my mother-in-law. I would love to stay there for a month or so. That way you'll be able to pop in at any time to help out too."

"Baby, thank you for giving me three beautiful children. I can't wait until Calvin can walk and talk. Watching him grow up with the girls is going to be the perfect gift," David told her.

David stopped by their house to gather some necessities for the baby and Loretta before taking them to the house. He called Victoria to let her know to get the room ready because Loretta had agreed to stay. Victoria hurried to get things prepared and to put together a quick pot roast in the Crock Pot. She wanted to make sure that everyone had food available when they got hungry. She told Keisha and Jada the good news as well. When David pulled up, he helped Loretta out of the vehicle. She was still sore and took her time getting inside.

Loretta was bombarded with family who had open arms and waited patiently to embrace her. David warned Asia and Aleyah to be careful because it was going to take their mama a few weeks to recover. They went from one extreme to the other in their excitement.

"Where's our baby Calvin at, Mom?" Asia asked.

"Yeah, I wanna hold my baby brother," Aleyah chimed in.

"Girls, your baby brother needs to stay at the hospital for at least a few more weeks. He came out of your mama's tummy too early and needs to be cleared by his doctors to come home," David told them.

The explanation seemed to satisfied the girls, and they ran off to play.

Keisha called Terrance and asked him to bring Natalia and the boys over. She told him that Loretta was home from the hospital and that she had some great news she wanted to share. Next, she called Megan so that everyone would hear the news at once. She kept Jada and Victoria company in the kitchen while they waited for the others to arrive.

Once everyone got there, Keisha announced that she wanted her family to help her celebrated her birthday by participating in a costume party just like the one Natalia had back in the day, an '80s theme too, and everyone was excited and thought it was a fantastic idea.

"Sorry, Natalia, but I had to copy it! Girl, your party was off the chain, and I want to repeat history, along with my brothers, godsons, and nieces. It's going to be ten times better. I can wait!" Keisha explained.

"Keisha, no worries; it's good to see your silly side, and besides, we can all use a little comic relief," Natalia admitted.

"Yeah, Aunt Keisha, Juan, Leroy, and I can come as LeBron, Coby, and Steph. I know it's not all that creative, but you know that we love basketball," Marco admitted.

Aleyah added, "Oh, I'll be a princess. This is going to be better than Halloween."

Keisha took a few notes, and they all competed to talk about who they'd be at the party. She almost forgot to tell them about the good news on the construction. The news was welcome, and the family spent some much-needed time bonding before winding down to go to bed.

It had been a long, exhausting day for Keisha. She realized that God really did work in mysterious ways, and she was loving her newfound hope for romance. Love was in the air, but only time would tell if love could sustain itself in her life.

# Chapter 22

## Wayward Changes

### (Complications & Blessings)

errance's life had greatly improved in so many ways since marrying Natalia, and him becoming the step-father of Juan and Marco and the placement of Leroy were just a few of those ways. He and Natalia had been following up with the state to find out when Leroy would be officially available to adopt. It appeared that his foster mother, who had him for a few years, never intended to adopt him after his biological parents' rights were terminated. The Child Services Agency did their best to find a "Forever Family" for him, but being that he was a teenager made it difficult.

Terrance received a call informing him that he and Natalia had passed all of their initial background checks for the adoption, and it was just a matter of months before Leroy would be their son. Juan and Marco were getting along with Leroy, and they jumped for joy, knowing that he would be their adopted brother soon. Leroy was grateful that they would be his parents, and the fact that he was gaining two brothers was icing on the cake.

Natalia was taken aback after Terrance told her that he desired to adopt Juan and Marco too. He explained that his intent wasn't to have them forget about and cut off all ties to their biological father, but it was more for them to experience inclusion and to be made whole. He said he hoped and prayed that Carlos was smiling down on them and giving them his blessing.

Natalia was in tears, knowing that Carlos hadn't always done the right thing, but he loved his boys and they loved him. However, she agreed that Leroy being adopted by her and Terrance could cause her boys to feel left out, and that was something that she would never want for them. After all, Terrance was a good and caring man who would stand by them through hell or high water and would make sure they became mighty young men of God.

"Terrance, I don't know what to say. You're such an amazing man, and I really can't believe that you are willing to adopt three boys who are not your blood. I would be honored for you to be their father, but it's really up to them at this point. I support them in their decision," Natalia told him.

"Baby, those three boys mean the world to me, and that's not to say that we can't have a baby together someday. I just see this as an unselfish way to pour into their lives as a father. I was a knucklehead who didn't see the value of my father's affection and his desire for me to be the best I could be. However, what I can say is that the Reverend was a wonderful father to us, and I want to be that for Juan, Marco, and Leroy," Terrance declared.

Natalia called the boys into the kitchen to talk to them and told them that Leroy's adoption would be finalized in a few months before asking Juan and Marco how they felt about being adopted too, "Juan and Marco, adoption could be possible for you too."

"Adopted by whom, Mom? We already have parents. I thought adoption was for kids who didn't have any parents," Juan said.

"No, not exactly, son. Adoption is for those needing one or both parents, but it's also for those in blended families to experience inclusion and the benefits of everyone having the same last name," Natalia told them.

Terrance explained, "I want to adopt all three of you, if you'll have me. I've been thinking about this for a long time. Juan and Marco, you guys are very important to me, and I want to share all your experiences, be your confidant, teach you how to be a man, and most importantly, show you fatherly love. I hope you'll allow me to, but I'll understand if you don't agree. I would never force a decision so important like this on you."

Juan and Marco were all choked up, and if the truth be told, they had considered what it was going to be like with Leroy becoming a Williams and not them. They too were seeking inclusion and agreed to be adopted

under one condition; they would like to hyphenate their last name —
Sanchez-Williams.

Terrance was the happiest man in the world, and so was Natalia, that
they would be adopted. It called for a celebration, and Terrance suggest they
go out to eat as a family.

Since it was her birthday, Keisha was running around the house like a
teen, and she was ready to party. Victoria and Jada had taken the lead and
ordered a beautiful birthday cake and made platters of finger foods. They also
hired a DJ to host the party in the backyard. Loretta was feeling stronger and
planned to participate in all of the festivities. She even decided to dress up
with David as Ike and Tina Turner.

Jada sneaked behind Keisha's back and contacted First Lady Jakes to
get Blair's phone number. She was hoping he would dress up for the party,
which would make Keisha's day. First Lady Jakes answered her call and was
more than willing to help out. With Blair's number in hand, Jada called him
right away.

"Hi, Blair. This is Jada, Keisha's little sister. She told me that you were
coming to her party. If so, I was wondering if you'd be willing to dress up. It
would make Keisha happy," Jada explained.

"Well, it's great to hear from you, and yes, I'd love to dress up. What time
should I arrive?" Blair asked.

"I can text you the address if you don't already have it. You may arrive
around 5:00 P.M.," Jada said.

Jada felt a little sneaky after calling Blair behind Keisha's back, but since
it was for a good reason, she didn't worry about it. She showered and put on
her Nicki Minaj pink Barbie costume and looked cute. She couldn't wait to
show it off. By now the guests had started to arrive and were ready to party.
Jada walked into the kitchen and found the lovely Aretha Franklin preparing
food in her short-tapered wig, long eyelashes, and plain dress. They look at
one another and laughed uncontrollably.

"Mom, you look great! I hope I don't embarrass you, but I had to wear
my push-up bra to show cleavage in this blouse so I can tap into my inner
Nicki," Jada joked.

"Jada, you look great! No judgement, as I can use all the laughs that come
my way this evening," Victoria admitted.

Asia and Aleyah ran into the kitchen. They were all dolled up as Elsa and Anna from *Frozen* and looked adorable. They heard someone clearing their throat, something David did before making his entrance. It was Ike and Tina Turner walking in. They had big smiles on their faces and had pulled off their notorious look with ease. David told Victoria to, "Eat the cake, Anna Mae," referring to a quote in the movie where Ike tried to force Tina to eat cake. David apologized for making Loretta laugh, knowing that she was still sore and that it hurt for her to laugh. Natalia made her appearance dressed as Whitney Houston like she did many years earlier, and she serenaded them in song. She was in the company of Coach Bobby Knight and his proteges LeBron, Cory, and Steph, who believed her voice was music to their ears.

The doorbell rang, and Cindi Lauper walked in still fit as a teenager in high school. With everyone there, including friends and family, it was time for the birthday girl to make her debut. David cued up the music for Janet Jackson's entrance, and they started singing the catchy words to the popular hit, "Control". Janet grabbed the microphone. It was her birthday, and she wanted to take more control over her life by having some fun. They admitted that the woman still had moves! They showered her with love after she finished singing. It was time to sing "Happy Birthday", and they did after she blew out the candles on her cake. Keisha was full of joy. Tears ran down her face, and she was grateful for her family and friends. Jada received a text message from Blair. He had gotten lost and would be there in a few minutes. Jada waited outside for him to amplify the level of surprise for Keisha.

Blair pulled up in his Land Rover looking sexy and dressed as Bobby Brown. He said it was his prerogative to date Keisha if he chose. Blair thought his outfit was fitting, since Bobby Brown and Janet Jackson had dated briefly. Jada greeted him and escorted him inside. She asked him to hold back while she went to get Keisha to bring her into the living room to see him all dressed up and ready to celebrate her birthday.

Keisha almost passed out but gave him a hug before introducing him to everyone. David and Terrance sized him up and agreed to give him the green light to date their sister. Victoria found Blair to be charming. The census was that Blair was a suitable choice for Keisha. Blair was paraded around like "Eye candy" by Keisha, but she was grateful that he was a man of his word. She pulled him off to the side to thank him for making it to her birthday party and his willingness to dress up.

While she was talking, he grabbed her hands and pulled her closer to plant a kiss on her lips. Not having been kissed in a long time, Keisha thought her knees were going to buckle.

"Happy Birthday! I hate that we weren't able to spend more time together in Dallas, but I'm here for a few days, so what would you like to do, spunky lady? I hope it's not running away from me," Blair said.

"I'm not sure how to do this getting to know each other stuff, but I must admit that I'm nervous and excited at the same time. I haven't been able to stop thinking about you, Blair. It was so sweet of you to travel to see me on my birthday," Keisha admitted.

"I'm scared too, but I really would like to get to know you. We should get back inside to your party," Blair told her.

When they returned to the kitchen, they noticed that most of the guests had gone out into the backyard. The Wayward Sisters agreed to show off their talents the same way they did years earlier to help make Keisha's birthday party a success. First up was Megan who morphed into her inner Cindi Lauper. She belted out the lyrics of "Girls Just Wanna Have Fun". Everyone sang the chorus and fun was in the air. In fact, they sang so loud that the neighbors on both sides came over to join the party. To break the monotony, Bobby Knight, better known as Terrance, held a two-on-two basketball tournament. He teamed up with Coby, while LeBron and Steph joined together. It was the perfect basketball game with all the antics and ball handling skills on display.

Juan, Marco, and Leroy had a great time dressing up as their favorite athletes and showing off their skills. Next up was a solo from Ike and Tina Turner. They lip synced to "Proud Mary", but Loretta had to curb her hip action because of pain, but the both of them were great. Elsa and Anna belted out the lyrics from *Frozen*, "Let It Go" and were adorable! Being in the junior choir helped improve their vocal abilities.

Finally, Bobby Brown danced around while lip-syncing to "Don't Be Cruel". Keisha was impressed by Blair's dance moves and his genuineness. She was happy that her family found him easy to get to know and liked him. He was funny too, which was great because a person had to have a sense of humor if they expected to hang out with the Williams family. Loretta served cake and ice cream, and of course they completed the evening by pulling out the old karaoke machine.

Keisha and Blair spent some alone time in Pittsford Park. She wanted him to see her favorite place. She told him about the history of the Wayward Sisters and their allegiance to the beautiful place. As they strolled around the park in their silly costumes, she explained that it was at the embankment where a lot of her creativity and spiritual revelations occurred.

Blair listened and was happy that she had let her guard down to get to know him. He believed it possible that they could share something special in their future, but the jury was still out. He took Keisha home and they planned to spend the next few days together.

When Keisha woke up the next morning, Victoria and Jada bombarded her with questions regarding Blair. Keisha blushed as she gave them all the juicy details. Loretta walked into the kitchen and asked who wanted to accompany her to the hospital to see baby Calvin. Keisha and Victoria accepted her offer, and Jada said she would stay home to watch the girls.

When they arrived, Loretta spoke to the doctor who said the baby was getting better every day and may be able to go home sooner than expected. Victoria admired her grandson's beauty and was saddened when she considered that the Reverend couldn't be there with her to share that special moment. Keisha explained that she needed to go to work and left Victoria and Loretta there since they planned to stay the majority of the day. On the drive to work, Keisha felt thankful that the sun was shining on her family.

# Chapter 23

# Wayward Dreams

## (Renewed Hearts)

It was a beautiful Sunday morning in October, and the weather had gotten colder. The pastoral team was taking turns preaching, and it was hard for the congregation to decided what location they would choose. Each one of the pastors was in their element, especially David and Keisha, and membership was at an all-time high. Today was a special day for Juan, Marco, and Leroy, as they were getting baptized, and baby Calvin was going to be christened. The boys' adoptions had all become finalized in late September. Needless to say, David and Terrance were proud dads. They agreed that Keisha and Jada would conduct the baptisms and christening, and Megan would deliver the Word. The church was packed, and Natalia and Loretta were nervous as expected.

Megan took her place at the pulpit. She had become comfortable preaching in front of hundreds. Her message was "Let God Wrap His Arms Around Your Heart", and she didn't waste any time getting started.

"Hello, men and women of God. It's good to be in the House of the Lord. If we listen to that small voice in our hearts, we will hear God asking us to allow Him to wrap His arms around us. In other words, He wants to protect those bold enough to trust Him from their pain and sufferings. When we don't pay attention to Him, hate our neighbors, cheat, lie, and steal, those things remind us that we are suffering from a broken heart. But trust me;

heartbreak is real, but when we allow our thoughts and behaviors to line up with God's will, He creates for us a clean heart that's perfect and protected. His loving arms are wrapped around our hearts, and we are better off for it," Megan preached.

Upon the completion, Megan prepared the congregation for tithes and offerings before the baptism celebration took place. She gave an altar call for those needing prayer or desiring to get baptized. To her surprise, Cory and his daughter Rhonda walked down to the alter. They requested to be baptized too. Megan's spirit yelled out, "To God Be The Glory."

She realized that there would come a time when Cory and Rhonda would accept God as their personal Lord and Savior. Keisha and Jada prepared for the christenings, and more than ten babies were christened, including baby Calvin. David, Loretta, Terrance, and Natalia couldn't stop crying after having four Williams males invite God into their hearts. The line for the baptism was even longer with thirty people waiting, including Cory and Rhonda. It was a beautiful day at Victory Baptist Church and for its members. The choir sang "Oh Happy Day" with Keisha, Megan, and Natalia to get everyone in a celebratory mood.

After church, everyone gathered at the Family Life Center for a catered meal and to continue to celebrate the lives that had accepted Jesus that day. Megan rushed over to Cory who was sitting at a table with his mother, Sister Alexander, who was beaming with pride. She gave Cory and Rhonda a hug and told them how proud she was of them. Cory squeezed Megan's waist and gave her a kiss on the lips. Megan was caught off guard, but he took it a step further by introducing her to his mother as his fiancé. Cory asked her to join them and said that he would explain later. Megan sat down at the table with them and couldn't stop smiling from ear to ear.

The Williams clan couldn't stop praising the boys for their willingness to get baptized. Victoria told Terrance and Natalia that she was honored to be the boys' grandmother and they shared a loving embrace. Keisha believed that the day was perfect with the exception of Blair not being there. They had been an item for the last three months, but Blair had joined his sister in Florida for a motivational conference. He had invited Keisha, but she wasn't able to go due to church business. By now, she had fallen in love with him and they had gotten engaged but planned to wait at least a year before making things official. They wouldn't see Blair until about Thanksgiving, when he could witness the groundbreaking ceremonies for the new church.

Little did Megan know that Cory had a trick up his sleeve and that David knew his secret. Today, Cory planned to propose to her even though the last time they were together he said he wanted to practice celibacy. Cory felt like he was ready to marry the woman he loved after three months of focusing on his relationship with God and helping Rhonda through her rehabilitation.

David walked up to the podium and cleared his throat, "May I please have your attention? Today is a great day full of memories that we'll never forget. My only son was christened, and my three nephews accepted God as their Lord and Savior, but now we have another major announcement. With that said, I'll turn things over to my cousin Cory," David told them.

Everyone tried to figure out what was going on. Cory stood up and gave his mother and daughter a kiss on their cheeks prior to taking the microphone. Cory turned toward Megan and got down on one knee to ask her for her hand in marriage. The Wayward Sisters and half the people in the building were in tears. Megan had never seen this coming. In fact, she thought she had gotten over Cory although she had buried her feelings for him to avoid being heartbroken.

"Megan, I knew I was going to marry you the first time I saw you. I've enjoyed the times we have spent together and the way you've always had my back no matter what. I love you, sweetheart, and I would like to make you my wife," Cory proposed.

"OMG, Cory! I don't know what to say, but... I love you, too. Yes, yes, yes, I will marry you," Megan replied.

Cheers filled the air as Cory presented Megan with a beautiful one-carat solitaire. She couldn't believe that she was finally getting her chance to get married, and now that Cory had accepted God and Rhonda was a recovering addict, she was more than willing to marry him and to enjoy a happy life as his wife.

The Wayward Sisters congregated in the bathroom and jumped for joy. They were reaping the benefits from all the good things that had happened over the past few months. They agreed to meet at the embankment in the morning to pray, show gratitude, and to ask God to keep them in this positive season. When they exited the bathroom, they found everyone celebrating and doing the Electric Slide like they were at a family reunion. The night was perfect, and even Sister Alexander was seen hugging Victoria and vowing to bury her grudge with the Williams family. Megan and Cory were inseparable. The Williams family had grown, and with the pending marriage of Cory and Megan, the Wayward Sisters were now related and no longer were they just best friends.

When Keisha woke up, she went through her normal routine and prepared protein shakes for her and Jada. They drove together to the embankment, where surprisingly Megan and Natalia were already waiting, with each of them basking in their own cloud of blessings, but collectively they were now family, requiring a deeper level of connectivity. They joined hands and allowed Keisha to pray, but she was too emotional, knowing that she was passing the baton to Jada. The others would be married, and with significant others, there could be distractions. Jada would be responsible for keeping them on track, which was something she was willing to do. She took the lead and prayed for the Wayward Sisters, their careers, their significant others, and their beautiful family.

"Dear God, our quadruple ministry has grown considerably, as you have blessed us to be a force to be reckoned with. It's by the Blood of Jesus that we are truly blessed. With grateful hearts and second, third, and forth chances, we thank You, Lord for who You are and for helping us to know *whose* we are. We love You, Father God. Thank You for bringing Terrance and myself home, for sparing the life of Mom, for blessing David and Loretta with a son, for blessing Terrance with a wife and children, for blessing Keisha, Megan and Natalia with significant others and a family that we can all be proud of. We thank You, Lord, for expanding our territory in ministry, for providing us with a second location, and the anointing You've placed in our hearts, a family of pastors prepared to do Your will. We praise You, Lord for these reasons and more. We ask that You continue to keep Your hands of protection on our family. In these things we pray. Amen," Jada prayed.

The Wayward Sisters embraced one another and wiped away each other's tears. They felt a quickening in their spirit, and with heavy hearts they joined hands and turned toward the murky water at the embankment. Jada was given the honor of conducting the countdown. They closed their eyes, and Jada counted, "10-9-8-7-6-5-4-3-2-1."

They opened their eyes to four beautiful silhouettes in the clear water staring back at them, and when they looked up, there was a beautiful rainbow sky. God was in their midst, rebirthing dreams and visions for all of their futures. God is good!

Once again, Pittsford Park could be credited for cementing their sisterhood. It would forever remain their place of reconciliation. They were ready to use their powerful testimonies as proof to all who had ears to hear that God never leaves or forsakes His people. Amen.

# Also by
# BENITA TYLER

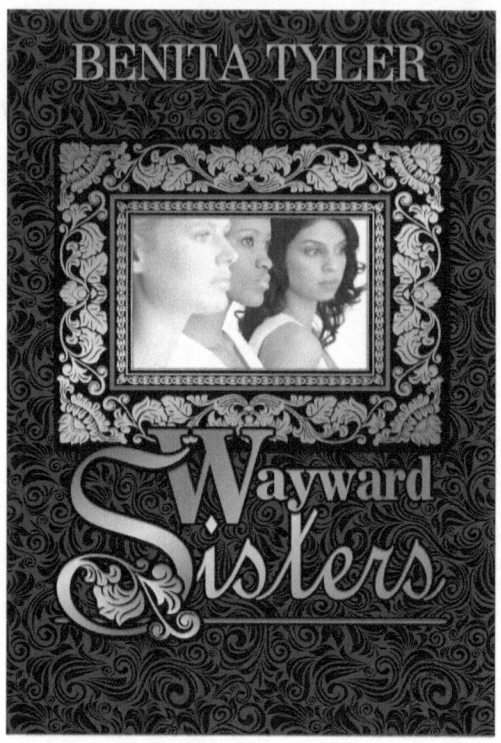

Imagine a beautiful place where secrets are told and reconciliation is at your fingertips. Boyfriend drama, parental disputes, and betrayal are the backdrop to the demise of a twenty year friendship. Keisha, Megan, and Natalia experience all this and more. Will the Wayward Sisters seek the path that God desires for them before it's too late? Come along on this captivating journey as good and bad choices are made that will leave you at the edge of your seat thirsting for more.

Softcover ISBN 978-0-9856964-5-0

Beloved Daffodil's Inspirations
700 E. Firmin Street, Suite 188 Kokomo, IN 46902
www.BelovedDaffodilsInspirations.com

***Addicted to Dysfunction: Released to Live Life Out Loud*** is the first book written that allows the reader to take an inconspicuous analysis of their own life's dysfunction through an honest account of the writer's sufferings and the lessons learned from them. This book is divided into five main character sections. The first section tackles disappointment. The second section stresses the importance of relational choices. The third section examines forgiveness. The forth section awakens our awareness. The fifth section challenges our acceptance of others. Collectively, these lessons will challenge you to let go and let God — releasing the reader to live life out loud.

Hardcover ISBN 978-0-9856964-0-5 • Softcover ISBN 978-0-9856964-1-2
eBook ISBN 978-0-9856964-2-9

***Put Up Or Get Shut Down*** is a bold and sassy "up in your face" excursion into the urban motorcycle world as the writer knows it. Salty Dog is a narcissistic brother with an ego big enough to match the horsepower of his chrome 1300 Suzuki Hayabusa. Throughout this epic journey, you'll learn about those scandalous women who lurk around the urban motorcycle community looking for a chance to get a "ride" in one form or another from the motorcycle brothers. This ride will be entertaining, and you'll either have to put up or get shut down for trying to flee from this urban tale.

Softcover ISBN 978-0-9856964-3-6 • eBook ISBN 978-0-9856964-4-3

Beloved Daffodil's Inspirations
700 E. Firmin Street, Suite 188 Kokomo, IN 46902
www.BelovedDaffodilsInspirations.com

www.ingramcontent.com/pod-product-compliance
Lightning Source LLC
Chambersburg PA
CBHW021145130626
46554CB00005B/1667